LAST HEIST

EMMA LAST SERIES: BOOK FIVE

MARY STONE

MARY
STONE
PUBLISHING

*This book is dedicated to those who've stared into cancer's darkness,
and the lights that refuse to let them face it alone.*

DESCRIPTION

Love's darkest gift carries a deadly price.

There's nothing like an old-fashioned bank robbery to get the D.C. FBI office moving, even as half the team are side-lined with the flu. But this isn't a normal heist, and Special Agent Emma Last is no typical FBI operative, something her partner, Leo Ambrose, is quickly realizing.

And he doesn't know the half of it.

As Emma struggles with her secret, a masked assailant stages a morning robbery, making off with forty thousand dollars and leaving a trail of chaos in his wake. Beyond the money, he forces the bank manager, a guard, and the only two customers—a mother and her young daughter—into the vault.

The loot? A safety deposit box containing nothing more than notebooks. The devastation? He murders the mother after cutting and collecting a lock of her hair. As a gift or a trophy?

Upon their arrival, Emma and Leo are thrust into a relentless chase, hot on the robber's trail. But just like the ghosts that haunt Emma, he vanishes into thin air.

As the team tracks down one dead end after another, they discover this wasn't the perp's first heist. Or his first act of murder. Driven by a desperate need for money, Emma knows he's on the edge of disappearing forever or striking again. The race is on.

Last Heist is the fifth book in the fast-paced new FBI series by bestselling author Mary Stone where you'll discover the menacing depths of a mind backed into a corner with nothing left to lose.

1

————

Chelsea Terrence sagged against the bank counter, fighting the urge to rest her head on her mom's shoulder. She used to do that all the time when she was little. But that was then, and she was twelve now. Way too old for that. Plague-infected or not.

Why did I have to get the stupid flu? It's the day before Valentine's, and all my friends are having fun guessing who's going to ask them to the school dance.

She drooped to rest her aching head on her folded arms, wishing she could just be home in bed. She didn't even have enough energy to get out her phone and check Snap.

"I'm sure it'll be just another moment, honey." Her mom ran her fingers through Chelsea's blue-tipped pixie cut. "I think the blue is making you look paler than you are in this light. Doing okay?"

"Mood, I'm so done standing."

Her mom patted her on the back. "Be patient, honey. I'm sure they're working as fast as they can."

Chelsea leaned heavier on the counter before forcing herself upright. If she fainted, they'd likely call an ambulance, and there went any chance of going to the dance tomorrow night. Of course, the ambulance would probably come for the crusty old bank guard they'd passed on the way in the door...

Damn this flu. She'd rather be in science class than at the bank or an emergency room.

At nine in the morning, her mom had thought they could be in and out in a minute's time before there was any sort of rush, but their little community bank, the People's Bank of Columbia, was like something out of the Stone Ages.

They only had one teller and some creeptastic manager, who kept eyeing Chelsea's mom. He sucked in his pudge and grinned with *all his teeth*, but her mom was oblivious. The temptation to pick up her mom's hand and flaunt her wedding ring skipped through Chelsea's mind right alongside a little wash of dizziness.

The teller was a sight to see, too, with her cheugy hair. What had she done that morning, electrocuted herself for funsies?

Chelsea and her mom just wanted to cash a check. But the teller was still waiting for the computers to wake up.

Three minutes after opening.

Chelsea bit off a yawn, and her mom rubbed her shoulder. A day off from seventh grade was grand and all, but Chelsea just wanted sleep.

"I'm kind of thinking..." The words left her, along with her awareness of the latest dizzy spell she'd been fighting. A shadow breezed past her periphery, and she could feel someone looming over her shoulder. Shaky, Chelsea snuck a peek. The security guard was there, along with another man, who stood behind him.

The security guard shook like *he* might pass out. He had beads of sweat on his upper lip.

"Mom—"

The security guard's veiny hand landed on her shoulder and gripped it too tight, pulling her away from the counter as a gun—*a flipping gun!*—speared the space between her and her mom, pointing at the teller behind the glass.

"Move." The man who'd been out of view gestured with his gun, and the guard stepped to the right, bringing Chelsea with him.

Chelsea staggered sideways. The old guard kept his grip on Chelsea's shoulder, and her mom reached out to help her too.

The robber shoved her mother in the other direction, keeping himself between them.

"You too. Move! Hands on that counter. Stay there, lady. I see movement out of you or your kid, I shoot you both, and she goes first."

A whimper, like that of a scared puppy, came up out of her mom's throat, and Chelsea froze along with her. That sound, more than anything, proved this whole thing wasn't some weirdo prank.

She could see the other man now. The bank robber.

He had one of those green screen masks on, totally covering his face. The top of his head was oddly smooth. Alien-esque.

The robber kept his aim on the teller. "Everyone, remain calm. I'm just here for the money."

The security guard wheezed something that sounded like, "You shouldn't do this, son."

Growling a response, the robber knocked the guy in the chest with the barrel of the gun. "Keep quiet, and nobody gets hurt."

With the robber at the center of their little huddle, Chelsea doubted he could be seen from the outside walkway. She breathed in deep, getting a waft of oil, like from their old truck that dripped on occasion.

Her mom stood frozen with her arms on the counter as Chelsea and the guard stayed where they were.

"Let's make this quick and quiet, everyone." The man tossed a duffel bag over the partition before tapping the glass with a knuckle.

Chelsea's attention was drawn to a messy sort of tattoo on the inside of the robber's wrist.

02/15/78.

"Fill it up," he barked. "I want everything in the drawers that's not rigged. Make sure none of those paint packs make it in."

A bank manager and the teller got to work, emptying the drawers into the bag. The security guard's hands shook harder against Chelsea's shoulders. The man had to be eighty.

Still, she leaned back into his grip a little, tightening her arms across her chest and staring forward. The man might have been using her for cover or trying to keep her safe, with her being tall and him being short, but at the moment, she didn't care. Any human contact to keep her centered was a good thing.

For a moment, she wondered if the flu could cause hallucinations, but then her mom reached for her, and the green-masked robber swatted her hand and growled.

Dammit, Mom, please don't draw his attention. Please.

The world got fuzzy, with tears or from the flu. Chelsea pinched her arm hard, bringing herself back to the moment. She wasn't hallucinating, she couldn't afford to pass out, and that gun wasn't a prank.

Chelsea met her mom's eyes where she stood rigidly down the counter from her, trying to convey that she was all right. They would all be okay, as long as nobody did anything stupid. She worried her mom might reach for her again. Her eyes were wide with alarm, and her fingers clenched the counter's edge.

When Chelsea's focus wandered back to her mom's face, her mom gave a firm shake of her head and mouthed, *Stay there. I love you.*

Chelsea swallowed the knot in her throat. She mouthed her own message back as tears streaked from her mom's eyes, tracking through her expensive blush. *Love you too.*

The bank manager had edged his way behind the teller, putting her in between him and the robber's gun. "Do as the nice man says, Vivian." Hovering at his teller's back, he stretched his fingers in the air and made a show of his hands.

The nice man's got a cannon, dumbass. And Vivian's way ahead of you.

Vivian was stuffing wads of money into the duffel bag, not even looking at what she was doing, just focusing on the gun and shaking like a leaf.

Chelsea's knees weakened, and she wobbled as the robber ran a hand through her mom's long dark hair.

"You got nice hair, lady. Somebody else'd get a lot better use out of it than you, I can tell you that."

Wtf?

And the robber kept petting her mom's hair. At least he wore gloves, but Chelsea thought she might vomit for real.

Her mom's face went slack, and she shuddered at the robber's touch. The security guard's grip tightened on Chelsea's shoulders, as if to keep her in place.

After carefully climbing onto the counter, Vivian lifted the heavy duffel full of money over the glass partition.

The robber moved his free hand from her mom's hair to collect it, and his sleeve pulled back, revealing his tattoo once more.

Zero, two. Fifteen. Seventy-eight. Zero, two, fifteen, seventy-eight. Zero, two, fifteen, seventy-eight. Got it.

Chelsea's eyes remained fixed on the tattoo, taking deep

and even breaths. That was what her field hockey coach always told her. *"When you're nervous, take good, even breaths, and the moment will be over before you know it."*

Coach Osborne had been talking about an opposing player coming right at you, ready to knock your socks off with their stick, but the exercise seemed to help in this life-or-death situation too.

"Dammit, woman!" The robber yanked some stacks of money from the bag and tossed them toward the corner, where they exploded in a shower of red next to Chelsea's mom. She shrieked, flattening herself against the counter.

Red dye now covered her mom's coat like blood. It was splattered on the floor, too, bright and angry against the basic beige tiles. It really looked like fake blood. Her mom looked down at it all, mouth agape.

We're never getting that out, Trisha.

Chelsea had to fight down a totally inappropriate laugh. Her mom never left the house without "hair and makeup," as she'd put it. She always looked perfect.

As the gun roared in the robber's hand, his elbow knocked into Chelsea. He'd shot beneath the glass.

Vivian fell backward, mid-scream, chest painted red with real blood. She collapsed into the bank manager then slid downward out of sight as the manager screamed over and over.

Chelsea's ears rang, but the robber was yelling now, barking orders, and swinging his aim back and forth at each of them. Every time the barrel passed in front of Chelsea, she expected to feel a heavy pain in her chest.

The guard pushed her forward, still holding her shoulders...

And then her mom was there beside her, gripping her hand...

"Security boxes! Where are they?" The robber's scream echoed off the walls.

The blood-splattered bank manager came out from behind the counter and headed toward a hallway. They all followed him at a stumbling walk. Chelsea fought to keep her feet in the little tug-of-war she'd been caught in. Her mom and the security guard both held onto her like she might either be bulletproof or need help staying upright.

At the end of the hall, the bank manager fumbled to unlock a big wooden door even as he begged for their safety, his desperate words beginning to break through the ringing in Chelsea's ears.

The bank robber wasn't speaking now, just muttering under his breath.

Now that they'd come to a stop, Chelsea couldn't take her focus off the manager. The side of his face and his gray goatee were red with blood splatter.

The robber shoved them all forward into the room, which was filled with security lockers, and had a little nook at the back with a curtain hanging half open across it. Their captor gestured with his gun for the group to head toward a privacy curtain. He pulled it partway shut behind them. Somebody was pushed into Chelsea's back, and she slammed into the wall of to the left of the curtain. Someone else—her mom, it was her mom—guided her to the corner and whispered, "Sit."

Chelsea scanned the ceiling. No cameras in this corner.

Her phone dug into her hip, taking all her weight as she slid to the floor beside her mom. The old guard slumped down next to Chelsea on the other side, apologizing under his breath for pushing her.

She shook her head to tell him it was all right, but the robber gave the guard a kick in the leg.

"Shut it." He kicked the man again, in the shoulder this

time, sending him sideways into Chelsea and crushing her
hip onto her phone again.

The guard righted himself and rubbed his shoulder,
giving Chelsea a sorrowful look. She had other things on her
mind, though, as she watched the robber stalk back and forth
in front of them.

My phone.

"All of you, stay still and let me do my business. You
understand?"

Chelsea played along, nodding hard just like her mom
and the guard were doing.

Taking them at their word, the robber turned his focus
back to the manager and gestured with his gun. He spoke too
low for Chelsea to hear him, but through the opening around
the curtain, she watched as the manager began searching the
safe deposit boxes. He wiped at his eyes, mixing Vivian's
blood with his tears as he looked about.

The robber took out a key from his pocket and slapped it
against the manager's chest.

"Open it, or the kid gets shot."

The manager blubbered something, then reached for his
own pocket, watching the robber's gun the whole time.

"Get moving, dumbass. I'll only shoot you if you pull out
anything other than your keys."

Finally, the manager drew a ring of keys out of his pocket.
He dropped them twice before finding the right one. The
robber kept tapping his arm with the gun, which wasn't
doing any good.

Chelsea angled her hand and tugged her phone free. With
her knees up, she set the phone on the floor between them
and widened her legs just enough to see it. She switched to
Silent Mode before it could give them away but then noticed
she had no bars.

They must be too deep into the secure section of the bank to get a signal.

She could hit record, though.

One eye on the bank manager as he opened the locker, Chelsea turned on her video.

She took aim with the phone, centering in on the robber and manager, who was moving things from a safety deposit box to the robber's duffel now. Before she could zoom in, her mom's fist darted between her knees and yanked the phone away from her, chucking it over into the corner of the room.

Mom!

Chelsea almost lunged for it but froze in place as the robber reacted.

Cowering at the sudden movement, the manager fell to the floor.

The security guard started praying in Spanish.

And Chelsea shrank backward into her mother as the man before them shoved the gun in his pants and yanked a hunting knife from his belt. The thing looked like a Gordon Ramsay knockoff, shiny and sharp and long enough to cut into a boar. He brandished it at her mother.

"Smart move, getting rid of your kid's phone." He eyed Chelsea, the green mask nodding up and down. "Dumb move on your part. But if your mom behaves, we'll call it even. Got me?"

Chelsea forced herself to nod.

"Say 'yes, sir,' you blue-haired brat."

Chelsea tasted blood. She must've bitten her tongue.

Her mom nudged her.

"Yes, sir."

"Good girl." The man's green nose pointed back at her mother, his knife waving in the air. "Stay still, lady. You hear me?"

Her mother nodded, a look of pure fury on her face.

The man took a hard hold of her mom's hair. He stretched it out and sawed the knife through it. Taking one chunk, then two, and then a third...until her long, beautiful hair had all been torn away. Not as short as Chelsea's pixie cut, but it had been a valiant effort.

He fisted the hair as he stood, muttering beneath his breath again. Then he sheathed his knife before focusing his blank green mask back on Chelsea. "Thanks for this."

Chelsea clenched her mom's thigh.

In another second, he was back at a table in the center of the privacy room, where the manager had placed one of the locker boxes. He pulled something or another from the locker, a couple of papers fluttering away from his grip before he snatched them up.

In catching the pages, his tattoo flashed from his wrist again. Chelsea wished she'd still had her phone out to capture it.

When he tucked the pages away and turned to his group of hostages again, the gun was back in his hand.

He lifted it, and the barrel swept in front of Chelsea's face.

She shut her eyes. "I love you, Mom."

Chelsea opened her eyes to see her mom had shoved herself between her and the robber. "You have what you want, so you can leave now. Leave us al—"

The gun roared.

Chelsea screamed as her eyes snapped shut, and she clapped her hands over her ears.

A heavy *thump* sounded beside her, followed by a hushed gasp.

Chelsea opened her eyes.

Her mom lay crumpled beside her with a dark stain blossoming on her chest. Blood soaked through everything. Into her coat, her blouse, and her pants, covering the floor beneath them.

Chelsea reached for her. "Mom! No…"

Her mother's blood spread all over Chelsea's hands and sleeves as she bent over her, searching for the gunshot and a way to stop the blood. But red oozed everywhere.

The security guard's prayers increased in volume as the bank manager screamed in the background. And, dimly, from somewhere behind her, Chelsea heard a door slam and knew the robber must be gone, but that didn't seem to matter so much anymore.

When Chelsea found the hole in her mom's chest, her own cries had ratcheted up, blocking out all other sound. Her mom's hand lifted, trailing along Chelsea's face.

"Mom, Mom, you're going to be—"

"Chel…baby girl. I—"

Her lips fluttered, and tears leaked from her eyes, but not as fast as those coming from Chelsea's.

"I love you, too, Mom."

The woman's mouth opened, but her eyes were already going flat. Her hand fell from Chelsea's cheek, limp.

Her mom was gone.

2

S pecial Agent Emma Last chucked the used disinfectant
wipe into the wire bin beside her desk and yanked out
yet another from the container. She attacked the phone on
her desk until it shined with disinfectant before going to
work on the desk surface, mouse pad included. The monitor
gleamed under the lights, and she'd already sprayed down
the keyboard before anything else.

Come hell or high water, she was *not* getting sick. This flu
could take down all of D.C., but not Emma. She had no time
for that BS. Or anything else.

"Get out of here!"

She closed her eyes and scrubbed harder. She refused to
think of her mother's words from beyond the grave. Or what
her mom had been so afraid of.

"Emma...go! She can see you!"

Had the voice really belonged to Gina Last? And if it had
been Emma's mom, why only show up to scream at her those
couple sentences and then disappear?

Why hadn't Emma listened to Marigold when the psychic

warned her about trying to reach out to her mother on her own?

"Understand that opening the door between this world and the Other, even with the purest of intentions and reasoning, can go wrong. It's a two-way portal we're talking about, and an infinite number of lifetimes exist on the other side. Your mother may not be the only one listening."

Yanking out two more disinfectant wipes, Emma attacked her chair. She might not be able to control the Other or the ghosts who appeared in her life, but she could damn well control the number of germs she came in contact with.

After all, she hadn't been skipping out of yoga for nothing. She'd gone to the studio on Saturday to try and clear her mind of her ill-advised séance only to come face-to-face with two coughing regulars. Hearing them both proclaim that no flu would keep them home from yoga had been more than enough of a wake-up call. Even if staying away meant no Oren.

Seeing him this morning would've been nice, though.

Emma grimaced at her own train of thought and refocused. The Bureau wasn't the place where she ought to be thinking about ghosts or fantasizing about a man, even if he was the hottest yoga instructor in town.

Instead, she pulled out another wipe and started scrubbing at the desk drawer handles.

This *flu-demic*—as the ever-so-creative news had deemed it—had already taken out about a quarter of the D.C. FBI office, including Agents Denae Monroe and Vance Jessup. Even Agent Sloan Grant in the Counterterrorism unit, who normally prided herself on staying away from germs, was sick in bed.

Leo's boots stopped beside Emma's desk. "You trying to make everything lemony?"

"You kidding?" Emma offered him only the briefest of

glances before returning to her chore. "Have you talked to Denae? Seen Vance's texts? Fevers, coughs…this thing is miserable. If a little cleaning'll save us, I'll bleach the entire building."

"Maybe we should just send everyone else on a get-well break." Leo flopped into his chair and leaned back, not bothering to take any of the wipes for his own desk. "Vance just got over a bug, and now he's out again? Flu season's pretty brutal up here."

"Missing Miami?"

Emma forced a smile to go with her quip as her colleague hummed in agreement. The last thing she wanted to do was encourage deeper conversation. Every time they ended up alone, she couldn't help worrying he'd confront her about the ghosts again.

Seriously, what was she supposed to tell him about the Other?

About the threatening ghosts? The wolf who'd made her fall out of bed? The Other-worldly call that lured her to the deck of a mountain at the B and B, where she very nearly leapt to her death?

If Leo hadn't saved me…I owe him for that.

Emma swept away the tightening in her chest with another scrub of a wipe, grateful that she could hear Leo's fingers ticking away on his phone. Maybe there'd be no questions so early on a Monday morning. Which meant she wouldn't have to make up any excuses.

She reached under her desk and ran the wipe beneath the edge of its surface, just for good measure. Then got on all fours under it. *What the hell.* Her fingers practically itched with the need to put more distance between her and Leo, but she told herself it was likely the disinfectant making her skin crawl.

Certainly not the echo of Mom's voice warning me that some unnamed "she" can see me from the Other. Certainly not that.

Maybe she'd been wrong earlier, thinking she'd rather have ghosts floating through the air than the germs from this flu.

"Emma, did you hear me?" Leo ducked his head beneath her desk.

She nearly bumped her head pulling back to sit on her heels. "No, sorry." She took a deep breath. "What?"

Leo's eyes narrowed as he casually slipped his phone into a pocket. "I said, I know you're helping Mia investigate Ned's death."

Licking her lips, Emma threw away the latest wipe and swept her hands along her pants, getting rid of the chemicals as she sought retrieval of her voice. "Wha—"

"I heard you two talking. I didn't mean to," Leo held out both hands, "but I did. And I want to help. I know how much Mia's brother meant to her, and I also know what it's like. To lose someone."

Leo's voice had gone a bit gruff, and he shoved one hand back through his curls, mussing them even more than usual. But his dark-brown eyes were all business, so Emma couldn't find it in herself to joke about the gesture.

She flexed her fingers, her nail beds actually stinging from the disinfectant sinking in. This was not the emotion she'd been expecting from Leo Ambrose today. And the way his voice had just gone heavy...she wasn't good at vulnerability. Showing it or seeing it.

And still, Leo's focus remained on her...waiting for some response.

"Leo, I appreciate it, but—"

"Don't do that." Leo sat forward farther, holding her gaze. "Don't put me off. I'm part of the team, and I want to help."

For a moment, Emma was shoved backward in time to their first case together, when he'd gotten a whiff of a girl being abused and gone off like a bull seeing red. That had turned out to be nothing, but the normally laid-back Leo Ambrose was anything but chill right now. She knew he was sensitive, but still, the man's layers kept throwing her off-balance.

Whatever losses he'd suffered, the experience engendered a strong sympathy for others going through their own grief.

She thought to joke about his intensity, in hopes of forestalling the inevitable just a little longer, but the shriek of Jacinda's office door being shoved open faster than usual stopped everything.

Their SSA stood at the edge of the team's shared workspace, near Vance's desk, with a phone in one hand and her Kevlar vest in the other.

"Emma, what are you doing on the floor? Get up!" Jacinda thumbed a text as she shrugged into her vest. "Vests and coats, now. Bank robbery at People's Bank of Columbia on the outskirts of D.C. Police are in active pursuit."

Leo was already throwing Emma a vest, and she had it on before she'd reached the door.

A bank robbery. Talk about a fast start to a Monday.

Jacinda held the elevator for the two of them as they rushed in beside her. "Mia's meeting us downstairs. We'll take one Expedition. You two take another and call me as soon as you're en route. I'll brief you on the way."

Emma glanced at Leo, her eyebrow raised for permission to hit the gas beyond his granny instincts.

"Yeah, yeah, I know. You're driving."

3

Leo typed in the bank's address as Emma swung the Expedition out of the parking lot, bypassing Mia and Jacinda on the road just a few seconds later.

"Police are in pursuit, you know." Leo grunted with the force of a turn. "It's an emergency, not an apocalypse." He double-checked his seat belt even as he dialed Jacinda for the briefing.

Emma shot him a fast glance before twisting back to the road. "Just call Jacinda so we can find out what we're dealing with, yeah?"

"Already ringing."

Leo held up the phone between them once Jacinda answered.

"You two hear me?"

"Loud and clear." Emma took a fast left, leaving Mia and Jacinda out of sight in the rearview mirror.

"All right, listen up." Jacinda was talking fast. "A masked man arrived minutes after it opened at nine and held up their only teller. He stole approximately forty grand in cash and shot her...a woman named Vivian Marx...in the process. She played dead after being shot and hit the panic button when she got a chance."

Smart woman.

"So no casualties?" Emma asked.

"I'm getting there. Vivian Marx is being transported to the hospital. Police are searching the premises for the manager she mentioned, but she went into shock after that, so we don't know who else might be inside. I'm waiting for an update now."

Jacinda muttered something on her end, presumably responding to Mia, before continuing.

"Police arrived right as the suspect tore out of the parking lot, driving a cherry-red Ford F-250. Pursuit is ongoing, as I said. Heading south out of the city, so we'll be in range in about ten minutes."

The Expedition jumped forward, ramping up with Emma's lead foot, and Leo grimaced. "Make that five."

Confirming the location of the chase against his maps and Jacinda's updates from the local police, Leo gripped the *oh shit* bar and kept his attention trained around them for erratic drivers. Well...erratic drivers who weren't his partner, that was.

"He didn't take hostages. Not as far as we know." Leo's lungs tightened as she took a fast exit and opened up the throttle. "Not worth an accident."

"And I won't get us in an accident." She hit the gas harder, but Leo refused to allow himself to look at the speedometer. Bank robbers tended to hit targets in a sequence, and if this man shot a teller in his first robbery, he'd likely do the same next time.

They needed to find the criminal now, not later, after he'd had the chance to exercise his trigger finger a few more times.

I don't know whether to be thankful she's driving like herself or not.

If Emma Last was one thing, it was a fast driver. Which wasn't exactly abnormal for an FBI agent with her track record of success. He only wished the rest of her behavior matched up with what he'd expect from someone in her position. Someone he'd come to trust for her professional instincts as well as her smarts.

From talking to people who weren't there, to reacting to crime scenes as if they were haunted houses, not to mention ending up on the ledge of a deck some hundred feet above a forest floor, Emma hadn't been acting normal. Even the killers they'd taken down recently seemed to notice it, going back to Ty Belloise at the circus. Emma had distracted him by pretending she could talk to the trapeze artist Ty had murdered.

Today, Emma was all business, but how long would that last?

What Leo believed was happening, he couldn't actually say. But *something* was making Emma act out of sorts and know things she shouldn't. He couldn't deny that any longer.

If anything, he hoped helping them investigate the death of Mia's brother would lead to some answers. About Ned, about Emma's behavior, and about his own headaches with wolves, if he was lucky.

Emma swerved around an expensive sports car fast enough to make the driver slam on the brakes, and Leo's heart stuttered in his chest. Horns honked in their wake. This was faster than he'd ever seen her drive.

The Expedition catapulted onto a rural highway with open road ahead. Under Emma's foot, the pedal hit the floorboard.

Thoughts of Mia, Mia's brother, and even Emma's odd behavior fled Leo's mind as scenery whizzed by in a blur. In its place, the faces of his parents fought for attention—remembered from pictures more than his own memory banks, they'd been lost so long ago.

Lost in a car accident.

Gritting his teeth, he broke down and took a glance at the speedometer, but then wished he hadn't. They'd passed the hundred mph mark, which explained the shimmying. Emma might just shake the damn thing apart with her speed.

"Emma, slow down."

"No."

Despite her words, she glanced at the speedometer, and the vehicle slowed perceptibly.

But then Leo saw why.

Ahead, a cluster of police cars blocked a crossroads.

Emma hit the brake hard as they approached, coming to a skidding stop on the shoulder of the road. A sheriff's deputy approached Leo's window without being called over, a sheepish look on his young face.

"Agents," he nodded at them, "we're thinking to set up here."

Leo glanced beyond the stopped police cars but saw nothing except dust and empty road. "You want to tell us why? What happened to the truck?"

"Uh, we think the truck went off-road. We were in pursuit, but all of a sudden, the tires kicked up so much dust in the dry fields that we couldn't tell what was what. Had to pull off, for fear of getting in a dustup with each other. We've been waiting for the dust to settle so we can see."

Emma made to grab the door handle—presumably to give whoever was in charge a piece of her mind—but Leo grabbed her wrist. "Emma, wait."

He pointed out to the left, across the field, where a cherry-red blur could just be seen in the distance. "He's on a parallel road. Cut across the field!"

Slamming the SUV back into gear, Emma tore the wheel sideways and left their sheriff's deputy coughing in her exhaust fumes. With the Expedition bouncing across the field, Emma maneuvered it expertly around an irrigation rig and tapped the gas again, angling after the truck.

Behind them, Mia and Jacinda arrived and went swerving around the collection of cop cars. They shot forward on the road, presumably to run parallel to their robber and cut across when another road gave the option.

Leo kept one eye on the rearview and one eye ahead but remained silent, letting Emma do her thing.

And for a few seconds, it seemed like they might catch up. The truck was moving at a steady, fast speed, but not suspiciously so. Clearly, the driver had seen the cops stop and thought he'd lost them.

But then their Expedition caught the driver's eye, and Leo realized they were done. The cherry-red truck leaped forward, even while they fought their way through the field. "The truck…" Leo bounced in his seat, his head almost hitting the ceiling. "Do you see that speed? That thing's engine has aftermarket parts. No way is that factory standard."

Emma grunted. "Your point?"

Leo didn't get a chance to answer. Her foot hit the gas—hard—and the SUV bounced ahead. He braced one hand on the dash and the other on the *oh shit* bar, gritting his teeth as Emma let up on the accelerator and leapfrogged a ditch, bouncing onto the roadway beyond it.

As soon as they hit the asphalt, Emma put the pedal to the floor again and brought the engine up to a scream.

He glimpsed the rpm gauge cartwheeling into the red and forced his eyes back to the road and the pickup…which, somehow, they were closing in on.

Going too fast, and still well behind him, but definitely short-ening the distance.

Staring ahead, Leo braced for whatever Emma might decide to do next. Now that they were on a straightaway, her leg was stiff with pressure on the gas, and he had to clench his teeth to avoid turning into a back seat driver.

"Emma, that's a classic truck. See how boxy it is? The angles and chrome lining?"

Emma practically growled at him, swerving around a stray bit of debris that was unrecognizable at this speed. "So?"

"So," Leo gritted his teeth, "this guy knows what he's doing. We're not going to catch him in an Expedition, for Pete's sake. Slow down. We know what he's driving, and they may have gotten a license plate—"

Leo cut himself off, white-knuckling the dash.

When they were within a couple of football fields of the vehicle, the F-250's brake lights suddenly flashed.

"Emma…"

"I see it!" Emma slammed on the Expedition's brakes, skidding forward as the pickup ahead of them reversed fast, backing up directly toward their vehicle ever faster. The pickup grew bigger as Emma got the Expedition under control and, at the last minute, swerved sideways around the approaching truck.

Leo hissed out a breath he'd barely been aware of holding. He'd never doubt Emma's driving again.

He'd not doubt their perpetrator's driving either, though.

Still braced, he muttered, "I got a license plate."

"Probably fake."

"Well, yeah. And I'm not trying to write it down now while your hands are still on the wheel."

In their rearview, the pickup skidded into a U-turn

worthy of a Michael Bay film and took off in the opposite direction, kicking up rooster tails in the dust.

Emma was already intentionally fishtailing the Expedition, grunting as she fought with the wheel. "This damn thing's top-heavy."

"Don't flip us."

"Why do you think I'm not going faster?" Her growl was punctuated by the squeal of their tires as she re-centered the Expedition on the road once more, but even as she hit the gas, Leo was biting back curses.

There was no sign of the truck. Farther down the road, local police had clearly attempted to assemble behind them and block off an exit, but they'd managed to tangle into one another.

Leo's grip on the grab bar loosened. "They weren't fast enough."

And there was no sign of Jacinda and Mia anywhere.

Emma slammed her fist into the wheel as she slowed their approach, coming up on the disabled cop cars and the red-faced sheriff's deputy they'd left in their dust. A road off to the side led back to where they'd met just minutes ago, and Leo couldn't help thinking they'd all have been better off if the cops hadn't tried to help.

Because as it was, their killer was flat-out gone. He'd disappeared just as sure as if he were a ghost.

4

_____

After losing the suspect in the wide-open farmland, Emma and Leo scoured the local byroads, trying for any glimpse of his trail. They'd found nothing, and Emma came close to uttering the first truly foul words to cross her mind in months. She'd even lifted her lead foot on the way back to town, bringing their Expedition to a stop beside the bank well after the SSA and Mia had arrived.

They had already been taking stock of the crime scene and any available evidence. Mia was in the process of assisting the small local police force, keeping onlookers from getting too close.

Leo unbuckled his seat belt beside her, stretching as he got out of the SUV. "This might be the smallest bank I've ever seen."

"That allows walk-ins anyway." Emma eyed the chaos of the parking lot, which was unnecessarily big by comparison.

The brick structure was about as nondescript and conservative as any she'd seen. Cream-colored accents and green lettering beneath a slate gray roof, with a parking lot lined with tired shrubs and one large shade tree. The whole landscape appeared exhausted from winter, on the brink of dying in a way that spring alone wouldn't remedy. More than that, though, the chill in the air spoke to disrupted calm.

Like this was a space that should've been safe, but the morning's activities had broken it into a million pieces. She suspected their little entourage of cops and ambulances and Feds was more action than the place had seen over the entirety of the last decade.

Emma pointed at where Jacinda stood near the entrance talking to a plainclothes detective she recognized only vaguely. "Let's see what they have for us."

While Leo marched ahead, Emma absorbed the organized chaos, on the lookout for any signs from the Other. So far, nothing…with any luck, maybe that meant no fatalities.

Mia had left crowd control to the locals and was making her way over as well.

"We had a security guard inside, and two bystanders." Jacinda grimaced, lacing her fingers through her red hair and pulling it into a loose bun. "They were found in the vault along with the bank manager. A preteen girl and her mom. The robber shot and killed the mother, but the manager, guard, and young girl are…as fine as can be expected."

A mom and her daughter. Of course.

Emma needed to see the girl, but revealing that urgency in front of Jacinda would be a bad idea. Hiding her clenched fists from the SSA, she kept her voice even when she replied. "Where is she? The daughter."

Jacinda nodded toward the nearest ambulance. "They just brought her out. She's there if you want to babysit, but we should wait for her father to arrive before we question her. He's on the way now."

With no further prodding, Emma turned and moved in that direction even as she heard Leo ask about the manager.

She wanted to speak to the girl before they took her to the hospital, assuming she was up to it.

Before Emma even reached her, though, she felt the change. The dip in the already cold temperature, the subtle shift in pressure that gave extra heft to the plumes of breath leaving her lips.

She braced herself but pushed forward.

At the ambulance, she found a gangly preteen, all knees and elbows, perched at the back end of the vehicle with an EMT, who seemed to be at her wit's end. She held a water bottle in one hand, extended toward the girl, but all she got was a shake of the girl's head along with a glare from her red-rimmed eyes.

Emma drew closer, noting a sickly pale sheen to the girl's cheeks that might've been due to the blue tips on her hair, but it read like more than that to Emma. Beside her, a ghostly woman sat with a bloody chest, hair that looked like somebody had hacked at it with a pair of lawn clippers, and white eyes.

The mother.

The EMT pursed her lips in Emma's direction and put a hand on the shoulder of the girl, who immediately shook her off. "Agent, I've been trying to explain to Chelsea that she needs to go to the hospital. Or at least drink something. She's had a rough morning, and she also has the flu. We need to get her checked out. She almost fainted on us once already."

"I did not," the girl bit out. Her glare could have melted asphalt. "I got dizzy because I stood up too fast."

The EMT grimaced. "You got dizzy because you have the flu, are dehydrated, your electrolytes are out of whack, and you're potentially going into shock."

Chelsea shoved her short blue-tipped hair behind her ears before stuffing her hands into her coat pockets and meeting Emma's gaze. "They need to bring my mother out. I'm not leaving without her."

Emma came within a foot of the trio, focusing on the girl rather than her ghostly mother, whose bloody suit coat oozed red all the way down to the ground. "Honey, to find the person who attacked you and your mom, the best thing we can do is let everyone do their jobs at their own pace."

Though the words were antiseptic and hard, even with Emma's softened voice, they were also true.

The EMT nodded, speaking to both Emma and Chelsea when she continued. "The forensic techs are inside with the...Mrs. Terrence."

Thank goodness she didn't say they were inside with "the body."

The EMT almost lifted a hand to Chelsea's shoulder again but caught herself in time to avoid another angry shrug-off from the girl. "I'm sure they'll release your mother as soon as they can, but we have to wait on the techs and the investigators if you want them to catch the person who did this."

Chelsea's gaze darted up to Emma's. "It was a man. He had one of those green screen masks on, like they use for movies."

Unfortunately, this wasn't the time for pushing. Emma held up a hand, holding her off. "I think we should wait until your father arrives before—"

"Why?" Chelsea scowled, her fisted hands bouncing in her coat pockets hitting her thighs with an anxious rhythm.

Emma traded glances with the EMT, whose frown probably mirrored her own. She didn't have the expertise to decide if Chelsea was going into shock, but she did look sick and like she needed a hospital sooner rather than later.

"He said somebody else would use it better." The ghostly mother leaned toward her daughter, attempting to run a bloody hand over her hair and failing as it slid through the strands without effect. "He cut it."

Emma swallowed her instinct to speak to the dead rather than the living. That was not what any of them needed right now.

Mrs. Terrence peered back at Emma, one hand still half buried in her daughter's hair. "You should listen to your mother, Agent Last. Stay away from the Other. She says it's not safe. She can see you."

The "she" in question being my mom? Or not? Great.

Despite Emma's frustration, though, the ghost's simple claim sent a chill through her blood that had nothing to do with either this apparition before her or the seasonal chill.

Her mom's voice from a few days ago—no, her *scream*—echoed in Emma's memory. Her mom had gone to pains to warn her of some danger, yet Emma didn't even know how or why.

The EMT reached up to feel Chelsea's forehead, and the girl let out a little wail as she batted her hand away. "That's what my mom does! Not you!" A sob broke out of her throat. "And who's caring about her now? Huh? Why can't they bring her out?"

Sorrow tightened Emma's chest. She knew just what this girl would be experiencing in the future, without her mother around to take care of her and be there. She was in for a lot of heartache in the months and years to come.

"And you won't even listen to me!" Chelsea twisted where she sat, near exploding with anxiety, and her mother let out a little groan beside her. "The other agent said to wait, and this woman said to wait, and you say to wait, but why can't we even talk about what happened to her? My dad wasn't there!"

"Chelsea, your mom's going to be taken care of, I can promise you that much." The EMT glanced backward at the street, apparently hoping the father would show up sooner rather than later, but no other cars were coming through the roadblock the police had set up. Not for the moment anyway.

She put her hand on Chelsea's forehead again, but this time the girl only sighed and clenched her eyes shut. When the woman lifted her glove away, she met Emma's eyes. "We should really get this girl to the hospital. Can you question her without her father or not?"

If we have to.

I mean, technically, we do have a parent present. Even if I'm the only one seeing her.

Emma gave the woman a tight nod. Ideally, they would have waited for the other parent—the living one—for fear of him raising a fuss about it later or this young girl becoming distraught. But there was no question that Chelsea was a witness, not a suspect, which meant questioning her now was better than nothing.

"Okay, Chelsea, let's do this your way." Emma waited for Chelsea to take a breath and look up at her, the girl's breathing seeming to even out now that the adults she faced had relented. "My name's Special Agent Emma Last, and my team's going to take care of your mother and find the man who did this. How old are you, honey?"

"I'm twelve. Old enough to know what I saw." The girl's red-rimmed eyes were clear enough, determined, and her mom's ghost patted her head ineffectually once more.

"And I understand you have the flu…are you on medication? Anything that might make you confused?"

The girl shook her head violently, nearly losing her balance in the process, but the EMT's quick hold kept her seated. "We picked up some stuff at the drugstore, but I haven't taken anything yet."

"I'm listening, Chelsea. What can you tell me?"

"We were just here so Mom could cash a check. At first, it didn't seem real. Especially with that green mask the guy was wearing. And I think stuff was...fine? I mean, fine for a robbery? But then the teller gave him dye packs, even though he told her not to. That's what they're called, right?"

Emma nodded, forcing a smile. "Yes."

Chelsea hugged herself, leaning more heavily against the ambulance. "He shot her for that. Just...just shot her. They said she'd be okay, but I don't know if they were just saying that. 'Cause I'm a kid, you know? I thought she...I thought she...like Mom. And then, then, we were moving and..."

The girl broke off as if the words wouldn't come out. Emma shifted in the heavy cold of the mother's presence, looking for her voice, but then she realized that Chelsea Terrence hadn't stopped only because she was lost for words. She was reaching into a lower cargo pocket. A moment later, she pulled out a cell phone with a glittery black case and a *No FOMO for Me* sticker. She thrust it at Emma.

"I tried to record what happened in the locker room. I don't know what I got, but you'll hear what happened, at least. I didn't..." She broke off again, eyes going a little glassy. "I didn't have a signal to call nine-one-one."

"That's okay. This is great." And it was. Anything could help. "By the locker room...you mean where the safety deposit boxes were?"

The girl nodded. "Yeah, sorry. The safety deposit boxes."

"And did the man have a key?"

Another nod. "After we went inside, he made the manager go to one box. The manager was nervous, and the robber kept telling him to hurry and stuff. When they were talking about the box itself, I didn't hear what they said. If they said anything...there was a lot going on."

"Did he ever take his mask off?"

Chelsea grimaced. "No. I took out my phone to record, but Mom grabbed it and threw it."

The white-eyed woman raised a bloody hand to her

mouth, running one finger along her lip. "He cut it. Said somebody'd get better use than me."

Emma kept her face flat even as the ghost ran her shaking, bloodied hand over the back of her own scalp.

"The guard started praying, and the man came over," Chelsea reached for, and found, the EMT's hand, "and he...he took out a big knife. Big like what I've seen on *Top Chef* when they're choosing teams, ya know?"

"It's called a chef's knife."

"And then he came right up to Mom and he...he cut her hair off. He was touching it earlier, before he took us to the vault, and he said...he said he knew somebody who would get more use out of it than her."

"He took her hair with him?"

"Yeah." Chelsea took in a ragged breath, and the EMT grimaced. "And then he went to the table at the center of the room again. I saw his tattoo again then too. *Oh...his tattoo!*"

Emma couldn't stop a smile from coming to her lips. "Tattoos are a great way to identify people in situations like this. What do you remember?"

"It was on his wrist. Really messy. I have an older cousin with homemade tattoos, and that's kind of how it looked."

Prison tattoo, maybe?

"I saw it for the first time when he...when he tossed the duffel over. And then he tapped the glass. Before he shot the teller." The girl's eyes went a little glassy again, and Emma reached out and touched her knee, bringing her back to the moment. "But I saw it clear. It was numbers, like how you write a date. With slashes, ya know? Oh-two, slash, fifteen, slash, seventy-eight."

Emma felt her eyes widen along with the EMT's. She hadn't expected that level of detail, and she scrambled for a pen and notebook. She scribbled down the date as Chelsea repeated it. *02/15/78.* Done, she held it up to the tween before her for confirmation.

"Yeah, that's it. I thought it might be important, so I kept saying it in my head to make sure I remembered it."

"You did really good, honey. And while I've got my notebook out, can you tell me the security code for your phone?"

Chelsea hesitated but then seemed to realize there was no reason to do anything but share it. "It's Milo's birthday. He's my dog. Ten nineteen."

"Perfect." Emma noted the code down and tucked her book away. "I promise we'll get your phone back to you as soon as we can. Now, is there anything else you can tell us?"

Chelsea tugged her hand from the EMT's and hugged herself. Beside her, Ghost Mom began to fade, and Emma realized there wasn't much left to the story. "He was putting stuff into the duffel bag with the money. My mom's hair too. And then he took the gun out again, and came back, and...and..."

"I get it." Emma's excitement over the tattoo died under the reminder that this girl had just watched her own mother killed. No need to make her relive that part. Certainly not right now. "Chelsea, I want to—"

"*Chelsea!*" A man all but bounced off a patrol car as he ran over and landed at the edge of the ambulance, where Chelsea fell into his arms. He wore a suit and tie, but his long limbs and angular chin matched his daughter's. She sobbed against him, and he pressed her tighter to his chest, eyes closed.

Emma stepped back from the pair, her eyes burning. Maybe her father had held her like that once upon a time, when she'd been little, but they hadn't grieved together in any meaningful way. Either because she'd been too young, or he'd avoided sharing his grief until she got old enough. Maybe both. And maybe this pair would at least have one another in a way that would help.

Finally, his eyes turned up beyond his daughter's shoulder and darted between the EMT and Emma. "I think I need to get my daughter to the hospital now."

Ghost Mom retreated into the ambulance, as if waiting to go along for the ride, while Emma gestured them inside as the EMT supported Chelsea on one side, Dad on the other. The girl was wavering on her feet now, all her energy used up with the conversation about the killer.

Emma raised her voice as she stepped closer, watching as the EMT buckled a strap over Chelsea's lap for security. "Your mom's always going to be with you, honey."

Chelsea eyed Emma. The girl appeared more shell-shocked now than she had before, but nodded thanks along with both of her parents.

That's enough, Emma girl. It's all you can do.

Backing off, she watched the mother lean over her daughter's gurney just before the ambulance doors were shut. It seemed the whole family would ride to the hospital together after all.

If that counted for anything.

5

———

Stopping their team in front of Vivian's teller window, Jacinda gestured to the surrounding area. "Our guess is the teller tried to include dye packs, the perpetrator caught on, and tossed them."

"That matches what Chelsea told me." Emma took a step toward the paint splatter. "She's the girl whose...her mom was killed. She said the robber told the teller not to put dye packs in with the money, but he found them and shot her."

Jacinda motioned for Emma to rejoin the group by the counter. "What else did she tell you?"

Emma gave the team a quick recap of the preteen's statements, including all the details of who was in the vault, where they stood, and how the robber had a tattoo on his wrist. "She's a champ, catching those details about the tattoo. And having the presence of mind to use her phone to record it all...that took guts."

"Has anyone considered her mother might be alive if she hadn't tried that stunt?" Leo wasn't quite as ready to give the young girl an award. "What if the robber killed the mother as a lesson to the daughter?"

Emma's entire body stiffened. "Then that would make him more than your average bank robber. It takes a special kind of evil to do something like that."

Clearing her throat, Jacinda motioned with her iPad to get the conversation back under her control. "Those are all good points, and we'll want to consider the possibilities going forward. For now, let's concentrate on the facts we do have. No paint near the teller windows here, or on the path to the vault, means the perpetrator probably avoided any of the dye hitting him, the bag, or the money."

Emma nodded toward the area back behind the counter where she could just see a puddle of blood smeared along the floor. "The teller got hit there?"

"That's right. Vivian Marx." Jacinda referenced some notes on her iPad. "Twenty-four, a longtime employee of the bank even at so young an age. Clean record. She's been taken to the hospital for surgery, and the EMT said he expected she'd survive."

"Not to be coldhearted about this, but same question as before." Leo pinched the bridge of his nose, as if exasperated with the world. "If she hadn't slipped in those dye packs, maybe our guy wouldn't have shot her. That could have been the act that spun him up."

Emma wheeled on him this time, unable to hide her irritation. "You're suggesting our victims are at fault for their own suffering?"

"I feel like nobody here acted the way people are supposed to. Keep your head down, comply. It's just money, and it's not worth dying over. The teller disobeyed the robber's directive. He shot her. Maybe the mother did something as well, and by that point, our perpetrator is already seeing red, so he goes for the kill."

Jacinda conceded Leo's point with a quiet nod. "You're right. The advice is always to comply and stay clear. We're in a small municipality here, and bank robberies are probably as frequent as celebrity sightings. My guess is, in the heat of the moment, despite training and intellectually under-standing what they were supposed to do, nobody present had any idea how they were 'supposed to' act emotionally."

Leo scowled, sending a glance at a man's hunched form behind the desk of a nearby office. The guy's hands shook as he struggled to fill out a form. "And him?"

"That's the bank manager, Addison Wright. Shaken and stirred, but not drunk yet."

And as far away from the blood as he could get, Emma noted.

Jacinda nodded at the gray-haired man. "He's unharmed. From what Emma said, it sounds like our preteen witness got more information on the killer than anyone else. The bank had one security guard, also unharmed. He's elderly and was taken to the hospital for observation. Heart palpitations and shock."

Emma and the team followed Jacinda to a hallway leading behind the counter. She could just glimpse crime scene tape cordoning off the vault.

"That's our safety deposit box room, where the homicide took place." Jacinda gestured with her iPad. "We should proceed on the expectation that it was the primary target since he had a box in mind. That's assuming our star witness...her name was Chelsea?"

Emma nodded. "Chelsea Terrence. Her mother's name was Trisha."

"Assuming Chelsea was correct about what she saw, our perpetrator had a goal in mind. He knew about something being kept in one of the boxes. It may not sound like much, but that narrows the scope of our search."

"We track down anyone connected to it," Emma sighed, "and until then we learn what we can from the scene here."

She glanced around the relatively small space of the bank before her eyes landed on the door. "We think our guy came in the front soon after opening, headed up to the counter to get what money he could, and then herded everyone back to the vault. That about the size of things?"

"So far." Jacinda frowned. "Our tech team is down to two people, so processing the scene isn't going quickly. They're in the vault now, and I'll let you know what they find. For now, let's focus on separate assignments. According to the local PD, a similar robbery occurred at a car dealership a few miles away. This was Saturday morning at a place called Crazy Barry's Car Emporium."

"What makes it similar? Banks and car dealerships aren't exactly birds of a feather."

That earned Emma a chuckle from Jacinda, but the SSA returned to her usual seriousness. "The perpetrator wore the same sort of green screen mask, and the business owner was shot in the shoulder. Emma, I want you to head over there to question him. We have an agent on loan from a nearby office en route. You'll meet at the dealership."

Emma didn't love the idea of working with someone she didn't know when a killer was on the loose, but she nodded at the SSA without arguing. At the very least, this meant she wouldn't be paired with Leo, which meant she could avoid more awkward questions.

"Leo," Jacinda pointed back toward Addison Wright, "question the witness still on scene. He's slowly pulling himself together. We need to find out who owns that security deposit box. ASAP. Mia, you're in charge of reviewing the bank footage...all security cameras...as well as Chelsea's phone."

Emma passed Mia the evidence bag containing the smartphone, thankful she'd remembered to get Chelsea Terrence's security code before letting the girl disappear in her ambulance. Anything to save time. "Code's ten nineteen."

"Mia," Jacinda swept a hand around her, "I also need you to cover for me as the team's liaison with the locals whenever I'm out of the building. I'll be coordinating the crime scene processing while also getting back out to where the truck was spotted. We have a couple tire impressions to collect in case they'll add anything of use, and based on what Leo and Emma told us of their vehicular aptitude, I don't want to trust the cops to collect the right impressions without supervision. With my luck, they'll have me looking for my own vehicle."

Mia nodded. "Yes, ma'am."

"When I get back," Jacinda continued, shutting down her iPad, "I'll coordinate removal of Trisha Terrence's body. Hopefully, the techs will be done by then. Emma, I understand you know the agent you'll be meeting."

"I do?"

"He's coming in from Richmond BAU. Keaton Holland?"

Finally, some good news. Having an old friend instead of a stranger at my side? Hell, yes.

"Keaton and I go way back," Emma nodded, barely holding in an inappropriate grin, "and I know he'll be a great asset on the case. Profiling is second nature for him."

Jacinda sighed. "Let's hope so. We can use all the help we can get with the rest of our team out sick. Which reminds me…" she turned her gaze around the group, scowling, "don't any of the rest of you catch this damn flu."

"Aye-aye, Boss." Leo gave a short salute and raised an eyebrow, waiting for their official dismissal.

Jacinda waved her hands in the air, giving her blessing. "You have your assignments. Let's get this guy before he hits another bank."

6

Mia sat forward at the desk, scrolling through the camera footage. She did her best to examine every detail, not simply to stare at the robber in his odd green mask. The disguise was weirdly effective. The mask's color, combined with the wearer's tendency to face away from any camera, made it hard to imagine any facial features. A ski mask would have at least given them eye color and the shape of his mouth to go on.

This guy is entirely featureless.

But tall. This guy is really tall. And creepy.

Freezing the view on the monitor, Mia zeroed in on Chelsea Terrence and their perpetrator, trying to get an idea of height against the glass running above the teller windows. She switched to a camera view that captured the bank entrance and scrolled through until she spotted the perpetrator entering the building. Based on the measuring tapes alongside the bank doors, he was a solid six two.

Unfortunately, that wasn't enough for an identification all by itself.

The outside security cameras showed nothing more than the man pulling into the lot and getting out of his truck, which remained running throughout the robbery. Placed as they were, the cameras didn't catch which direction he'd come from—presumably the same direction he'd fled in—or his license plate. He'd approached from an angle, and parked in a position that ensured his plate would be obscured by landscaping.

If he's trying to hide the plates, maybe they're real. That gives us a chance at catching this jerk.

Switching to the inside camera feed, Mia watched as the robber stuck his gun into the elderly security guard's back, prodding him forward behind the mother and daughter. The poor man was probably just trying to supplement his retirement and had nearly died in the process. Mia thought she could actually see the skinny guy trembling where he held onto Chelsea Terrence's shoulders.

Mia found herself shivering at the memory of how Emma had talked about the man cutting it off before killing her. Whoever this man was, he had a screw loose, and she couldn't help being glad the preteen had worn a pixie cut. Her short hair might have saved her life today.

On screen, the robber got creepily close to Chelsea and then her mom. He even petted Trisha's long dark hair.

The view on the wounded and bloody teller was pretty good from one of the cameras. Mia could just see when Vivian Marx shifted and hit a panic button beneath the counter with her foot. This happened after the robber and the four innocent victims had disappeared into the hallway.

We're lucky he didn't kill her. If he had, who knows how long it would have taken us to get here?

The bank had no security camera in the vault, which Mia found odd, given what the room was used for. But it was a small bank, reasonably distant from nearby highways, so this was probably the most activity that vault had seen in decades.

Mia's only resource for the rest of the robbery was Chelsea's camera. She hesitated before hooking it up to a monitor that allowed her to enlarge the footage. The last thing she wanted to see was a mother being killed in front of her own child, but from what Emma had said, the camera was mostly aimed at the ceiling. Taking a breath, Mia hit play.

Initially, she only had a view of Chelsea's shoes and the underside of her legs. Then the view rotated to show the robber at the center table, holding a gun to the manager's head as he moved the contents of a deposit box into his duffel bag.

Mia backed up the footage and watched on half speed, trying to make out what was being taken from the box. Flat, flexible items, less than an inch thick. Manila envelopes, or notebooks, maybe? She couldn't tell, but those were her best guesses.

And then there was the flash of a hand and a whirling chaos of nothing as the phone flew through the air before it hit the ground.

Turning the sound up, she got only muffled white noise along with reverberations from unintelligible commands. She guessed the phone must have landed near a vent when the mom had thrown it and caught airflow more than anything useful.

The robber's hand entered the view. His sleeve had ridden up slightly, showing the blur of a tattoo before his hand left the screen again. Muffled words and louder pleas overtook the recording, nothing showing in the phone's view for a full two or three minutes. Thinking back to what Emma had reported, Mia could guess what was happening.

The man was taking out a knife, stealing Trisha

Terrence's hair, and then finishing up emptying out that safety deposit box.

Thinking of the shell-shocked girl she'd seen in the security cam footage, Mia fought down a snarl of anger at their perpetrator and waited for what she knew was coming. Before that, though, the girl nearly broke Mia's heart open with her cracked-voice *I love yous*...all the more because it made something else absolutely clear. The girl had seen her mom's death coming and maybe thought she was about to die as well.

The man we're hunting is a monster.

Despite knowing it would be coming, the sudden, violent report of the gunshot startled Mia. She jumped in her seat, her heartbeat pounding with alarm as screams overtook the roar of the weapon. The rapid thump of footsteps and a slamming door were quickly replaced by the sobs filtering into the camera feed.

Mia held in a sob of her own as she stared at the ceiling tiles on the monitor.

She switched back to the camera feed showing the still-running pickup truck outside the bank. The man exited, climbed into the vehicle, and bugged out. With a surprising amount of calm, though, for a guy who'd just shot two people and stolen who knew what.

He's done this before. Or something like it.

Barely a second later, the flashing of blue-and-red light swirling across the parking lot verified that cops had seen him leaving and had taken up the chase. An ambulance pulled in mere seconds later, along with more police cars.

Grimacing at how near a thing the timing had been, Mia turned her focus back to the cell phone footage, but a knock straightened her up in her seat before she could review it once more.

Leo leaned against the doorframe behind her, his coat folded over his arm. "You find anything?"

She stretched her shoulders and wiped at her eyes, glancing back at the stilled monitors before answering. "Not much. I'd say the guy was calm...too calm not to have done this before. I confirmed the presence of a tattoo, but it's a good thing Chelsea caught the numbers. The video isn't great. You?"

"Not much. Our bank manager, Addison Wright, kept his head on straight, but with that mask...?" Leo shrugged and folded himself into the seat next to Mia, raking one hand through his curls. "He did say that what the robber grabbed from the box looked like nothing more than notebooks, whatever that gives us. I'm waiting on him to get us the name of the box's owner. We should have it soon. Meanwhile, the license plate traces back to one reported stolen weeks ago, so that's no more help than we guessed it would be."

"Huh. When he pulled up, it looks like he went right to a place where the plate couldn't be seen by the exterior cameras, and his route into the lot looks planned as well. He knew where the cameras were."

"He was planning this for a while, then, or at least had enough foreknowledge of the bank's security to devise a quick in and out with minimal chance of being identified. We should review surveillance footage over the last couple weeks at least."

"This much planning for a bunch of notebooks?"

"That's what Wright says."

Mia disconnected Chelsea's phone from the monitor and tucked it back into the evidence bag. They'd transfer the footage to an Agency computer back at the office, but she doubted there'd be anything else useful on it unless computer forensics could decipher more from the sound.

"Hey, you mind if I ask you something?"

Mia stopped what she was doing and turned back to focus on Leo. His eyes were on hers, unflinching. "Yeah, of course. What's wrong?"

His smile came out smaller than usual, less self-assured as he leaned forward and lowered his voice. "Have you ever noticed anything strange about Emma's behavior? Like... maybe seeming to, uh, see things? Talk to...herself?"

Shit.

He didn't mean "herself" at all. *He's seen her talking to thin air. To ghosts. So much for her being careful.*

Mia forced a small laugh. "Our Emma? What's not strange? Have you met her?"

Her colleague's smile still didn't reach his eyes. "Come on. Don't avoid the question."

"Emma's Emma." Mia turned her focus back to storing away the cell phone and then rewinding the cameras so she could review them one more time. No way was she going to gossip about Emma with Leo, no matter how well-intentioned the man might be.

But if she was slipping up and letting Leo see her interact with the Other...that didn't bode well for how she was doing. *Dammit.*

Mia settled herself with a deep breath, then another. "Emma's secrets are hers to share. If she's going through something...and I'm not saying she is...then you have to talk to her about it."

Leo huffed a sigh. "I'm worried about her."

You and me both.

But Mia couldn't say that. Not without risking the conversation going way past what was acceptable here and now, without Emma present and with a bank-robbing killer to catch.

"But listen." Leo took a seat beside Mia, making the

plastic creak and drawing her gaze back to him. "I want you both to know I'm here for you. And whatever's going on with Emma, I'm glad to help you find out what happened with your brother."

Mia's throat tightened, an image of Ned's smiling face flashing into her mind. Before she could stop herself, she answered him. "We thought he died in a car accident...until recently."

Leo nodded. "I couldn't help overhearing you and Emma talking about him. I'm so sorry. And I know...I mean, I've lost people. I can't imagine how you must be feeling, trying to process that the car wreck wasn't what you thought. I want to help."

Rather than trying to reply, Mia gripped Leo's forearm. He was a smart agent, and they could use his help. She trusted him to help, now that he'd made the offer.

"Thank—"

"Agents." Addison Wright appeared in the doorway and held a sticky note out to them. "The owner of the safety deposit box is a man named George 'Georgie' Treadway. I've written down his contact information for you here, but you'll...I'm afraid you'll need a warrant to search customer records."

"Great. That's great, Mr. Wright." Leo couldn't seem to hold in his frustration. "We'll just hop on down to the local courthouse and get a judge to put a rush on that warrant."

Mia had her phone out and was searching for the name they'd been given. "Let's see if Georgie has any public records first."

She got their answer in a few minutes, and it wasn't one that put her at ease.

"Looks like Mr. Treadway shouldn't be hard to find after all."

Leo glanced at her phone. "You're kidding. He's in prison?"

"Yep. We know who our bank-robbing killer *isn't*. But maybe this Georgie knows who he is."

7

Emma parked on the street, settling in to pass the time across from Crazy Barry's Car Emporium. Three rumpled salespeople hung around the entrance, standing on the concrete curb that ringed the building like vultures waiting for carrion. She had no desire to entertain their pitches while waiting for Keaton.

When her old partner did pull into the lot in a plain black fleet sedan, she sat still for a few seconds more and watched one of the salespeople stumble off his perch by the door, nearly tripping over his own feet to reach him.

Keaton looked the same as ever. Smartly dressed in a black suit that hugged his slim frame even though it was likely right off the rack. His pale skin practically glowed in the sunlight.

She grinned as she got out of the Expedition, enjoying the view of him patiently sitting through the salesperson's pitch before pulling out his identification and stopping the man in his tracks.

Anybody with her and Keaton's training could spot a

scam a mile away, and this place screamed, *Come let us take advantage of you. We'll make you think you got a deal!*

"Well, look who I've gotta deal with this week." Emma stopped a foot away and smirked, curbing the urge to hug her best friend in greeting since they were in full view of a bunch of smarmy car salespeople. "You made good time."

Keaton pointed to his vehicle. "Guess they told you I was coming? And here I was hoping to surprise you."

"SSA Hollingsworth isn't really one for surprises. Shall we?"

He grinned brightly, gesturing for her to lead the way as he shoved a wave of hair behind his ear. "Looks like D.C. just can't function without me, huh?"

Emma's step faltered, but she laughed off the quip and kept going. No need to tell him the VCU had been functioning better than ever, at least to her way of thinking. She'd missed him desperately after he'd left, but lately...lately, she was doing okay. In a manner of speaking. If you discounted the whole Other thing.

"Shit."

Emma glanced behind her to see Keaton hopping on one foot, using a tissue to slap mud off what looked to be a very expensive loafer. "Step in something?"

His nose crinkled with annoyance as he made a show of walking around the puddle of sludge he must have stepped in. Funny how she'd forgotten that about him. How he could let little things get to him and was just generally clumsy.

She nudged his elbow as he came alongside her. "Need me to clean your shoes, bestie?"

"Ha." He straightened his coat, but then his signature smile came back. "You know me—"

"Always wanting to be the center of attention." Her joke didn't quite land.

Was it really only a few weeks ago when I last saw him? Why does this feel awkward?

Nonetheless, Emma forced a laugh and turned back to the entrance to the car emporium, where the small group of salespeople were eyeing them as if they were vermin.

So what if she and Keaton weren't quite as simpatico as they'd been when working together every day, like she was with Leo now? They'd get back on track soon enough. For now, it was time to get to work.

Inside the glass entrance, the man who'd initially spoken to Keaton gestured them past a couple of souped-up muscle cars. At the edge of the space, a large glassed-in office sat partially obstructed with a cheesy cardboard standee showing a picture-perfect family throwing cash in the air. Below their image, a greased-up salesman looked on approvingly beside a gleaming sedan.

The model for the salesman's photo apparently owned the place. Emma caught his eye through his office windows, where he sat behind an oversize desk. One arm lay across his middle, cradled in a sling. The other held a cell phone that he waved around as he carried out a conversation on speaker.

When Keaton knocked on the door, the man took a few long seconds to end his call and put down the phone before waving them in. His attention fell on Keaton first. "You here about the guy who shot me? Took long enough for things to escalate."

"Barry Meldrum?" Emma shut the door carefully behind them, wishing she could leave it open and forget about privacy. The smell of cigar smoke hung thick in the office, probably from years of soaking into the cheap rug and institutional office chairs.

"That's right." The man used his left hand to gesture to the sling holding his right, but his grin had gotten a little toothier when refocusing from Keaton to Emma. "I survived a gunshot just so I could meet you, pretty lady. What's your name?"

Keaton coughed behind his hand as he perched on the seat closer to the door, forcing Emma to walk deeper into the office.

"Special Agent Emma Last, Mr. Meldrum. And this is my colleague, Special Agent Keaton Holland. And yes, we're here to talk about the man who robbed your business and shot you." Emma waited for the man to say something, but he seemed content to leer at her. *Talk about creeper vibes.* "Would you mind telling us about the incident?"

"Well, sure." He leaned back, making a show of adjusting his sling. "And then maybe we can talk about brand-new cars for you folks?" He focused all his attention on Keaton now. "That, uh…very fine vehicle you have outside looks like it's seen the backside of its glory days. Why don't you let me show you something more your style? I'm seeing you in something like a…a Jetta? Maybe an Integra. Yeah, a little sporty. Good around curves."

Keaton adjusted himself in his seat, pulling out a notebook. "Maybe another day. And you'd have to talk to the taxpayers first."

"Huh?"

"I'm driving a government vehicle, Mr. Meldrum. It's not for sale or trade, and no, I'm not interested in any lease options you may have to offer me."

Meldrum's gaze swiveled to Emma, one eyebrow raising to meet his greasy hairline. "Well, Emma, I bet you—"

"Agent Last," Keaton interrupted him, "asked you a question. Sir."

Emma shot Keaton a quick glance. What ever happened to his policy of attracting flies with honey? If this dirtbag wanted to flirt with her, she could pretend to go along for the ride as long as it got them answers.

But Keaton's expression was flat and annoyed—totally without nuance—as if he'd completely forgotten that Emma knew how to handle herself. So much for them falling into their old pattern together, even if this was just his big brother mode kicking in. She'd have to get used to that if it came up again.

"Sure, sure." Meldrum sat straighter, a little sneer on his lips as he eyed Keaton and then turned back to Emma. "I'm glad to go over it all again…for you. You two are just lucky to find me at work. This being my first day back and all."

Emma forced a smile. "Let's take advantage of that luck, then, shall we? Tell us about what happened?"

"Well, we were hosting our Pre-Presidents' Day Sale. Big deal around here." Meldrum plucked a flyer from the side of his desk and slid it toward Keaton, fast enough that the page slid off the edge and fell into his lap. "We offer the best deals around, buying used cars for cash, so I started the day with about a hundred and sixty grand sitting in our safe."

"And the robber came in…when?" Emma prodded, resting her notebook on her knee.

"Came in soon after opening, Saturday morning. Wearing a weird green mask. Man drove a blue pickup truck onto the lot, pushed his way into the office—"

"I'm sorry," Emma leaned forward, one hand up, "you said he drove a blue truck? Are you sure?"

Meldrum's eyes narrowed at her. "You see what kind of business I run? 'Course I'm sure. Thing was an older model, early seventies. Made more noise 'n anything I'd have on my lot. All souped up, like you'd want to do if you were gonna drag race or shit. Manual, too, so I'd never sell it."

Keaton glanced her way.

She shrugged him off. "You know he was driving a manual how?"

"I watched the guy drive in here. Could tell he was

shifting manual from the way he jerked his shoulder. Plus the sound of the transmission." He patted his sling. "When did his drivetrain become more important than me getting robbed and shot?"

"Everything's important." Emma sighed. "Please go on."

"Well, like I was saying, he pushed his way in here." The man gestured toward where the salespeople still loitered near the front door. "Demanded we give him the whole take in the safe. Locked my guys in the storage room and followed me back there. Forced me to put the money in the bag and watched me the whole damn time to make sure he got all of it. And then? Then that fucker told me to keep my hands to myself and shot me anyway!"

Meldrum sat back in his seat, a mix of injured pride and frustration radiating from him.

Keaton slipped the flyer back onto the man's desk. "And then?"

"And then? Hell if I know." The salesman grunted and closed his eyes for a long second before refocusing on Emma. "Gunshot hurt like a bi...like a...well, it hurt. I heard the guy's engine revving, so I figured he was taking off. He shifted like a race car driver, ya know? Didn't even let up on the gas and burned up the asphalt, squealing out of my lot."

"What did you do then?"

"I crawled into the front office and called nine-one-one."

Emma was about to stand when the man leaned forward, staring at her.

"You talk to Davy yet?"

Emma froze in her chair. "Uh...Davy? And who's that?"

"Who's that?" Meldrum spluttered, glancing between her and Keaton. "Those damn worthless cops didn't even take me seriously? You mean they came to my hospital room and questioned me and then they didn't even check into their main lead?"

Keaton sat forward, one hand on the edge of the desk. "Well, we're here now. Who's Davy?"

Meldrum went to cross his arms over his chest, wincing when the sling reminded him that that was a bad idea. He sat back in his chair again. This time, he finally focused on Keaton when he answered.

"Davy is Davy Delko. An *ex*-employee of mine. Tall-ass motorhead who's half-baked most of the time. I caught him stealing vehicle parts from our auto repair shop...oh hell, must've been three months back. Kind of stuff he'd use to build big, fast engines on the side. And whatever the hell he wanted to do on his own time was fine, but when he started stealing from me and trying to do business on my lot, that was another thing. I always knew he had a side hustle selling parts, but I didn't know he was getting some of 'em from me."

"Can you give me an address for this Mr. Delko?"

"Yeah, yeah, sure. Guy lives by the junkyard out near that strip joint. You know the one?" Meldrum peered at Emma over the folder he'd begun hunting through.

She didn't smile. "No."

"Well, I bet your partner here does."

Keaton shifted in his seat but didn't acknowledge the comment, so that was something. Leo might have opened his coat to reveal the sidearm on his hip.

Finally, Meldrum jotted down an address and passed it across to her. Emma gave it a fast once-over to make sure she could read the writing. "And you recognized his voice?"

"Well...no." Meldrum grimaced, running his good hand along his expensive desk. "But he could've disguised it. People got all sorts of technology now. I wouldn't put it past him. Plus, he hasn't shown up since the robbery. You tell me...what kind of man doesn't show up to check on an old employer when he hears he's been shot?"

I guess that depends on the employer.

Keaton stood up from his chair, not bothering to reach out and shake the man's hand. "We'll look into it, Mr. Meldrum. Thanks for your time."

Emma stood up even as Keaton was pulling open the door. She still took an extra second to smile and nod a goodbye at the man behind the desk. Slimeball or not, he was a victim they might need to talk to later.

And in the meantime, she might just have to remind Keaton she could take care of herself.

You get flies with honey, Emma girl. Better remind your new old partner of that bit of the equation also.

8

Emma climbed into the passenger seat of Keaton's fleet sedan, rubbing the chill from her hands. Without waiting for him to turn over the engine, she dialed Jacinda.

"SSA Hollingsworth a good boss so far?" Keaton settled back into his seat, leaving the car in park since they'd have to drive separately when they left. "Or getting better since she called me in?"

"Ha. She's been—"

"Hi, Emma. Keaton and you meet up okay?" Jacinda's voice was loud in the space of the small car, and Emma cut off a chuckle as she turned her volume down.

"You got us both here, Jacinda. We just interviewed Barry Meldrum. He gave us the name of an ex-employee. David 'Davy' Delko." Emma spelled his name, filling Jacinda in on everything Meldrum had said. "Meldrum's a character. He says he gave Delko's name to the cops, but it's hard to tell what he remembers while he was hopped up on pain meds in the hospital."

Jacinda consulted with someone on her end, and then a sigh came through the speaker. "I checked the report.

Meldrum couldn't remember a last name while he was in the hospital. He just ranted about a pothead. They were going to follow up with him this week."

Keaton shook his head and mouthed, *Figures*.

"So updates for you..." Jacinda's voice trailed off as a car engine revved in the background. "Sorry, I'm outside. Okay, so we got the tire impressions to forensics. They're running them through the database. Mia and Leo will interview the owner of the safe deposit box. It was associated with a Georgie Treadway, who, get this, is a felon who's been in jail for the last six months. Any guesses about what he's in for?"

"We're not going to like this, are we?"

"Oh, you might. Bank robbery."

"No kidding?" Emma rolled her eyes at Keaton, feeling for a moment like it was old times between them when she saw he was doing the same.

"No kidding. Meanwhile, I'll work on getting you that address for Delko. Why don't the two of you take an early lunch and get to work on a suspect profile?"

"Sounds good to me." Emma thumbed her phone off as Keaton buckled his seat belt.

"So lunch?"

She opened the door with a smile. "Yes, Keaton. Lunch. I'll let you choose where, seeing as how you've been out of D.C. for a while, but let me guess...the Paul Revere Diner?"

He grinned. "You know me too well, Emma Last. And hey, it's close by, right? What else could we do?"

A minute later, Emma was relaxing into her Expedition's seat, letting Keaton pull into traffic ahead of her so she could follow. So much about working with him felt familiar. Just like she knew it would feel with Keaton sitting across from her and gorging on a chicken parm sub, probably splattering marinara sauce all over the table as he did.

Yet...today, she couldn't see their conversation going anywhere but around the same old circuits.

Back when they'd last seen each other only weeks ago, she'd wanted desperately to unburden herself to him, to tell him everything she knew about the Other. But now that idea hit a wall inside her.

More than that, she actually wanted to talk to Leo about it. Now her chest ached a bit with the realization that even though Keaton was supposedly her best friend, she didn't have that same urge to confess to him. Not like she had with Mia and like she wished she could do with Leo.

Whatever that meant, though, she'd have to think about it later.

Despite the coffee, which bordered on being undrinkable, the Paul Revere Diner had been their go-to lunch spot whenever they'd been nearby.

Emma slid into one side of a beige booth and ran her gaze over the menu while Keaton traded pleasantries with the owner, who'd hurried out upon seeing him. Everyone loved Keaton, just like everyone loved Leo. But this was Keaton's home turf.

She offered him the menu, but he waved it off. "Chicken parm sub, I assume?"

He closed his eyes and gave a chef's kiss gesture. "You?"

The server was already standing by with a grin, so Emma made a quick decision. "I'll have the Cuban and fries. And bring my friend here some extra napkins, would you?"

She jotted the order down and glanced between them. "Waters?"

"Please," they said together. Emma tucked the menu back to the side of the table, smiling at Keaton as she did. "Okay, before work, fill me in on whatever I've missed. How's your sister doing?"

"She's good. The Richmond PD's treating her well, and I think she's adjusting just fine."

"With you there to help." Emma probably wouldn't have been able to keep a bit of bitterness out of the comment a few months before, but Keaton's move was old news now. And she had to respect that he'd wanted to transfer to offer his sister support as she started a new job. "And how are you doing with it? Her being on the street and all?"

He frowned, and that usual little line appeared on his forehead, marring his otherwise perfect skin. "I'm...getting used to it. Hard not to worry about her patrolling at night, or any time really. Richmond's not exactly small-town America where the worst thing to worry about is bar fights and shoplifting."

Scoffing, Emma sucked down some of the water that had just showed up. "You do remember that the last few towns I've visited have hosted axe murderers and arsonists, right?"

"Touché, touché."

Much as he looked abashed at the reminder, though, Emma couldn't imagine how he would've felt if his kid sister were chasing down criminals like the ones they faced in their line of work. The way he worried about her was classic, textbook big brother, and almost made her wish she had someone nervous about her safety. Not posturing and protecting her from idiots like that Barry Meldrum...just worrying. A little bit.

She fought down the wish, moving on. "And how about Sarah?"

Keaton blushed, almost spitting out his water, and Emma hid a grin. "You...uh...mean Autumn's sister?"

"Yes, Autumn's sister." Emma rolled her eyes. "You know, the bartender you spent half the night watching the last time I visited you in Richmond?"

"I...uh...go to her bar sometimes."

Before she could tease him further, their food showed up, and Keaton made a show of taking a gigantic bite of his sandwich. True to form, the marinara sauce dripped down his fingers and splattered well beyond the confines of his plate. He'd taken his coat off before eating, though, and managed not to make a mess of himself as he dug in.

Emma ate slower, noticing the little differences in how she felt about her best friend. On one hand, Keaton was so familiar, making the same noises and mess as he ate. But she'd forgotten what it was like to be on a case with him. He could be all business one minute, and then perfectly at ease the next.

Unlike Leo. Leo always seemed...well, a little bit haunted when they were on a case. Like the job never quite left his mind, no matter the food or the friends or the banter going on around him.

More like me on a case.

Emma thought back to their perpetrator's driving and his brazen behavior in general. "We had him in our sights for the blink of an eye this morning, and he reversed toward me and Leo like it was a game of chicken."

Raising an eyebrow, Keaton swallowed a bite. "Leo? That your new partner?"

"Yep. I promise you'll meet him later." Emma's promise felt awkward, even to her, and she rushed past it. "Based on that driving, though...which came after he buzzed through a field in his overcharged pickup...I'd say we're looking at someone with a rural upbringing. He'd have needed space to practice driving maneuvers like that without getting hauled in by the cops every other day."

"And you said it was an F-250, souped up. Older model or newer?"

"Older, Leo said. I trust him on that, though I'm no

expert. And, not that I'd consider Barry Meldrum all that reliable when it came to most things, but…"

Keaton nodded and finished the thought for her. "Cars are his business. He said it was an older model he saw the man driving on Saturday morning. That fits with him driving one today, too, different color or not."

He took a bite, chewing as he thought, and Emma gave him space. Keaton's aptitude for profiling had already earned him high praise with the Richmond BAU.

Might as well let him have room to run.

"Older model probably means we have an older driver. Manual transmission would suggest that as well. Let's say he's over forty, since favoring an older model like that would mean he's used to that style. Younger drivers mostly drive automatics. And he must have multiple vehicles since we've seen at least two different colors on the trucks. Or he's stealing them. But how many older model trucks are still on the road around here?"

"Or it's the same truck, and he has the space to paint it and repaint it as needed."

"That seems kind of far-fetched, but you could be right."

Emma jotted the ideas down in shorthand then scribbled *40+* into her notebook, just below where she'd written the tattoo number Chelsea had given her. "This is the tattoo Chelsea Terrence caught sight of during the robbery this morning, just above his wrist. In the video we got, which wasn't great, it looked messy. He took the contents of a box registered to someone doing time, so we're probably looking at a prison tat."

Keaton stared at the numbers. "If it's an important date… maybe a wedding day? Day he lost someone? Or the day he entered or was due to get out of prison, if you're right about it being something he had done inside."

Emma stared at the number. "Backs up the idea that he's older, if that date is relevant to a prison stint."

Keaton stuffed a few fries into his mouth, frowning at the notebook. "And then you've got the violence. He shoots Meldrum after saying 'keep your hands to yourself,' whatever that means. Meldrum didn't lay a finger on him."

"Unless he conveniently left that part out."

"Point to you, Agent Last." He made a downstroke in the air with a forefinger. "And that would match up with the women he shot this morning. They both *disobeyed* him or upset him in some way. He either meant to kill them or didn't care if he did."

"Comfortable with violence." Emma's Cuban turned a little in her stomach as she thought back to the shell-shocked preteen she'd met that morning and the blood on the bank floor. "Definitely another sign he's done time. Real time, for real crimes."

Keaton licked the sauce from his lips, eyeing the remains of his sandwich. "The food is just too damn good here." He took another bite before looking back at Emma. "And then you've got the fact that he wanted access to a prison felon's safety deposit box and had the key for it. It'll be interesting to find out how old our guy on the inside is, but either way, that key didn't come to him by happenstance."

Emma sighed, sitting back in the bench seat and shifting her plate toward her friend so he could finish off her fries. She'd lost the rest of her appetite. "I still feel like we're missing some big pieces here. He's picking and choosing who he's killing whether it bothers him or not. He didn't shoot all the witnesses…just the car dealer, the bank teller, and Trisha. He left those other salespeople alive, along with Chelsea, the guard, and the bank manager today."

Keaton shrugged—again making Emma consider how

casual he was right now, even given what they were talking about. Leo would've been radiating focus.

"So figure the dealer and the teller got shot for resisting." Emma tapped her still-wrapped straw against the side of her water glass. "Barry said he did just what the guy told him, but who knows if that's entirely true? If nothing else, he was probably talking back, griping about what was happening."

Keaton swiped another fry through a drop of marinara. "I'd take that bet, given what we saw of Meldrum today. And the teller added booby-trapped packs even though he told her not to. He shot with reason, not without."

"I don't know about Trisha Terrence, though."

Keaton quirked an eyebrow in question.

"The mom, Keaton. He stole her hair, but Chelsea didn't say anything about her resisting. She got in his face a little right before he shot her, but the girl said it sounded like her mom was begging him to just leave. If anything, she was more compliant than her daughter. She saw the girl trying to record with her phone and tore it out of her hands. She threw it across the vault."

As Keaton waved for the bill, his eyes went a little glassy in thought. "Okay, so…assuming he knew the phone was the daughter's and not the mom's, maybe he was punishing the daughter by killing her mom in front of her? Or he was punishing the mother because he thought the phone belonged to her? None of our other victims had family members or loved ones close by, so this was his only opportunity to punish someone by killing a loved one."

"That's dark." Emma sipped from her water, not bothering to argue as Keaton made a grab for the bill and began fishing out his wallet. She knew him too well to waste time on that argument. "How about…how about if it was something about Chelsea? As in, something about her kept him from shooting her, either in addition to her mom or separately. Plenty of cold-blooded killers out there wouldn't balk at killing a kid. The teller he shot today was young, mid-twenties."

"And she's also survived so far, but it may be that he didn't intend that."

"Or, if he did, maybe it's because he can't bring himself to kill a kid, or someone young enough to basically be a kid in his eyes. He'll punish them if he has to, but he won't kill them."

"He might have a soft spot for children, or even have children of his own. Maybe a daughter, maybe not. Maybe someone Chelsea's age, but I don't think we could guess that far. I feel like we're spitballing here, and it may be getting us further from the truth. We could just be dealing with a guy who knows how to drive and likes to watch the world burn."

Emma thought back to the ghost of a father she'd seen on her last case, defending his bomb-triggering daughter even after death. Parenthood's bonds meant something.

"Something tells me there's a child involved. Maybe not his, but somewhere close to him, there's a kid he wants to protect. Bank robbers are usually people who act from desperation these days. What if he has a kid who needs money for college, or a new car, or...the hair."

Keaton's eyes went wide. "What did he say to Chelsea's mother? Somebody else will 'get better use out of it,' right?"

She'd already added the line to her notebook. "I mean, you're right, we're spitballing. But somebody who needs hair...it could be a child battling leukemia or another form of cancer."

"We'll have to check every hospital's cancer ward for anyone with a parent who's done time. I can only imagine how easy that's going to be."

"HIPAA allows it, but it'll take a lot of time. We also have to consider the amount of money taken."

Emma's phone buzzed, and she glanced down at it absently. "We have Davy Delko's address. But the money. What're your thoughts there?"

"Our perpetrator got a hundred and sixty thousand dollars on Saturday." Keaton sipped down some water, frowning. "That's a big haul. And then he turns around and robs a bank today?"

Emma nodded, her own mind on the exact same question. "Why's he pushing so hard, so fast? There's desperate, and then there's this guy."

"Too fast for casual stockpiling. You may be onto something with the kid angle. We'd have to look up costs for cancer treatments to know if we're on the right track there."

"Or he's just grabbing everything he can because he's frantic for his kid's health."

Keaton conceded the point with a second downstroke through the air. "Or he has another reason for needing a ton of cash and fast." Keaton tapped his fingers along the side of the table. "You thinking what I'm thinking?"

Emma swallowed but was forced to nod. One of two things was about to happen. Either their guy was about to disappear, or he was already making plans to hit another location, which meant the clock was ticking down.

9

"Nice and easy does it. Nice and easy."

The glossy paint went on in a smooth grassy green across the unmarred metal. I'd washed the trucks just that morning, and they'd soon look brand-new. Brand-new to anyone who looked, including stoplight cameras, federal agents, and the average idiot witness.

With the first coat already dried, this second coat was turning out to be a gorgeous spill of green that mirrored the *go, go, go* of the green light that had been pushing me on that morning. My blood still buzzed from that damn chase, but I'd gotten the best of 'em.

Just like old times.

I filled in the green downward across the driver's side door. My second truck stared at me from across the garage, its first coat still drying. The sight of these two beauties side by side lit up my insides. Love might have been the thing driving me on, but I'd missed *this*. Working on trucks, and better still, playing games with the Feds on the open road with fresh paint jobs and phony license plates.

"Back to business, baby. Just like old times."

That's what I was working on telling myself, at least. No one's body made it over four decades without showing time, let alone six. I'd done my best to stay in shape over the years, but exercising in a cell, and sometimes a yard, only did so much. The muscles I'd retained as a kid were long gone, as was the six-pack I'd once shown off to Mary Karen.

Now, I might not have extra weight, but I didn't have the strength or the full head of hair either. Hell, my hand strength wasn't even what it had once been, given how I kept on taking breaks with the damn spray nozzle.

But what I did have, in spades, was my old driving know-how.

Sure, after forty-five years in the joint, I'd figured I had some rust to shake off, even if I didn't admit it to Mary Karen. No point in worrying her.

Those cops had been as turned around as a two-headed dog with one wagging tail, and the Feds hadn't been a damn sight better.

Maybe I'd give the one Fed some credit for their driving...but credit didn't translate to handcuffs on my wrists.

Another panel done, I moved on to the large side panel, eyeing the roof to make sure it wasn't dripping anywhere. It was perfect. This truck would be as professional in appearance as anything else on the road once I drove her out of our garage.

No more candy apple red. It's green for go from here on out.

Thinking of all the green lights ahead, my throat just about clogged up with paint fumes, mask or no mask. The exhilaration of this morning went beyond all my wildest dreams in that cell all those years. I'd been itching for a gas pedal and some long stretches of asphalt.

Even now, the gasoline practically pumped in my veins, my instincts and reflexes as fired up as ever. Every sweet

turn of those wheels, every little twitch of the transmission—
I could feel them swimming in my future.

Our future, for as long as I had my Mary Karen.

"Throttle might as well have been an extension of my
arm, baby." I couldn't stop picturing all those cop cars piled
up behind me as I'd hightailed it off the main road, leaving
even the Feds in the dust. Literally.

Behind bars, surviving, I'd almost forgotten what it felt
like to *live*. But no more. We were in the homestretch now.

Once I got this second coat finished on the trucks, my
workbench'd be waiting for me with the contents of
Georgie's safety deposit box laid out just for us. That idiot
had done so much of my work for me, I owed him a helluva
lot more than the small cut he'd negotiated. Not that he'd be
getting even that.

"Thank you, Georgie boy." I grinned, thinking of all
those meticulous notes. More detail than I'd ever drummed
up for my own hits in previous years, that was for sure.
And considering how things had changed when it came to
security cameras and features—going all high-tech on me—
that kid in the joint had done me and Mary Karen a real
solid.

We had the layout and security features of six different
banks...six different *targets* now. And once I cleared those
safes, it would be on to Belize, where we could live the high
life for all the time we had left together.

She deserved it. She deserved everything.

The woman had been through the wringer, doing her
own time, but it hadn't changed her in any way that mattered
to me. I still saw the bubble-gum-popping, drop-dead-
gorgeous, loud talker I'd fallen in love with when we were
kids.

The paint swept the truck's back panel, faltering in my
hand. When I thought of what Mary Karen had sacrificed for

me, I wanted to scream at the whole damn world to let up on her.

Get a grip, man.

Belize, that was our future. Living somewhere tropical like that was exactly the break she deserved, and she'd have it before the cancer killed her. If I could give her the rest of her days on some gorgeous beach, a drink in her hand and no worries in her head, then that was sure enough what I planned to do.

Living the straight and narrow life wasn't for me anyway. That had never been in the cards. And with Mary Karen losing her fight...no, there wasn't no use playing it safe. It was well past time to make a whole lot of money real fast, and then spend the rest of our days with our asses in the sand and our eyes on the horizon.

I checked my paint levels and was just about to move around to the tailgate when the garage door clicked behind me. Mary Karen's house slippers flapped on the metal of the step down a moment later. Glancing up, I caught her smoothing down her old sweater over her jeans, a hint of nerves in the movement.

That was one thing the joint had changed for her. Or maybe it had been the cancer diagnosis? Either way, she'd lost some of her old confidence. I aimed to make sure she got it back in short order, though.

"Brought you a sandwich, baby. You ready for a break?" Her smile was a little crooked today...probably the pain pills getting to her.

I bit the thought back and grinned, focusing on her pretty eyes. "You know me so well."

The sandwich and chips could wait. I set them down on the workbench beside our future fortune and turned back to her, holding out my arms just like I'd done every day since getting paroled.

Her kiss tasted like the grape soda she loved, and I lingered in it for a minute. My hands stayed firmly on her shoulders, never straying to her hair. She was too sensitive over it lately, and it'd been days since I'd seen her without a kerchief over the ratty blond wig she'd had to put up with these last few years.

But I had a fix for that.

When I pulled away, I went right for the front seat of the other truck rather than the bologna and ketchup sandwich. That'd have to wait, much as it had me salivating.

"I've got something for you. Close your eyes."

With the bag of glossy dark hair in hand, I moved right up in front of her and just gazed at her for a minute. Alopecia, and now cancer, might have kept my woman from taking pride in her own hair, but she was still as gorgeous as she'd ever been, far as I was concerned. Petite, more than a foot shorter than me, she could pass for twenty years younger than her sixty-five years.

And the cancer couldn't have her yet. Not yet. She was mine.

Mine!

"Look what I got for you." I fanned out the clear bag of hair in my hands, and her eyes went wide.

"Oh, baby, it's gorgeous. I can make a beauty of a wig from this as soon as we get settled." She opened up the bag and touched the hair, running two fingers along the strands. "The last bank?"

"All for you, baby. You like it?"

"I love it." She held it up beside her old Red Hot Chili Peppers kerchief, which hid most of her itchy blond wig, and batted her lashes at me. "What do you think? Maybe I'll do a long bob, like old times."

"Not if you want me to ever let you out of our bedroom and onto the beach."

She blushed and came in for a hug, the hair gripped tight in her hand. "Tell me about the woman who had it. Please, baby."

I thought back to that bitch of a mother. She'd done me a favor batting her kid's phone away but should've been smart enough not to let her take it out. And the woman couldn't have been much of a mother. Dragging around a daughter in public when the girl should have been home sick in bed. Letting the girl dye her damn hair blue. What kind of a parent allowed that shit?

The woman had deserved every drop of blood my bullet drained out of her. And one of these days, that girl would appreciate what I'd done for her too. Maybe she wouldn't have had blue hair if she'd had my Mary Karen as a decent mother instead of that long-haired bitch with the expensive makeup.

On some level, though, I was glad the daughter's hair hadn't been prettier. I'd have hated to hurt her.

You couldn't have hurt her, old man. Not really.

Well, maybe not. Maybe not the kid. Kids were something sacred if ever anything was, I guessed. But the mom...

"She wasn't as pretty as you." I pointed at the bag of hair, glad for the bright garage lighting showcasing the silky locks. "The woman was crabby, paying more attention to flirting with a bank manager than her own daughter. But I knew you'd love her hair."

Mary Karen stilled, hesitation clouding her eyes just a touch. "She had a daughter?"

Shit. The stuff I let slip out.

"A troublemaker." The assurance came out easy, a little white lie to help my woman sleep. "She'll grow up to be a bank robber or a movie star who never takes no for an answer. Don't you worry about her. She was practically grown."

Mary Karen took the words as I'd willed them, tension releasing from her shoulders as she hugged me. "I just wish I could be with you for the jobs." Her voice was a whisper against my chest, reminding me of that catch in her throat that she'd get when we used to run from the cops together. She'd put one hand on the dash and one hand on my shoulder, urging me along like I was her white knight at every turn.

I am your white knight. Still and always.

I thumped one fist against my chest. "You're with me where it counts."

She hugged me tighter, and I felt a little moisture wetting my t-shirt. The cancer made her more sentimental every day, just about. Me, too, maybe.

"You remember when we met, baby?" A sniff, and then that throaty whisper again... "You kept drooling over that truck at my dad's dealership. And then, when you came in to buy it with all that cash, you swept me up right along with the pink slip."

"And where'd we go?"

"Right where I wanted to." She leaned into me, fingers clenching the back of my shirt. "You asked me where I'd like to go, and I told you I wanted to go to the beach. You drove us all the way to Chesapeake Bay before I believed you meant it."

That had been a perfect day if there'd ever been one. We enjoyed the sand and the surf. And just when I thought the date was over, we stripped and went skinny-dipping beyond the public pier. Just us and the moonlight because it had been so late in the season.

And we never looked back.

Oh, how I enjoyed how she still fit against me all these years later. "Mary Karen," I leaned down and whispered, "you know you're the only person on this earth I adore."

"You old flirt." She laughed into my chest before turning her head sideways and waving at the garage wall. "Hey, which license plate you gonna use this time?"

I eyed the wide wall of them, where we had plenty to choose from. Spanning three states, vanity and government issue just the same. Mary Karen had stolen plenty of 'em for us over the years, and lately she'd been making sure they were up to date on their inspection stickers as well. Always preparing for her white knight to come back to her and pick up the cause once again. "You pick."

She hemmed and hawed but pointed at the one I'd known she would, ever since I'd caught sight of it. "Use that Virginia Is for Lovers one that's got my initials in between the numbers, would you? It'll be like I'm there with you after all."

10

Leo unholstered his gun and placed it on the prison counter as Mia signed the registry beside him. She fidgeted while the guard examined her ID, yet another instance of her acting nervous ever since they'd parked. Her customary smile had been pulled into a tight line of tension.

He leaned down beside her, keeping his voice low. "You look uncomfortable." No point in acting suspicious when walking into a place like this, even if they were legit. He handed his own identification and weapon to the grumpy guard across from them.

"It's this place." Mia stood back and gestured for him to sign in. "Kind of gives me the heebie-jeebies."

Having locked away their guns, the guard handed back their IDs with a shrug. "You're not alone, Agent Logan. This is one of the oldest federal max units in the country. They didn't build these places to feel friendly, not back then. You ever want a tour, it'll tell some stories."

Leo could agree with the guard's sentiment, but he understood where Mia was coming from just as well. This was, put simply, an uncomfortable building. Low to the ground, gray, and surrounded by domineering, obnoxiously high metal fencing, not a green leaf or tree for miles. Inside wasn't any warmer than the February air of the parking lot. "There's certainly a gravity to this place."

Mia shot him a grateful smile as the gate opened before them, and then they were in.

The guard led them down a cinder block hallway and through an open area with concrete tables that sat completely empty. "This space is close to the entrance, but while it's comparatively comfortable, we don't use it much. Mostly for guards to congregate before and after duty. No point in letting the inmates out around here when we've got other options."

Forcing a nod, Leo kept his steps even. Nearby, a guard cage housed a few men staring at video monitors. They raised hands in greeting, but barely looked up.

The whole place was oppressive. Darker than any prison Leo had ever seen.

He hoped he didn't hear any wolves howling. The same threat of violence echoed with their footsteps along the claustrophobic halls beneath caged lights.

"Dim lighting part of the psychology of this place?" Mia's voice didn't tremble, but also didn't carry the confidence it usually held. "I don't remember it being this dark in here."

"Saving on energy. This economy and all. You can see we switched to LEDs last year, but they don't seem to reach the corners like the old-fashioned bulbs did. Damn inspector was wrong about it being 'just as bright' around here. Fitting, I guess, but the lights do the trick. Not like we're running a library." The guard's voice remained flat, as if he didn't even realize how dim their surroundings were. Leo could barely see ten feet in front of them.

He stopped behind the guard as he unlocked a room. "Doesn't quite seem safe, keeping it so dark."

"Yeah, well, that's why we keep the inmates in their cells and keep the extra rooms locked. Use just the space we need for their *activities*." He opened the door wide and gestured them inside. "You need me to bring an extra light bulb? Flashlight maybe? Light a bonfire for your comfort?"

Leo flicked on the light switch and met the guard's smirk with a polite, "No, thank you," rather than something more colorful. Not that "color" would have worked in this environment anyway. The walls probably ate it for breakfast.

The room was small and dim, just what he'd expect of a maximum security prison. A small table in the center was welded to the floor, with two seats on one side for him and Mia and one seat on the other. A little bolt in the table pinned down the open cuffs waiting for their interviewee.

"I really don't remember this place being so dark." Mia adjusted herself in her seat, scowling at the small space. "Heck, I think there was even a window last time I came to question someone here."

"Hard to imagine sunlight in this room." Leo eyed the wall and then the door, fighting the urge to get up and pace. "But did you see those guards' faces? I wouldn't have put it past this place to lose the windows just to discourage any more visitors than necessary."

Footsteps in the hallway quieted them moments before Georgie Treadway stood in the doorway. The man was tiny, thin, and just over five feet tall. If that. He carried himself with a larger man's attitude, shoulders back and steps wide, but the effect was more comical than threatening.

The guard escorting Treadway nudged him in the shoulders with his baton. "Get in there, Treadway. I ain't got all day, and neither do your visitors. Show some respect for once in your life."

He grunted something that might have been a response, or maybe just indigestion, and plopped himself in the chair.

His wrists came out in front of him without a fight, and the guard cuffed him to the table before stepping back and looking at Leo and Mia.

"You need anything, I'll be right in the hall. Give a shout. Or just sit on this bug 'til he behaves."

Treadway scowled as the guard made his way out the door and closed it.

"Mr. Treadway, I'm Agent Leo Ambrose, and this is my colleague, Agent Mia Logan. We're hoping you can help us with an ongoing case."

Georgie Treadway stared at Mia rather than meeting Leo's introduction. "You're pretty, Agent Logan. Got a boyfriend?"

"Mr. Treadway," Mia met his gaze, "we're prepared to put in a good word with your warden *if* you'll help us out today. I understand you're generally on good behavior and hoping for eventual parole."

The felon's jaw twitched, his rough stubble giving the impression of a hungover frat boy more than a bank robber. Maybe that was how he'd gotten away with robbing three banks in the D.C. area...he didn't look like he was dangerous enough to carry a Zippo, let alone a gun.

"*Eventual*'s the word, ain't it? But all right, yeah, whatever." He pulled himself straighter in his seat, adjusting his wrists in their cuffs. "But you want information on anyone in here, you got another thing coming. I ain't endangering my beauty sleep just so you can clear your fucking desks."

"Noted." Leo waited for the man to meet his gaze, then got started. "How about you tell us why you're in here?"

See how he meets a softball question we know the answer to.

Treadway shrugged, one shoulder rolling upward like he aimed to perform a dance. "I'm a bank robber. I robbed banks. I got caught. End of story."

Mia huffed and leaned forward. "Tell us about your

process, Georgie. What did you do to prepare for those robberies?" She lowered her voice into a soft purr that fitted her personality better than her black FBI attire. *"Please."*

"Since you asked nice." He sat silently for another minute but then came to some decision for himself and did his little dance-move of a shrug again. "Whatever. Security and shit'll probably be a whole different ball of wax by the time I'm out of here anyway. My time's done out there. So…yeah…my *process* is that I played the long game."

Mia nodded him on, leaning forward just a touch. Maybe unconsciously, Treadway mirrored her just a smidge. Leo marked that as a temporary win in their book.

"Most guys get caught because they don't prepare, so I do the opposite." Treadway's youth showed for a moment in his proud grin. "I over-prepare. Mom taught me to be meticulous, and that's how I work things. I'd get a job as a part-time security guard in target banks and scope everything out. Most banks want top-tier security for low-budget pay, so if you show 'em you can carry a gun without shooting your own foot off and give 'em enough 'yes, sirs' and 'no, sirs'… well, they'll hire just about anybody."

True enough, unfortunately. For a moment, Leo thought back to the elderly security guard in the bank lobby that morning. Georgie Treadway might not look the part of a security guard any more than he looked the part of a bank robber, but he was certainly more able-bodied than that man. And he had the ego to make up for anything else he lacked, clearly.

"Anyhow, I'd work there awhile. Few months, usually. Easy enough to write down all the information I needed in notebooks. Schedules, passwords, layouts, you name it."

Leo imagined it would be for anyone willing to work weeks rather than days. "And you always worked alone?"

That dance move reared its head again. "Wouldn't trust anyone else."

"And did you keep the notebooks anywhere specific?" Mia's voice was measured, far from betraying that this was the first real question on their list.

Treadway squinted, just a touch. Barely discernible in the dim lighting. "My notebooks were seized."

Leo focused on Treadway's face...the man could lie, but not well. "*All* the notebooks?"

Another shoulder roll. "You're the Feds. You don't know what your own people seized, fuck am I gonna do about it? File a complaint? That's your lookout, man."

Mia cleared her throat, bringing the robber's gaze back to her. "How many banks did you case, Georgie?"

That squint again, followed by a shrug and a smile.

Leo fought back a sigh. "Do me a favor and remember how we offered to talk to the warden on your behalf, okay? And then tell me this...do you own a safe deposit box?"

The man remained still—suspiciously frozen—and somehow refrained from moving his shoulders. "Maybe. Hard to remember little shit details like that about life on the outside. Prison's got a way of making it all fade into the background. Fuck me if I remember the security code on my own mom's front door."

"Georgie," Mia leaned forward, softening her voice a touch beyond her earlier register, "we know you have a security box. It's been paid up years in advance. The question is, do you know your box was robbed?"

He licked his lips, but no shrug came to suggest the truth. "Well, that's a weird synchronicity, ain't it? Me being a robber and getting robbed. Must be karma."

Leo sat back in his chair, torn between relief that they were about done here and frustration that they'd bothered coming. "And if you didn't remember you have a security box…"

"I surely don't remember what might've been inside it. Could be nothing, could be something. You tell me." Treadway shoulder-rolled a shrug again, a glimmer of a smile visible even in the room's dim light.

Mia hummed beneath her breath. "Okay, Georgie, but you know how your friends are, right? Who would know you had a security box? In here or on the outside?"

The convict focused on her more closely, eyes roving up and down until Leo wanted to reach across and throttle him. But then he went back to his dance moves, shrugging a shoulder as if he were nudging flies off it. "No idea. Most bank managers I knew talked like fuckin' comedians. Who knows who they'd tell after recognizing me on the news? I'm better at keeping secrets than most." He leaned closer to Mia. "Give you any ideas, maybe? Of the personal sort?"

To her credit, Mia let out a laugh that could have chilled ice. "Guard, I think we're done!"

Mia's shout brought in the guard within seconds, and he glanced between them while undoing the felon's cuffs. "He any use to you?"

Leo just barely resisted rolling his shoulder. "Not much. No need to tell the warden anything on our behalf."

Treadway remained silent as he was guided out of the room.

Leo stood and stretched as soon as the guard's and felon's footsteps faded. "So whatever robberies were planned, but not yet attempted, were probably laid out in Treadway's notebooks and kept in that safety deposit box."

"Meaning, there'll be more robberies soon. We knew our robber took some notebooks, but this confirms why." Mia paced to the door, darting a glance into the hallway. "And

Treadway didn't seem surprised, so that at least tells us he knows who robbed him. Gave him the key, probably."

"Agreed."

"We need to look into his employment history. See where Treadway may have worked while playing his 'long game.'"

Leo typed out a quick text to Jacinda to that effect. "We could just get it out of him now, couldn't we?"

"Maybe, if we threaten the likelihood of an additional sentence for withholding information. Bet you lunch he'd just cry *lawyer*. He's covering for someone. You saw how he clammed up when we told him the box was robbed."

"All the more reason to press him now. He probably had a partner on his long game, and now little Georgie's sweating because his partner isn't playing the way they laid it out."

Mia shook her head. "He'll lawyer up, and then we're looking at another bank being robbed while we're shuffling papers and getting subpoenas."

Leo added those thoughts to the text thread with Jacinda just as the guard reappeared.

"He says to tell you thanks for talking to the warden, only he spells 'thanks' with an *F*."

Mia giggled at the comment, but Leo could only sigh.

"We can probably tell the warden that Georgie Treadway remains as exemplary a candidate for incarceration as he was when he arrived. We'll want a list of his outside contacts for thirty days before and after today's date. Anyone who's called him and anyone he's called. Think you can make sure the warden gets that request?"

The guard was already waving them out of the room. "Anything for the Feds."

Right. Meaning that I'll make sure Jacinda follows up with the warden. Twice, maybe.

11

———

E mma pulled the Expedition to a stop across from Davy Delko's apartment building, unable to do anything but stare. The ex-employee of Barry Meldrum's dealership was looking guilty already. "This...looks like a chop shop."

Keaton scoffed but seemed to agree with Emma's assessment.

The apartment building was a three-story affair abutting a junkyard. Muscle cars rested on cinder blocks, stacks of tires sat in every corner of the property, and car seats posed as lawn chairs. Not to mention the junkyard itself.

Garages for rent took up most of the first floor, many of them with junker cars or trash blocking the doors. One had *Knock here to talk to James* graffitied across the front, and another had a row of coolers in front of it, as if to mock the winter air with whatever they held. The junkyard, sprawled out beside and behind the complex, sprouted metal car parts that had to go back decades.

Parking on the street, Emma glanced between the junkyard and the first-floor garage spaces. "I wonder if this is all connected, like if the junkyard actually rents these spaces or owns the complex. It's like the apartment building grew out of the scrap metal."

"Wouldn't surprise me. Whole place reeks of grease. And our windows are up." Keaton's nose crinkled, as if to give the comment emphasis. He hopped out and was already leading the way toward the staircase closest to the junkyard. Not even a chain-link fence separated the properties, and as Emma climbed the stairs behind Keaton, she found herself scanning the landscape of scrap.

Anything—or anyone—could've been hiding in there. She still remained unsure where the main office or entrance was, the place was such a mess.

"Either way, this is an ideal space for a chop shop." Emma gestured over the graveyard of cars. "Nobody would look closely at the ins and outs of whatever organized chaos this counts for. We could have ten different bank robbers planning their heists while they build their makeshift getaway cars."

Upstairs, they dodged discarded trash and a couple of worn plastic chairs to stand in front of Delko's door. Keaton pressed the grimy doorbell button, and a tone-deaf chime bleated out what had once counted for a melody. The door opened seconds later.

Emma normally considered herself a pro when it came to keeping a poker face, including body language, but this time...

A cloud of marijuana smoke hit them harder than the Other had ever pressed in on her, and Emma fought to breathe through the attack.

They were greeted by a man wearing Emma stumbled a step back to stand against the opposite wall and raised her hand halfway to her nose before she caught herself and lowered it. Beside her, Keaton coughed unapologetically.

The man in front of them reeked of pot. Like he bathed in

it and rubbed himself down in it and washed his clothes in it. Emma wouldn't have been surprised to find the stuff sprouting from his head instead of hair, the way he smelled.

At least he's too baked to notice our reactions.

The lanky motor head leaned on his doorframe, as tall as a pro basketball player and as baked out of his gourd as a granny who hadn't realized she'd been given pot brownies by her hippie niece.

"Davy Delko?" Emma flashed her identification, but the man's red eyes barely shifted.

"Yuh. Uh, yeah. What?" He propped a thumb in one of the holes in his t-shirt, and Emma could only be glad he hadn't seen fit to prop his thumb in the hole at the front of his boxers instead.

Keaton coughed again, glancing her way. His look said it all, and she agreed…she did not want to go inside this man's apartment. They'd drive around the rest of the day smelling like cheap weed, if they didn't already. Besides that, Davy wasn't feeling the cold, high as he was, so they might as well avoid it.

"Mr. Delko, we're here about a recent robbery that occurred at Crazy Barry's Car Emporium—"

"Shithead deserved it." Davy glanced down as a calico cat nosed between his feet, then nudged her backward before looking back up, his red eyes as hazy as any Emma had ever seen. "But I didn't do it. Not me, no sirree. Hey, mind if I smoke?"

Emma opened her mouth to respond, not quite sure what she'd say. "I—"

"Anxiety. I got anxiety. Bad." He yawned. "So mind if I smoke?"

"Please don't. We'll only take a minute of your time." Keaton held up a hand, patting the air, and Davy watched his fingers move as if they were a cartoon bug waving hello.

Emma tried not to laugh.

"Yeah…uh…all right." The motor head shrugged, nudged his undoubtedly high cat back inside the apartment, and stepped out onto the cement walkway in his bare feet.

He shut the door behind him, and Emma could only pray he hadn't locked himself out. Would they be duty bound to let him sit in the warmth of her SUV 'til a locksmith came if he had? She didn't want to think about it.

Davy leaned into the door, swaying just a tad until he seemed to steady himself on discovering an enormous amount of the world to consider in Keaton's paisley power tie. "What do you want?"

Emma bit her tongue to hold in a groan before answering. "Crazy Barry's—"

"Yeah, yeah, yeah. Right." Davy stretched his arms up to the ceiling of the walkway, cracking his elbows and shoulders. "Right, right, right. He got robbed. Man, that's a nice tie. Oh, hey, I didn't do it."

No kidding.

This guy was young, not a pinch like their profile, and didn't seem remotely smart enough to get away with one robbery. Let alone two. Although, that didn't mean he didn't know their robber personally.

"Tell us about working for Barry." Keaton leaned against the wall.

"Guy's an asshole, and working for him sucked. Sucked the big one, like, a big fat one. You understand, right? Yeah. Ask me, he's a sexual predator to boot." Davy chanced a look at Emma, focusing on one sapphire earring when he missed her eyes. "Sorry to bring that kind of thing up in polite company, Agent Lady. Sorry, can't remember your name. But yeah, Barry. Low kind of scum. Whatever they took from 'im, he had it coming."

Emma blinked. She couldn't quite tell if her confusion

over that long-winded answer came from the pothead's way
with words or from the beginning of a contact buzz.

Shit, we need to get this over with before we're both high for the
next car chase. Wouldn't Leo love that?

"All that aside..." Emma pulled out her notebook,
watching the way Davy's red eyes roamed the air. With any
luck, he was too high to play games with them. "Anything
you can tell us could be of use. Do you know how much cash
Barry kept on hand? I'm wondering how common that
knowledge is."

"Yeah, I know. Too much. Always too much."

Keaton coughed yet again, apparently unable to help it.
"And you know Barry was robbed and shot on Saturday
morning?"

"Yuppers. It's that...the, uh, subject right now. Served the
dude right. Anything else? Oh, hey..."

Emma waited and waited some more. The man seemed to
be doing heavy calculus, based on the way his muscles flexed
and his eyes roamed the dead air.

"Hey?"

"About Barry, right?" Davy craned his neck to the right,
cracking it hard enough to make Emma want to call a chiro-
practor on his behalf.

"Right," she agreed, "about Barry."

"Told you he's a perv, right? Gotta say that. Case in point,
yeah? Barry was flirting with this older woman a few days
back. Or weeks. Something like that. But not far back, right?
Woman had a wig on. Blond. Fifties-like?"

Keaton raised an eyebrow nearly to his hairline. "You
mean the wig was fifties-styled?"

"Nah, dude. Sorry, Agent. You're an agent, right? Yeah,
that. Lady was older, wig was younger. By a little. Fifties,
right? Not her." Davy barked a laugh and coughed himself
near to his knees before he stood upright again.

Emma slipped her notebook away. Whatever non sequitur of a story this man was telling them, it would be easy enough to remember without her taking notes. Assuming Davy could get the tale out of his system.

"Okay, so Barry tried to stroke her hair." The twentysomething pothead patted the air beside him as if to mime the act, baring his teeth in a grimace before he continued. "You believe that shit? A customer, right, and he's trying to pet her like she's a fucking poodle. You ever see poodles all done up? Stupid dog owners. Oh, and hey, worse? Idiot Barry accidentally pulls her wig off. Clear off her head! Landed in the parking lot like a fucked-up squirrel. Her husband went apeshit, man. Threatened to knock Barry's block off, and I didn't blame him."

Emma tried not to imagine the embarrassment of the poor woman involved, but she had no problem imagining Barry causing such a scene. "And you're bringing this up because—"

"Because," Motor Head Davy emphasized, "maybe Barry's ass deserved what he got. But hey, I had nothing to do with it. Yeah? Hey, you mind if I smoke? Anxiety, right?"

Keaton shifted on his feet.

"And then you were fired? By Barry, not the woman." Emma bit her lip to hold in a groan.

Davy shrugged, propping his finger back in that hole in his t-shirt. "Yeah, Agent. Claimed I was selling parts on the sly while I was working for him, but what'd he expect? Dude pays pennies. *Pennies*. Wants me to keep my side gig as my side gig, he needs to act like he's my main gig, ya got me? Yeah, right? But he's not now. Anymore, I mean. Better off without him, you get me? That perv. He's not now, not ever...right."

Emma inhaled and immediately regretted taking in any

more air than absolutely necessary. Her brain hurt from the gymnastics required to decipher his pot speak.

Red-eyed, Davy cocked his head as if he'd managed to confuse himself, and Emma actually waved to call his attention back to her for her next—and hopefully last—question. "Davy, have you sold parts for older trucks? Say, seventies-era trucks? Maybe dealt with any shady characters lately?"

Davy's tongue poked out of his lips as if to taste the air, and then he grinned. "You get me, Agent Lady!"

She blinked and traded a glance with Keaton, who looked just as befuddled. "I...*get you?*"

"Yeah, yeah, you catch my meaning! Knew you would. Hey, mind if I smoke now?"

What the hell just happened here?

"Davy, try to focus for me. I asked about parts you've sold, shady—"

"Characters, yeah! All over the place, here and at Barry's both." Davy leaned toward her and winked, but nearly fell over and had to catch himself on the doorframe.

Keaton muttered beside her. "I think we're done now, aren't we, Agent Last? Before Mr. Delko injures himself on our behalf?"

"Injures?" Davy's eyes went wide. "Hey, who got hurt? Oh, Barry, right? Dude fuckin' deserved it. Shoulda seen that lady's wig, man."

This was absurd. Emma couldn't find the benefits of the interview at this point. They could always come back, right? Or better yet, send Leo and Mia over to deal with him.

"Okay, Davy," Emma waved again to get his attention and gestured to the side of the apartment complex, "can you at least tell us where we can get footage of the scrapyard for the past couple of weeks? Assuming there are cameras?"

What it would show them, she wasn't sure. She had no cause to suspect the motor head at this point, but whoever their bank robber was, he liked souped-up engines, and he was getting parts from somewhere, if Leo's diagnosis of that engine was correct.

And, hell, maybe the robber's connected to this pot smoker, somehow. Taking revenge out on Barry for firing him and cutting out a method of dealing parts. Or if nothing else, we'll break up a chop shop, based on how things look now.

Davy blinked, looked around, and then leaned forward, taking his marijuana-tinged stink with him. "Did I tell you about this couple Barry had a fight with? This woman—"

"Yes, we heard, Mr. Delko." Keaton pointed over at the scrapyard. "We're talking about *cameras* now. Not the woman with the wig. Could you tell us where we could find camera footage for the scrapyard?"

"Yeah, dude. At the scrapyard." Davy chortled, actually clutching his gut and tearing the hole in his shirt wider.

"Thank you, Mr. Del—"

"Can I go smoke now?"

Emma stopped with her mouth open, hard-pressed to find words. Finally, she did, since Davy was clearly waiting on them for permission. "Yes, Mr. Delko, you may go—"

The door slammed shut, and she actually heard him calling, "Mary Jane, Daddy's home!"

Keaton wiped his hands on his pants as if to clean them of the air. "Think he's beckoning his stash or his cat?"

"I wouldn't dare to guess." Emma turned, almost stumbling as she did. Dammit, had she gotten a buzz? Talk about a wasted afternoon, in more ways than one.

Yet the back of her neck tingled with the edges of that conversation. Something was strange about the way that man had fixated on the couple and their altercation with Barry. Strange enough to look into, maybe. True, the man was pot-addled...but a place like Barry's Crazy Car Emporium had to attract its fair share of characters, and altercations right along with them.

Especially so if Davy had been dealing chop shop parts out of his back pocket while working in the grease shop.

"Despite how confusing that character up there is, and the fact that we don't know if there's camera footage to be had… I don't know, Keaton." She stopped there, trying to get a handle on her thoughts. "I actually feel like this trip got us somewhere. If we can figure out where."

Keaton laughed. "Don't ask Mr. Mary Jane for help, that's all I ask. But if he's gotten us somewhere, I'll eat my mesmerizing tie. He's too baked to know how to find a gun, let alone use one. You really want to get sidetracked looking at his 'side gig' in this junkyard?"

Emma paused on the stairwell, peering out at the property beside them. "Davy may be a mess, but places like this usually keep track of what's coming and going. And since we're here…feel like making our way through that maze of scrap to try to find the office?"

"Lead the way." Keaton coughed again. "But if Davy's twin shows up, I'm going back to the car and leaving the questioning to you. I don't even know how that kid could breathe once he closed his door."

A dry laugh escaped Emma's throat. "He's probably too high to remember he needs to."

12

Back at the Bureau, Emma swallowed down another sip of coffee and flexed her fingers, fighting to remain focused on the computer screen in front of her. It was a shame she'd gotten so little sleep last night, as this particular assignment would have been boring as hell on the best of days.

Instead, for more than an hour now, she'd been reviewing footage of what had to be the most inactive scrapyard in America.

At one point, a week back, a group of teenagers jumped the fence to smoke what Emma guessed was probably weed.

You goofballs could've just knocked on Delko's door. Or stood outside and huffed all the secondhand smoke he produces.

The elevator door opened, and Mia offered her a wave. "Coffee hot?"

"It is," Emma held up her cup, "and I'll take some more if you're getting some. You guys finish at the prison?"

"Yeah." Mia hung her coat on her chair, taking a quick glance at the footage on Emma's computer. "Leo's off to cover for Jacinda at the crime scene, supervising and all that, and hunting up background on Georgie Treadway, the deposit box owner."

"What did you learn from him?"

"Only that he's probably not going to see sunshine without bars in front of it for a long time. He might be partnered with our perpetrator, or at least has a really good idea of who it is."

"But...you didn't get a name, did you?"

Mia shook her head. "Treadway wanted to play hardball, and we can get what we need without his help." She proceeded to explain what she and Leo did get from Treadway, including the details of his "long game." While it wasn't much to go on, Emma had to agree it gave them a lead to follow.

"So Leo's looking into where Treadway worked? To try and pinpoint where the next robbery might happen?"

"Yep. If we set up stakeouts at each possible location, the next time our guy strikes, he'll have a welcoming committee and free transportation off-site all rolled into one. What about you and Keaton? Get anything good for us? Where is he anyway?"

"He went to meet Jacinda at the field where we lost our guy. See if he can bring any new insight into how the morning went down. As for what we found being good, I want to say yes. We thought we might be looking for someone with a child suffering from a cancer diagnosis."

"That would explain the need for a sudden infusion of cash and the bizarre haircutting performance. So why the hesitation?"

"The car dealership that was hit last Saturday had an employee who was fired a few weeks back. Davy Delko. He said Meldrum, that's the dealership owner, got handsy with a woman wearing a wig, and the woman's husband flew off the handle."

"But we only have one perpetrator at the bank. A man. So we're looking for a husband and wife, possibly, with the husband doing the jobs because his wife has cancer."

Emma *mm-hmm*ed. "That's our best guess anyway. We still don't know who they are."

"I'm glad we're not talking about a child with cancer." Mia flopped into a chair. "That could still be relevant to this case, but I'm hoping it's not."

"It might make it easier to track our perpetrator. A search for families with child cancer patients is a lot narrower than the roughly two million new cases the American Cancer Society expects each year."

Once Emma took the last sip, Mia picked up her coffee cup and disappeared into the break room. A minute later, she reappeared with fresh brew for both of them and perched on the edge of Leo's desk. "While we're alone, I want to talk to you about something."

After Emma glanced up while sipping her coffee, she slowed the footage of the scrapyard a tad. She'd keep one eye on it, but Mia's pursed lips suggested that the most boring footage in the history of the world could be afforded a breather. "Shoot."

"It's about Ned."

Emma waited as Mia only stared at the empty scrapyard shown on the computer. The expression on her face had gone wary, empty of its usual light. "And...what is it? Spit it out, Mia."

"I received the electronic files I requested from the Richmond PD, covering car accidents over the last few years. I compared the files with my copy of Ned's report, looking for any similarities I could think of. Type of car, rural roads, questionable circumstances. You know the drill."

Upon hearing the nerves coming through in Mia's voice, Emma felt her gut go sour. "And you found something."

Mia gulped her coffee, wincing at the heat, and met Emma's gaze. "I did when I finally entered Ned's place of work into my search terms. Ned was the CEO's right-hand man...I can't remember if I'd told you that...and the thing is, Ned passed within three months of the CEO's wife and brother. Both of whom died in separate tragic accidents, after Ned. The CEO retired immediately after his wife's death. He moved to some secluded cabin in the woods."

Emma put one hand on Mia's jittering knee. "Three accidents involving people that close...that's no coincidence. It's a lead we need to follow."

A sigh erupted from Mia's lips, and she seemed to wilt with relief. "Thank goodness you agree. I was worried I was imagining things, looking too hard—?"

Emma held a hand up to stop her. Unfortunately, this wasn't the time for a personal conversation.

Their footage had suddenly gotten a lot more interesting.

A familiar-looking truck had pulled onto the scrapyard lot. Same make and model, and probably the same year. But brown instead of red.

They even had a clear shot of the license plate.

13

I *don't know if bank robbers live in neighborhoods like this. Not until they retire anyway.*

Beside her, Mia seemed to be thinking the same thing as she frowned out the window at the pretty neighborhood surrounding them. The license plate from the scrapyard's footage had led them here, but Emma had expected anything but this. Even if she'd tried, she couldn't have come up with a place that looked more opposite of Davy Delko's apartment building and that labyrinth of junk.

Sure, plenty of cars lined the street and made homes of the driveways, but those cars all rested on their own fully inflated, attached-to-their-vehicles tires. The houses were in good repair, and the yards well cared for. Their license plate had brought them into picture-perfect suburbia.

"Middle-class D.C." Emma pulled up in front of a two-story home with light-blue siding and red shutters. "Which means above-average incomes. But this is the address for our Eugene Brauer."

Their brown truck sat square in the driveway. Ahead of it, the garage door was closed, which either meant that someone was unconcerned about the truck being seen, or far more concerned about hiding something else.

Mia stretched in her seat. "Shall we?"

A mat on the front step announced a welcome to dog lovers. Country music played beyond the door. George Strait, Emma thought. Ringing the doorbell produced a sweet, charming chime that interrupted the music.

This place did not scream "bank robber." It didn't even scream "jaywalker."

"Smart homes. Gotta love 'em." Emma kept listening. When the music stopped, she took a small step back as the door opened. But almost immediately, she felt sure that this was *not* their guy.

The man in front of them was at least ninety years old, with hunched shoulders and the frail look of someone who'd been surviving for years despite his doctor's best guesses. His eyes were sharp, though.

"Yes, how can I help you ladies?"

"Mr. Eugene Brauer?" Mia held up her ID, only slipping it back into her pocket when the man had finished squinting at it.

"I am. And what have I done to catch the eye of the FBI, if I may ask? Don't tell me I was playing my music too loud again." He grinned.

"Sir, is that brown truck in the driveway yours?" Emma stepped sideways, giving him a view of his own vehicle just in case he needed the reminder. At his age, it wasn't impossible.

"It is. Bessy's my work vehicle."

No way should this man be crawling in and out from under cars at his age.

"And, uh, do you like working with cars and trucks? Rebuilding engines, I guess?"

The man let out a cackle of a laugh that could've given the

Wicked Witch a run for her money. Then he waved them inside, stepping back to welcome them in. "Oh no, no, no. You give me far too much credit. I couldn't change Bessy's oil if my life depended on it. I take her to the scrapyard to load up on material for my art projects. I'll show you."

Art projects, Emma girl. The man has...art projects?

Mia smiled so that her dimples showed. "Sir, there's no need—"

"I insist!" The man waved at them again, speaking over her. "You can come see my art projects and enjoy a glass of iced tea while you're here. Come on."

With that, he headed back into the house, leaving the front door open behind him. He moved quick for a nonagenarian and was halfway through the living room before Emma had made the decision to follow. *But...why not?*

Trading a glance with Mia, Emma stepped inside what could only be described as a neatly kept home straight out of the eighties. From there, they followed Brauer through his living room and kitchen.

He opened the door to a large backyard surrounded by metal privacy fencing that was far from empty. Aside from the picture-perfect Irish setter that lounged near the patio furniture, the yard was littered in surprisingly lovely sculptures.

Metal had been bent and turned and twisted into wind chimes that Emma guessed sounded beautiful when a breeze blew through. One section of the yard was devoted to near life-size welded figurines playing musical instruments. Still another section was full of animated metal dogs playing with metal bones and Frisbees and balls. Nearby, a metal cat watched a metal bird fluffing itself in a metal birdbath.

"You're an artist." Mia said so simply, the truth being clear to both of them.

Brauer beamed. "In my retirement, indeed that's what

they tell me. Oh, my name's not famous, but my metal-ines, as I call them, do pretty well. Now, can I offer you some tea?"

The Irish setter raised its graying muzzle as if it wanted some tea as well, but Emma shook her head. "Thank you for your time, Mr. Brauer, but we don't want to disturb your dinner hour. We have to be on our way since we're just here looking into the scrapyard. Your truck came across our footage. I'm so glad to have seen your work, though. I don't suppose you've seen anything suspicious while out that way?"

As Brauer gestured for his dog to come in, the creature slowly got to its feet. "Can't say as I have, though it wouldn't surprise me. That scrapyard is a perfect place for me to find material, but I admit it's probably more for the likes of gear-heads and their classic muscle cars. Car thieves, too, I guess, given the world we live in today. I hope you find who you're looking for."

With the old dog following, they made their way back through the house. And as Emma might have guessed, Brauer spent the time assuring them he would have called any suspicious activity in to the police if he had seen something, despite the scrapyard being his favorite hunting grounds for art supplies.

Outside, with the old man and his dog behind the closed door at their backs, Mia gestured to a wind chime hanging from the lamppost by the sidewalk. The setting sun's rays glinted along the metal, setting it off like a sort of prism. "They really are pretty. I didn't even notice this one on our way in."

Emma nodded agreement, but already had her phone to her ear. The hour was getting later, and her stomach was grumbling with hunger as well as frustration at this point, so she saw no reason to belabor the bad news. "Hey, Jacinda.

Nothing to see here. We spoke to Eugene Brauer, but he's a dead end."

Jacinda blew out a breath on the other end. "I was afraid of that. Dead ends seem to be the order of the day." Muffled conversation sounded on the other end of the line, and Emma thought she heard someone mutter something about pizza. "Look, it's nearly five. You and Mia head out for the day, and we'll regroup early tomorrow morning."

Emma ended the call and looked over at Mia as they climbed into the Expedition. "You hear that?"

"Indeed." Mia slid her seat belt on. "How about we pick up the cars from the office and get an early dinner? Catch each other up?"

Emma sighed with relief. The last thing she'd wanted was to head home to her empty apartment and eat a frozen dinner. *Now to convince Mia that a quick drink is also in order after this virtual nonstarter of a day.*

Losing a car chase with a bank robber and viewing a bunch of footage that had gotten them nowhere? Not to mention the confusion-laced conversation she'd had with a weed-addled motor head. Hell yes, she deserved a drink.

Ideally, one without ghosts crashing the party.

14

Emma took another satisfying bite from a piece of bruschetta. The sharp tang of balsamic vinegar, decadently melted cheese, and perfectly ripe tomatoes did a fine job of taking the edge off the day. And her sweet Riesling, though not a fruity mai tai, worked like a charm too.

Rather than opt for a full-on dinner, they'd decided on appetizers at the little Italian bistro near Emma's apartment, which she'd been meaning to try ever since it opened. They'd overshot their promises of a light dinner, though, by sharing nearly every app on the menu, from the fried calamari right to the tomato and mozzarella salad ringed by stuffed mushrooms.

So far, the place lived up to its reputation and was most certainly on her list as somewhere to bring Oren in the near future. She still had to make up for canceling their last date because of work, after all.

Mia popped a prosciutto-wrapped olive in her mouth and followed it with a few crumbs of the feta that had been scattered around the edge of the appetizer plate. "You never told me about your day with Keaton, except for that stoner,

Delko. What's it like running around with your old partner again?"

Emma forced a smile. "It was fine."

The comment died between them, more damning than anything. Emma winced at the frown that stopped Mia's next olive midway to her mouth.

"Fine? Emma, a hot cup of coffee out of the breakroom is fine. A new pair of work pants is fine. A visit from your best friend and longtime partner is supposed to be a helluva lot more than *fine*. What on earth happened between you two today?"

Emma sipped her wine, wishing for something stronger all of a sudden. She couldn't exactly tell Mia that the problem was, simply enough, that the man wasn't Leo. That didn't even make sense to her own mind. Yet...Mia was Mia. The understanding showed on her face in a sudden blush of awareness that dimpled her cheeks.

"Here I thought you'd never get used to Leo, and now you prefer working with him." Mia pushed the bruschetta closer to Emma when she noticed her refraining from taking the last piece—it was Emma's favorite Italian app—and Emma gave in to the offer, plucking the cheesed-up bread from the plate.

"It's not that I don't love Keaton. He's my...he's one of my best friends." The correction felt awkward, even though Mia had the grace not to react. "But I'd forgotten how casual he is. Leo's so focused on the job, and as much as he rags me about my driving—"

"Which you deserve."

"Which I maybe *sometimes* deserve," Emma scowled, "and which catches us bad guys more often than not. But, yeah, I guess Leo and I have been in tune with each other lately. I like...his passion for the job. His work ethic. And working with Keaton again was..." She trailed off, taking a bite of her appetizer rather than forcing a word that didn't quite fit.

"Uncomfortable?" Mia's voice had gone quieter and a little too knowing, but Emma shook her head. No way would she admit to herself or anyone else that the day had been that off.

"Awkward." Emma nodded as the server passed by. He pointed at her glass to see if she wanted another, and she waved a *yes*.

"Isn't that Keaton's middle name? Keaton Awkward Holland. I thought we'd agreed about that."

Emma tried to laugh, but the bubbles of humor died on her lips. "It's just because he's better at the work-life balance than the rest of us, and I'd forgotten that. It'll improve tomorrow. We'll get our old mojo back. I'll be back to missing him when I'm on the next case with Leo, and you'll be rolling your eyes at me all over again. Today was just...strange."

Though Mia raised an eyebrow, she sipped her own wine rather than argue. "Well, I told you about the claustrophobic prison and how horrid it was, but speaking of Leo and strange..."

Emma felt her composure wobble just a touch. She'd been hoping not to keep talking about Leo. Not tonight anyway.

"What?"

"Leo's worried about you. Thinks you've been acting strange."

Almost without thinking about it, Emma closed her eyes, following an instinct to shut herself away from even Mia. If only for a moment. That damn man was just too perceptive. She should've known he'd see something he shouldn't, and she still didn't know what to say to him. Her voice finally came out in a hesitant whisper when she asked, "You didn't tell him, did you?"

Mia's mushroom-greased fingers snaked over and gripped Emma's, steadying her. "Emma, hon, of course not. Your secrets are yours to tell. But he's going to figure it out... well, figure out *something's off* anyway. He thinks you're seeing things, and the idea of..." Mia lowered her voice, "*ghosts* may not be the most obvious conclusion, but I can't rightly say what he will think. Seriously, that man's like a bloodhound. When he gets a sniff of something out of the ordinary, he's inexhaustible."

Chuckling, Emma gripped Mia's fingers back. "I know. And I'll figure it out. Just...thanks for giving me the time to do it."

Mia's lips quirked. "Like I want to be the one to tell him ghosts are getting involved in our cases? Oh, hell no. But also..." She paused while the server refilled both their wine and water glasses. "Also, he said he'd help us look into Ned's death. And like you said, he's so focused."

"He could be a real help." Emma nodded, sipping her wine. "But it'll be tough to have him help us if he doesn't know why we started suspecting foul play to begin with. And I have to admit...this whole Other situation is feeling more dangerous lately."

Again, Mia's eyebrow lifted, and as they kept eating, Emma filled her in on her last experience with her psychic, Marigold, and then, more importantly, her mother's warning. How, despite the psychic's warnings, Emma had connected to the Other by herself with nobody there to anchor her. How things had gone cold, and how her mother had chilled her deeper than any February night when offering Emma that warning. That some mystery "she" could see her.

Just the memory was enough to sober Emma and make her wish she wasn't facing an empty apartment that night.

"*She can see you?* That's what your mom said?" Mia gulped

another swallow of wine, frowning into the dusky liquid. "She *who?*"

Emma shrugged, feeling all the more helpless in doing so. *That's the Other-loving question...*

"What do you think about telling Leo my secret too? Should I? I mean, maybe it would be good to have more backup...but what do you think?"

After darting her tongue out to lick her lips, Mia bit into another mushroom stuffed with feta before replying. "You just have to trust your gut. A secret like yours? It's way too big for me to tell you who you should be bringing in on it. I can't make that decision. Leo can ask me whatever he wants until he's blue in the face. Your secret is yours."

Emma wanted to argue that Mia might well be thinking more clearly than she herself was. Before she could, though, her phone rang.

She glanced at the screen, and her heart picked up speed. "It's Oren. You okay with me answering?"

"Only if you put it on speaker." Mia dimpled and sat back in her seat, gesturing with her wine for Emma to go ahead.

Emma kept the call private. Mia would just have to keep up with a one-sided conversation.

"Hey, Oren. How are you?"

"Glad to hear your voice."

Emma cheeks warmed, and she hid at least one of them behind her glass of water.

Across from her, Mia batted her eyes.

Praying she wouldn't laugh out loud at the antics, Emma swiped a hand at her.

But when she answered Oren, she couldn't stop herself from being just as cheesy. "I'm just as glad to hear yours." And she was, it occurred to her. Oren's deep voice was the stuff of dreams. Hers anyway.

"I'd like to ask if you're available for Valentine's Day. No pressure, but if you are?"

Shit, what day is that?

He read her hesitation for what it was, thank goodness. "That's tomorrow for us mortals."

Emma grinned into her phone, pretending she couldn't see Mia leaning forward in interest. "You reading minds now?"

"Just yours, I hope. What about it?"

Emma swallowed. When had she last been on a date on Valentine's Day? College? Was there added pressure?

And do I care if there is?

"I'm free." The words were out before she'd thought about them. "What do you have in mind? I mean, I can't quite promise, but—"

"I know, I know," Oren broke in. "If work calls, and you must save the world rather than entertain your besotted Oren, then you must go and save the world. But if the world doesn't call, would you do me the honor of meeting me at Edelweiss on Leigh Avenue at eight?"

Emma thought of the romantic little German restaurant she'd seen pictures of in advertisements. "I'd love to."

"Well, I'll let you get back to your evening and call to confirm our reservation."

Emma's mouth dropped open. "Wait, you already made it?"

"As soon as we met, Emma." Oren chuckled. "See you tomorrow."

The line went silent.

Mia leaned over 'til her chest nearly rubbed into the emptied plate of fried calamari they'd demolished earlier. "Well?"

Half hiding behind her wine, Emma grinned. "It seems I have a Valentine's Day date with my yoga instructor."

Mia clapped her hands loudly enough that a woman at the next table stared, but neither of them apologized. "Your *boyfriend*, you mean. Yoga instructors do not take their students out on Valentine's Day. Face it. You've got a boyfriend."

Emma bit into her lip hard enough to leave an imprint. The idea was sinking in. "Yeah...I think I do." A giggle far more fitting of her friend bubbled out of her throat, and she drowned it in some water.

"This is kind of next-level, you know?" Mia's voice was gentle as she leaned forward, prodding. "Don't hate me for bringing it up, but I know you, and I know you don't want to lead this guy along. Are you ready for that?"

Any remaining giggle died a quick death. So much for easy girl talk.

Swallowing, Emma told herself it was the wine as she nodded. "Maybe so. I mean...someday, it'd be nice to have a family. You know...and someplace to really treat like a home. Love."

Mia's brown eyes went wide, sparkling with sympathy. "That was way more honest than I expected of you, Agent Last."

Emma's cheeks went a little warmer as she nodded. "I'm a cheap date. You give me one more glass of wine, and I'll dance on the table in my underwear."

The quip didn't quite ring so true as what she'd said before, though, and although Mia laughed and pretended it did, Emma couldn't do the same.

Her mind darted to the picture of her mother holding her, so close in appearance to the way Emma herself looked. But Emma didn't have a husband, let alone a baby. Her apartment was barely furnished beyond the basics.

But as much as she wasn't honest with herself when it came to thoughts of the future...the future felt closer than ever, nonetheless. It seemed possible in a way she'd never imagined.

She did want a family. A real home. Love.

She'd just never quite expected those things to come her way.

15

Despite the cold, Emma cuddled on her balcony in an old blanket, her mother's photograph gripped in one hand. The honesty she'd let out of her heart at dinner still hurt. To think about a home, family, and even love wasn't something she allowed herself often. All those things had seemed out of reach for so, so long.

Sure, her dad had loved her in his way, but they'd mostly spent their lives apart even when she'd been a child, going to boarding school after boarding school while he worked himself to death. And then he died. Although, she never felt like she had a real home before his death either.

Not since Mom died, really. Which is to say, not ever.

Flurries swirled from the night sky, and Emma tugged the blanket tighter around her shoulders. Across the way, the ghost of Madeline Luse waved at her. The woman hovered over her family in death, just as Emma assumed she must have in life. Her two young children had inherited her blond hair, making Emma sometimes wonder if they resembled their mother like Emma did hers.

Emma's hair was shorter than her mom's had been and

more flyaway than straight, but their eyes were the same, and they could have been sisters if one went by pictures of the two of them at the same age.

Shaking the thought of her age away, Emma simply sat and watched the snow and Madeline Luse. If she dwelled on the fact that her mom had died of a brain tumor at twenty-eight, Emma's current age, she'd never get any sleep.

The ghost of Madeline bent at the waist, peering into her family's home from the balcony, reminding Emma of how Trisha Terrence's ghost had hovered over her daughter Chelsea that morning.

Had her own mother ever done the same?

The thought sent a warm shiver of hope down Emma's spine, but it wasn't necessarily comforting. Until recently, she'd always thought her mother was ignoring her or had gone somewhere unreachable. She'd had moments in childhood where she'd hoped for her mother's ghost to make an appearance or dreamed of her looking down like a guardian angel…but as she'd grown up, she'd let all that go.

And then, when the Other had intruded on her life, she'd been forced to come to the conclusion that Gina Marie Last had either willfully left her side or had simply gone somewhere else after death, another Other.

Now she didn't know what to think. Hearing the woman's direct warning, in a voice she'd never be able to mistake after years upon years of seeing it in home movies, had thrown Emma for a total loop.

It seemed her mother was here, but Emma simply couldn't see her.

And the sad fact of the matter was, she felt more alone than ever after having heard her mother's warning. Her mother's actual voice.

She'd tried to shake off the vulnerability she'd shown Mia that night, but even after the wine and a night spent with her friend, her nerves felt stretched taut and thin. Like she could laugh or cry for no reason at the drop of a dime.

And the hope she felt for tomorrow night and some possibility of a future with Oren felt almost too painful to be real.

But all of it's in danger. Mom wouldn't have come out of her silence after all these years if not. That warning isn't something I can ignore.

Leo's earnest face flashed across her vision, jarring her away from Madeline Luse and her children. He'd saved her that night at the B and B when she'd been following some half-baked directives from a wolf she'd dreamed up. Somehow, he'd known she was in trouble, and he'd managed to save her.

Maybe she should tell him.

Tears roiled up as Emma looked at her mother's picture.

And then Madeline's French accent drifted across the distance between their apartments. "She can hear you. If you want to speak to her."

The ghost was leaning out over her balcony, focused on Emma now. Cuddled in her blanket and with the picture gripped nearly tight enough to break, Emma could only stare. Madeline rarely spoke to her. Before Emma could think to answer, though, the ghost disappeared.

Okay, then. Okay. Maybe that'll help if nothing else will, Emma girl.

Emma pulled up her blanketed knees and rested the picture against them, staring at her mother, where she sat frozen in time, holding onto baby Emma. Sky blue eyes shining, light-brown hair gleaming, vibrating with life, even across the distance of twenty-six years and old photo paper.

"Mom, I love..." Emma's voice broke, and she coughed out some tears before breathing deep and beginning again. "Mom, I miss you so much."

Tears welled in her eyes again, but she didn't fight them this time.

"Dad did his best after you died. I know he did. But we needed you so badly. Seeing my friends with their moms, seeing the way they had...*families*. It was hard. I had a therapist who thought I'd hate you for leaving, but I swear I never did. I just missed you. I want you to know that. I missed you so, so much. And Dad did too. I hope..."

Emma choked on her tears, pulling the blanket tighter around her shoulders until it felt constricting, almost smothering.

"I hope he's with you. I hope...I hope you have some happiness. You deserved so much more life than you had, Mom." She closed her eyes, wondering if her mom could indeed hear her. And if she could, what she must be thinking.

"I don't want you to feel bad for me. I love my life. I love my work. But I met a girl today. Her name is Chelsea Terrence, and her mom, Trisha, died in front of her during a robbery. They were at the bank for a quick errand, and everything changed for them. Everything."

Memories of nights spent crying in bed over her mom's absence hit Emma like a physical blow. She pressed one hand against her stomach, starting to rock in her chair.

"Chelsea's never going to have her mom there to tuck her in again. To pick her up from school when she's ill. No bedtime stories, no talks about first dates and first dances and first boyfriends or college visits. No relationship advice." Emma shuddered. "No hugs."

Some flurries drifted across her face, but Emma didn't even feel chilled by them. Her old blanket and the emotion had warmed her.

"And someday, Mom, I know she's going to be where I am. That's what hurts. I know someday she's going to be sitting on her balcony, alone, wishing her mother could be there with her or at least hear her." A sigh dragged more tears from Emma's eyes, where they froze against her cheeks. "I love you, Mom. That's all. I hope you know that, somehow. Wherever you are. I hope you know I still miss you and I love you."

Emma pulled the picture to her chest and hugged it beneath the blanket, ignoring the cold of the glass against her sweater. The cold, at least, felt real. Realer than the possibility of family or love at the moment.

Minutes passed, and a warmth slowly began settling into her bones. Maybe from the effort of holding herself together...or maybe, somehow, from some slip of effort from the Other. Emma wanted to believe that so badly, she allowed herself to sink into it, nestled in her blanket.

When her eyes started to close, she didn't fight the exhaustion. She only pulled her mother's picture closer to her chest and let herself fall into a sleep that took her away from the cold of the world around her.

L eo's hand fumbled for his ringing phone before he fully opened his eyes. After he'd spent three years as an FBI agent, the reflex was as natural as scratching an itch or drawing breath.

He glanced at the device just long enough to confirm whether it was Jacinda—it wasn't—and then lifted it to his ear, still lying prone in bed. "Hello?"

"Agent Leo Ambrose? This is Warden Payne of Jackson Federal Max. I understand you spoke to one of my inmates yesterday and requested more information regarding his connection to a crime. I apologize for the early call, but I may have something for you."

Leo sat up in bed, rubbing his eyes as he glanced at the clock. Just after six in the morning. "I appreciate the call, Warden. And don't worry about the hour. This is the only way I ever want to wake up on Valentine's Day."

"Funny. Too bad my wife doesn't feel the same. She'll have my dinners burning just for spite if I forget to get her jewelry, a fancy dinner out, and flowers. But I didn't call to tell you about my Valentine's woes. I'm sending over the recording of Georgie Treadway's phone calls over the past twenty-four hours. Is the email you wrote down at intake the best one for you?"

Already standing, Leo ducked into his home office to make sure he'd left his laptop on. He wanted to be on those recordings the second they came through. "Yeah, that's perfect. Thanks."

Next up for chores, coffee.

"You'll have those files shortly, then. Mostly, they're short and don't cover much, but one might be interesting to your investigation. The call is to a burner number and doesn't appear to be traceable, but I've highlighted it in the email so you can jump right to it. I'll stay on the line until the email's come through. Meanwhile, we'll keep on top of Treadway's calls. You'll let us know if there's anything we should be aware of regarding his activities or communications with persons outside the prison, I hope?"

"You've got my word." Leo leaned over his desk, refreshing his inbox until the warden's message popped up. "And I've got your email. Thanks."

The warden clicked off, and Leo poured sugar and creamer into the mug sitting on his Keurig, even as coffee streamed in. Patience wasn't his strong suit when it came to evidence waiting on his laptop.

As promised, the warden's email was short and sweet with one number highlighted. It did look like a burner, but Leo would look into that later. First, he pushed the sound bar on his computer up to thirty and grabbed a notepad before hitting play.

The mechanical operator's voice came on first. "Do you accept these phone charges?"

"Yeah, yeah, yeah."

Gruff voice. A smoker? Either way, that's a deep voice. Definitely male.

Georgie Treadway's familiar voice came on next. "Listen, you gotta hurry up and finish your homework. Dad's gonna be on your ass soon."

"Homework," even without the notebooks, had to mean whatever circuit of crime he was completing. Not like a guy this age actually had homework for a class to worry about seriously. And it was clear enough "Dad" probably meant the Feds.

A pause followed, long enough to make Leo wonder if the call had been dropped, but then the deep-voiced smoker came back on.

"Did you talk, Georgie?" Venom dripped from the man's voice, chilling Leo as surely as those wolf calls from his nightmares had. "Because if you did, then you're never going to get your—"

Treadway's whine cut into the other man's threat. "I wouldn't talk! You know I wouldn't! And if I had, why would I call you, huh? I wouldn't! I told you, you can trust me—"

They made a deal. That has to be it, and he's threatening Georgie's profit margin, or life, if he talked.

"Don't interrupt me, you ass. Because like I said, if you do talk, you won't get your cut. But you might *get cut*."

A shuddering breath came from Treadway, and his voice trembled when he spoke again, shaken. "You listen too. My cut's doubled. You hear me? *Doubled*."

The man on the other end of the call laughed, low and dark.

Leo fiddled with his Saint Jude pendant, suddenly feeling sorry for the young felon behind bars. If there'd ever been a lost cause, he might well be it, and this older man had taken full advantage.

He sounds like he's enjoying Georgie's fear. Enjoying toying with him.

"Georgie boy, listen to yourself. Maybe, just maybe, you

want to call your mommy and tattle on me? That sound like a plan?"

Treadway's breath shuddered, and whatever he was about to say was cut off by a, "Fuck off, Georgie." Without another sound, the man hung up.

Leo reached for his phone and sat back in his chair. SSA Jacinda Hollingsworth wouldn't care about the early hour either.

"Jacinda?" She grunted in the affirmative. "I just got a call from Warden Payne. He sent over the call log for Georgie Treadway, and I've got a call here that we need to get the team on. Treadway called an unknown man on a burner this week and warned him the Feds would be on his tail soon. Mia and I suspected it, but this confirms he knows who's behind these robberies."

"We can use this to compel a subpoena, and I'll get working on that. Meanwhile, get Mia and head back to that prison. I want to know who the hell this guy was talking to, and I'd rather not wait for the subpoena if we don't have to."

Leo shot to his feet, coffee forgotten as he headed to his room to dress.

Interrogate a prisoner with a lead. That's my kind of Valentine's Day date.

17

Though Mia had visited this prison more than a dozen times, she couldn't shake the ominous feeling the place gave her, which seemed worse than ever this week. Sure, she'd never liked coming here, but something about the low-to-the-ground squares of felon housing felt more oppressive than ever before.

Maybe because she now knew the Other existed?

She didn't even want to think about what sort of ghosts this place could lay claim to. Hadn't that serial killer who'd haunted D.C. drugstores for targets back in the nineties just died of a heart attack here recently? And what about the kidnapper who'd kept those poor twins in his van for nearly a month? He'd died by suicide at this prison before trial. And those were just the ones who immediately came to mind.

There have to be dozens. And if any of them are lurking around here still...

Shit. I cannot think about that. I just cannot.

Almost without meaning to, she edged a step closer to Leo. Maybe he was lucky not to know Emma's secrets after all.

Inside, the guard who took their weapons and examined their identification this time was a mean-faced man named O'Connor with an ironic twinkle in his eye that suggested he knew exactly how dangerous he appeared. Mia saw right through him and bared her dimples. His bravado vanished instantly.

O'Connor led her through the same dimly lit halls and into the same claustrophobic room that she and Leo had enjoyed the day before. But at least the space was familiar and small enough that she could avoid wondering what haunted the darkest of its corners.

Leo's foot bounced beneath the table. "You want to take first run at him? Your dimples worked on that guard."

Refocusing, Mia lifted one eyebrow. "Are you asking me to flirt our way into information?"

A small grin shifted his lips. "You think we'd have a better chance if I did?"

Mia shook her head and fluffed her hair as footsteps sounded outside the door. Georgie Treadway appeared just as he had before, if a little bit more racoon-eyed, and a little less round-shouldered.

Nervous, maybe? I can work with that.

Mia leaned against the table as O'Connor cuffed their petite prisoner to it and backed out, making the same assurances the other guard had but minus the wisecracks.

"Back so soon?" Treadway's nose crinkled, somehow making him appear even younger.

"Tell me you didn't miss me?" Mia gave him the smile she usually reserved for Vance.

"Right." But the man preened a little, adjusting in his seat. She'd gotten to his ego, even if he didn't want to admit it. "Bet you say that to all the boys in orange."

At her side, Leo shifted in his chair but maintained his silence as she kept her gazed locked on the prisoner. "Looks like you haven't slept, Georgie. Something bothering you since we talked yesterday?"

Treadway's shoulder rolled in that same dance move as before. He couldn't have lost weight in the past twenty-four hours, but his uniform seemed looser. He certainly wasn't carrying himself in the same fashion.

"Well, I slept well." Mia pulled her notebook from within her coat, settling it in front of her with a casual plop before she uncapped a pen. "Well enough to think maybe we finished up too soon yesterday. I'm hoping you'll tell me which banks you robbed."

Treadway's eyebrow raised, disbelief shading his face. "You already know that. You trying to trick me into telling you about robberies I didn't get caught for?"

Mia let her dimples shine. "Would I do that?"

"Well, it won't work. You caught me on all of 'em." The man *harrumph*ed, but when Mia didn't say anything, he went on. "I robbed three. The D.C. Green Community Bank, Union National over on State Street, and Sundial Trust near the Capitol." He scowled, staring down at the table. "Sundial's the one that bit me in the ass. I shouldn't'a gone so near the damn capitol."

Though Mia jotted down the names, all three matched the banks named in his arrest records, which she'd dug up after their previous visit. She looked up and waited for Treadway to meet her gaze before speaking again. "And which ones did you case besides those? Where else did you work?"

Treadway's Adam's apple bobbed once, then again. His shoulder did that dance move. His eyes shifted away from hers.

"Georgie, you know if we have to, we can start digging through aliases. Mining through your social security records and those of your family. We can find out where you used to work, but that's time we'd rather not have to spend when you can just tell us. This is where talking to the warden on your behalf becomes a reality."

The man clicked his tongue against his teeth, shoulder rolling hard enough to pop right out of its socket. "All right, fine. Yeah. There were a few others I worked at. Davidson Union, down on Eighth Avenue. Manager there was too smart for his own good and fired me fast. Municipal Bank of Reading was another. Coffee there was good."

Mia waited, but Treadway's gaze had gone elsewhere, glazed and tired. "And? Where else?"

"Hell, I don't know. Some little bank near the fairgrounds that I don't remember the name of." He swallowed again, Adam's apple doing enough work for ten. "Union City, also over near the Capitol. That's all I remember. Banks all look the same. Blur together."

Mia took a moment to gaze down at her list. He'd named another bank "by the Capitol," and his whole manner revealed a man doing his best to stay hidden. Treadway was feeding them crap so far, but if Mia pushed a little harder, or nicer, he might start singing.

She smiled, softening her voice. "Try to think of any—"

"*I can't!*" The eruption rang in the air, and Treadway sat back as if he'd surprised himself. "I mean…I mean, there are no others I can remember. They've blurred together. That's all I've got for you, *Agent* Logan."

Rightly, Leo took that as a sign that her dimples had gotten them about as far as they could, and he pulled his phone from his pocket. "If that's all you've got, let's have you listen to something, Mr. Treadway."

Mia had heard the recording once on their way over to the prison, but the other speaker's voice still bothered her. *That man* was a killer. One who enjoyed it, too, and enjoyed the act of threatening others. Hurting others, as well, she had to guess. They'd concluded from the bank video that their fast-driving robber was all business, but now she thought he might just be having fun when he killed.

Across from them, Treadway's face had gone slack. "Lots of people named Georgie."

Leo barked a laugh. "Don't be an idiot. Every inch of this place is on video, and you do not want me to waste the warden's time by making him drag up the video of you making this phone call and timing it to our recording."

Mia glanced at Leo, fighting her own amusement as she leaned back toward Treadway and softened her voice. "My partner's right, Georgie. We already know it's you on this call. What we don't know is who you're talking to. And what cut are we talking about? A cut of what? What are you owed by this guy, and what do you even need the money for?"

He shook his head. "Fuck off. You ain't worth it."

"Worth what, Georgie?" Mia stared, focusing on the little twitch of nerves at the felon's mouth. The way his eyes were darting away from her. "Are you scared of this guy?"

"Of course he is." Leo laughed again, but this time Mia read the insincerity in it.

If the guy on the call was a shark, Treadway was a freakin' harbor seal ripe for being torn apart. And they both knew it, even if their job meant they needed to goad him past that feeling.

"Look at him," Leo said. "Safe as safe can be behind bars but twisting in his seat like he's a kid on a rope swing that got pushed too high."

Mia kept her eyes on Treadway. "Is he right, Georgie? Because you have a lot of friends in this prison, from the sounds of things." *Liar, liar, pants on fire.* She waited, and when he didn't look up, pushed harder. "I wouldn't think you'd have cause to be afraid just because some dude's blustering at you. You really want to let him get away with all those threats?"

Treadway swallowed, the little dance move appearing again.

Leo sat back in his seat, pulling out his phone and beginning to tap away at nothing, just for show. "Maybe we should tell the warden you're refusing to cooperate. See how hard he can make your life. You have friends, right? Like to talk? So you wouldn't want to be in solitary confinement. And this place is already so dismal, I bet the guards here have plenty of ideas for how to make your life harder. You like sports? Bet you won't be watching those if we file a complaint."

"Threats about sports and solitary won't work on him, Leo." Mia leaned back, playing the game in return and following Leo's lead. "But, Georgie, you do realize your guy outside is getting pretty violent, right? We prove you're helping him, you'll be in all kinds of trouble. Was the plan all along for him to murder people? Leave a trail of bodies with each bank heist?"

Treadway's eyes met hers, narrowing. "I never killed nobody."

"Until now." She leaned in. "Because if you've helped this man rob banks, you've helped him kill. I need you to understand that. This isn't your old bank robbery M.O., Georgie. This is new territory you're in. And if you don't help us, you'll end up regretting it in front of a judge who's adding to your sentence rather than granting you parole."

The felon opened his mouth, about to protest, but then clamped his lips shut and shook his head, seeming to melt into his seat. His shoulders hunched, his eyes going to his cuffed wrists before him. Stuck.

"He'll kill me. You might keep me in prison. But he'll kill me."

"Not if we catch him," Leo sat forward, "which we can do

if you help us. And my colleague here asked about your plans for your cut, but this guy's robbing places awfully fast, Georgie. Maybe you can tell us what he needs the money for. That could help us."

Another shoulder roll. Another head shake.

"Georgie." Mia pasted sympathy onto her face, waiting 'til he looked at her to continue. "Do you know what obstruction of justice is?"

The man jittered a head nod.

"So let me spell it out, to make sure we're clear." Mia spoke slower. "Because I wasn't lying to you about that judge. There'll be a judge in your future who sees you as partly culpable for this man's murders. You'll be considered an accessory after the fact to murder. Now, the warden tells us that your mom visits you regularly. That most of your phone calls go to her. Georgie, if you don't help us, you'll never see your mother again as a free man."

His head jerked up. "No!"

"Not with the long sentence you've already got and the potential of these new charges coming down on you. Whatever you were hoping to score as your 'cut' is gone. And this guy you've been talking to is no joke."

Treadway had winced backward in his seat upon mention of his mother, but now appeared more shell-shocked than anything. Scared...but not of them.

"Georgie, you're in over your head." Leo pointed down at his phone, where it remained sitting on the table as if threatening to replay the phone call. "All we need is a name, and then you'll be home free. No new charges."

"I can't, man. I can't." Treadway stared at the table, and Mia glanced sideways at Leo. She could see in his face that they'd both come to the same conclusion. This man was breaking apart in front of them and had been ever since this phone call he'd had, but that didn't change the fact that he feared the unknown robber more than he feared a lengthening of his sentence.

Or anything else, maybe.

"Okay, Georgie."

Nodding, Leo called for the guard to come get him.

Mia didn't say anything else. There was no point.

As O'Connor escorted Georgie Treadway back to his cell, an older man in a worn suit peered in the door at them. "Agents. I'm Warden Payne."

Leo stood and walked over to shake his hand. "Leo Ambrose. We spoke this morning. Thanks for your help."

He nodded, frowning. "I heard about your robber on the news. Treadway of any help?"

"Some." Leo tucked his phone away. "Time will tell, I guess."

The warden slid one hand into a pocket, fidgeting with something there. "I've been watching video of his movements since yesterday. Guy's walking around like he's just been put on death row. That man he spoke to scared him. And I haven't seen Georgie Treadway anything but cocky since he darkened the prison's doorstep."

Mia stepped forward and held out her hand. "Warden Payne, I'm Agent Mia Logan. I'm wondering if you could get us a list of other inmates Georgie's had real contact with. I realize there may be a lot, but perhaps there've been some he's been especially friendly with? Maybe someone who was recently released?"

The warden leaned against the doorframe, his frown going deeper. "Nobody comes to mind. Treadway's the type who survives and passes his time in here by making friends… of a sort…with just about everyone. But I'll talk to the guards on his block and get you a list. Anything I can get you, I'll have it to you in the next hour. I know how important this is."

"And if there are any recent releases on that list," Leo stepped through the door, following the warden's gesture to exit, "it would be ideal if you could get us their parole officers and other assigned parolees. It's looking like we might have to start going door to door here soon."

Payne gave a firm nod and waved down O'Connor, who was on his way back from delivering Treadway to his block. "I'll get on that. You'll hear from me soon."

Leo remained quiet beside Mia as they were ushered back outside, and the first sound between them was a deep sigh gushing from Mia's throat as they reached the Expedition.

"I really hope we don't have to come back here anytime soon." Mia pushed her hair back from her face once she'd settled herself in the driver's seat.

"You and me both. Let's see where this interview gets us. I'll call Jacinda while you drive."

Mia passed him her notebook open to the page of bank names and listened in as she drove.

"He just gave you those seven?"

"That's it. Three that he'd already robbed, and four more he says he worked at. But, Jacinda, he could've been blowing smoke. We need to check his employment history to narrow down banks he's *actually* been inside and possibly scouted."

Jacinda hummed distractedly. "Assuming he wasn't lying, which I know is most likely the case, did he give you any indication of which bank might represent the biggest take? Our perpetrator has a hunger that he clearly needs to keep fed."

Leo glanced at Mia, who shrugged. She'd been unable to read Treadway either way, except he was scared for his own life if he gave them the perpetrator's name.

"He knows who the robber is, but he wouldn't tell us anything more than that. And we had to pull the last four banks out of him. Even the threat of being named an accomplice after the fact didn't loosen his tongue."

Leo slapped a hand on his leg. "He could just give us the name and we could put out an APB. But he's more scared of this guy than having his sentence doubled. What do you think, Jacinda?"

"I think we're shorthanded as hell and have more leads than we have agents." Another few seconds passed as Mia and Leo gave the SSA time to consider options. "Okay, we'll focus on confirming his employment at the unhit banks first. Assuming he lied, it shouldn't be too hard to find out which ones he actually worked at."

"Jacinda, two of the banks Treadway hit are basically on our way back to the Bureau. We can check in to make sure there hasn't been any strange activity." Leo glanced at Mia, who nodded.

"Sounds good." Jacinda muttered to someone on her end of the line, then continued. "Emma, Keaton, and I will each take one of the banks that hasn't been hit yet. You two check the ones on your way and put in a call to the last two. Call me when you're done."

Leo was about to confirm the plan when the call ended. A sure sign that Jacinda was in a hurry.

But she wasn't the only one. Clearly, their robber was on a timetable, which meant the rest of them had better start working on catching up to his pace.

Or else they'd all be walking around like Georgie Treadway. Under threat from a deep-voiced smoker who, if history was telling, had zero concerns when it came to dealing out death.

18

I parked on the side street beside the bank, gentling my baby out of first gear and sitting back to wait. I still had a few minutes before opening time.

The Municipal Bank of Samson Creek looked just like it had back when Georgie cased it. A green metal roof over that cozy white siding, like it was actually someone's home instead of a bank. They even had a drive-through that almost took up more space than the building itself. This place was small, like the last one, so the bag, at most, would be around fifty grand.

Still enough to make a difference in retirement. No question about that.

Most importantly, Georgie's notebooks laid out all the bank's details like an engine rebuild kit. Every piece lined up in a row and waiting for me to slot it in. Georgie'd done his homework, all right.

I repeated his notes from memory, going over each detail. But I stopped mid-sentence as a lone car pulled into the small parking lot.

Opening operations. Assistant manager and manager come in

together, about a quarter to nine, to open up and get the teller drawers out of the vault.

There should've been two of them, but I saw only one person in the car—a woman, as far as I could tell from this distance. That matched what Georgie's notes said.

Manager is an older lady. Drive-through operator comes in around nine thirty, checks the ATM, then opens up the window. Security guard shows up around ten.

If only one person was showing up, I'd expect it to be one of them. But I wasn't planning on sticking around that long. Today, however, it seemed only the manager had arrived. Maybe this was one of those banks that didn't play by all the rules about what should be done security-wise.

The lady got out of her Honda Accord, and for a moment, I couldn't breathe. It wasn't some 'older lady' at all, but a mid-twenties beauty who stood almost as tall as me.

Was she a new manager? Had the bank set up some new policies, making Georgie's notes useless?

I had my hand on the keys, ready to turn over my engine and get out of there, but my worry quickly turned to relief. The lady who now stood at the bank door was a long-legged creature in turquoise pants and a cream-colored winter coat. Plenty nice to look at, but it was her hair that put a smile on my face as wide as the Mississippi.

Against the light fabric of her coat, her hair gleamed so dark a red that it almost looked deep purple in the morning light. Hanging to her waist like a waterfall, straight and well cared for.

Mary Karen could make a fucking masterpiece with locks like that.

I thought back to that black-haired woman I'd killed in Georgia, the one with the hair stretching straight down to her ass, practically past her miniskirt. Mary Karen had gotten two wigs out of her, both of them beauties. One had been long, cut like Cleopatra. Mary Karen had made the other into a cute little bob befitting a go-go dancer.

That particular teller had put up a helluva fight, though. She'd stamped her stiletto on my foot hard enough to leave a bruise, and "accidentally"—or so she'd claimed—dropped half her drawer's take over the floor rather than stacking it in our duffel.

She'd even tried to call the cops when I'd turned away and shot out their one security camera. Thinking about it almost made me grin.

Sure, I'd shot the spirit out of her after taking her hair, but everyone in that lobby had seen it as revenge. Me and Mary Karen's jobs had been twice as easy after that, with that pretty teller's face plastered all over the newscasts.

She hadn't known it, of course, but her little stunt shifted the way banks did business. That woman had taken pride in her job and gotten killed for it.

Georgie said things changed. Jobs were jobs, and nobody was stupid enough to die for them anymore. Nobody had Clint Eastwood for an idol these days, which seemed to be true for the most part.

Except somebody was stupid enough to hit an alarm and throw in dye packs when told not to. That dumb teller at the last bank, and the blue-headed teenager. I hadn't seen anyone with the impulse to play hero for so long.

It'll be interesting to find out if this lady is a throwback to old times or not.

Assuming she was the bank manager, I might still need an assistant manager to show up to open the vault. If that person got here in the next five minutes, I could still pull the job. And if not, I'd just have to make do with coming in for a trim.

With the lady shuffling in the front door and locking it again behind her, I checked the clock standing on a post beside the parking lot. Still fifteen minutes until showtime, so I might as well use it.

Gotta give Gorgeous Hair time to prepare and her lackey to show up.

Truck in park with the engine off, I went over Georgie's notes for the other banks still on my list. Even if this one didn't work out, Mary Karen and I could pull in plenty to set us up good for the rest of our lives.

I gave myself until the count of ten to feel sad about how long that might actually be, and then went back to reviewing my notes for the bank across the street.

Two girl managers, one girl sec. guard. Vault opened by managers dialing locks at same time.

Five minutes to showtime and still no sign of another car or anybody looking like another girl who might be the bank manager.

There was just no professionalism anymore.

"Fine, the hell with the money. I'll just go in for a little off the top."

I pulled on my gloves first. They fit snug, with no extra fabric to mess up my grip. Next, I tugged the green screen mask from my glove box and gave it a once-over.

Times sure had changed. Nowadays, looking around for lady's stockings was just about impossible. Women simply didn't wear them. Nylons didn't work the same way either. They ripped too easily. But I'd found these special effects masks in a discount tub at a big-box store, and they did the job better than I could have dreamed. Green screen masks, whatever that meant.

The material didn't snag, and once I "went green," as Mary Karen called it, nobody could see a single detail to tell the cops later.

With just two minutes remaining before the bank opened, I scanned the parking lot and street, just in case the manager was showing up extra late for some reason. I got nothing for my effort.

Pulling the mask on, I let my eyes adjust to the changed view. Green-tinged, definitely, but it wasn't like I was missing much when it came to February in D.C. Seeing the sky was a welcome change, sure, but it was gray as stone. I took a moment to remember I cared more about the open air above me than its color.

Mask in place, I picked up my gun.

Today was Valentine's Day, after all, and it was about time to go get my Mary Karen a gift she'd remember forever.

Roses are red. Violets are blue.

I'm about to take that hair away from you.

19

Work was just about the last place Assistant Bank Manager Lorena Diaz wanted to be today, but she disarmed the bank's alarm and began flipping on lights anyway. Teddy, her teller, and Moira, the security guard, should get here any minute now to back her up, so she wouldn't have to be alone too long with her thoughts.

And her thoughts were loud. Her mind buzzed with regrets. After fighting with her boyfriend, Angelo, the night before, she'd woken up with only one desire—to crawl back under the covers and sleep until the fourteenth of February had come and gone once more. But that wasn't an option.

Stupid holiday'll give me a migraine again this year. I can't believe I don't have a date. And how many guys are going to come through to pick up cash today, crowing about their plans for the night? I should've called in sick too.

Nancy, the branch manager, had texted that she was hit with a flu bug and wouldn't be in, but that Lorena should just open up anyway and she'd call Teddy in.

They kept the teller stations stocked with adequate bills and coins to operate for a day without opening the vault.

Unless somebody came in for an unusually large withdrawal, she'd be okay for a few minutes.

With a quick glance in the mirror at the side of the entrance, she straightened her blouse—turquoise, decidedly *not* red or pink for this cursed day—and forced herself to smile.

Her phone buzzed in her pocket. It was from Moira, the security guard. *Feeling super sick this morning. Can't get out of bed. Sorry!*

Lorena frowned but typed, *Feel better*! and hated the world a little more on this most romantic of days.

Seriously, doesn't anyone wash their hands anymore?

She'd have to look up the security agency's number to get a replacement. Moira couldn't be counted on to have called for a backup. Lorena made a mental note to give the agency a piece of her mind.

Then she unlocked the doors and hurried back to her spot without looking outside. A *ding* signaled a customer who must've been waiting. She called out a quick, "Good morning," as she used her fob to buzz through to the teller area behind the counter.

When she landed at her station, she turned to see a tall man in a green mask, standing just across the glass. *What the hell kind of absurd Valentine's Day costume is this?* And to make things worse, he stank of cigarettes and something like paint or grease.

Her mouth opened to say something as a gun rose up. The weapon pointed through her window with its gaping hole of a barrel staring right at her.

Shit. Shit, shit, shit, not today.

"Sir, please don't hurt—"

"Shut it and put up your hands." He gestured with the gun, and she thrust her hands up to shoulder height in response.

Her pulse raced, but she tried to breathe deep before answering. Panicking wouldn't do her any good right now. Not with a gun pointed at her chest. "Anything you say, sir."

The green fabric shifted around his lips, maybe hinting at a smile, and the tall man nodded. "*Sir.* I like that. Now, you stay still for me, darlin'. I'm going to come around the counter, and I'm going to watch as you dump whatever you've got back there in this bag. Understand?"

He hefted a beige canvas bag up beside him, and she nodded. "I understand, sir."

I can do this. We did that training last year, and I've thought about it hundreds of times. I just have to stay calm, and I won't get hurt. He doesn't want to hurt me.

The man kept his face turned toward her as he moved down the counter and hollered at her to buzz him through the swing door.

"And don't even dare think about touching that alarm button, little lady."

Lorena reached a shaky hand to her key ring where she had her fob. She pressed the button on it, and the buzz from the door lock sounded as loud as an air horn.

The robber yanked the door open and stormed into the teller area. When he was still a good four feet from her, he flung the bag her way, and she stumbled to catch it, dropping her keys to the floor.

Her hands shook as she hung one of the bag's straps on a nearby drawer handle to prop it open. But she could do this. She'd always been the best at her job, taking pride in her work, and this was simple. *Just ignore the gun, get the money in the bag, and survive. Easy as frying bacon on a Sunday.*

The masked man waved the gun at her. "You finish with your drawer, you move to the next, and then we'll be done."

One drawer and then the next. Don't ask him questions about anything he doesn't mention. Remember the training. Bank robbers are dumb. He wants to be in and out. Chances are, he didn't plan ahead.

I get through this, get him what he wants, I'll be fine.

She wavered where she stood, weak-kneed, but reached for her keys.

"I need to unlock the drawers, sir. I need my keys."

"Go on. Get 'em. And keep the other hand away from that alarm button under the counter."

Lorena nodded, scooped up her keys, and set to work, first unlocking the drawer in front of her, then pulling the elastic key ring onto her wrist. The keys jingled as she worked.

The sooner she got this over with, the better. And bank robberies were fast. What had that trainer said, three minutes? So she only had to live through this terror a little bit longer, and she'd be good to go.

Soon, Lorena, soon. You got this. Just be nice, and don't say anything you don't have to.

Filling the bag from one side to the other, she kept her hands as much in view of the green-masked man as she could. And she avoided the dye packs, too, as well as the alarm button that was just a little bit too far out of reach.

Let Nancy complain later if she wanted to. Her old ass hadn't showed up to get robbed this morning, and Lorena was not risking her life for this bank or this job.

She got through the last teller's drawer and swallowed. "That's all I have access to, sir."

There you go. Call him "sir" and be respectful. Like the trainer said. Be nice and stay alive.

"Put the bag down on the ground and zip it up."

Lorena did so, proud that she managed to zip up the bag without fumbling the job. Her hands still shook, but not so much as they had. Standing, she kept her eyes on the man's feet rather than chancing a look at the gun or the mask. If she looked at the gun again, she might just lose it.

"Now I want you to turn around and face that wall at the end of the counter."

Tears suddenly welled in Lorena's eyes, but she did as he asked. This was either over or it wasn't. Maybe if she turned around, he'd just leave.

If I cooperate, I'll be okay. That's what they always say. I just have to cooperate.

Face nearly touching the wall, she kept her hands up and rested them against the surface, in between the two boring landscape paintings that Nancy loved so much. She fought the urge to lean in and close her eyes, not wanting to appear any weaker than she was.

Predators preyed on weakness, and there was no doubt that this man behind her was more than willing to do so.

She'd get through this, though. And after the cops came and took her statement, she'd call her boyfriend and tell him what had happened. Angelo would feel so protective, their fight would be forgotten. He'd come running back to her side, freaking out, and they'd spend the night cuddling in front of the television.

She'd let him turn on one of those horror movies he loved, he wouldn't complain about how much wine she drank, and they'd end the night with those tarts she baked yesterday. And with some lovemaking, of course.

Everything would be fine.

His steps came closer, heavy on the carpet, and the sound of fabric shifting told her he was taking something from a pocket.

And then, in the span of a breath, her hair pulled tight at the nape of her neck, fisted hard in one gloved hand.

"Ouch! Please—"

"Shut up." The growl was accentuated by a tug at her hair,

like her sister might have yanked at her when they'd fought in grade school, and she clenched her fists against the wall. Willing herself not to move. Not to ask what this psycho wanted from her.

This isn't the way the trainer said it would go.

The grip tightened, coming closer to her scalp, and tears began sliding from her eyes. His hold on her *hurt*.

Behind her neck, the fist gripping her newly dyed hair angled against her head so that the man's knuckles dug into the back of her neck, drawing an unintended moan out of her throat. And then a slow, sawing *rip* seemed to lessen the grip centimeter by centimeter, her pain finally relenting as the man's hand came away from her.

But when the truth hit her, the relief from the pain stung worse in the aftermath.

He cut off my hair.

This pendejo *just stole my hair!*

Her hands came away from the wall before she could think, fisting down at her sides as she whirled on the robber, unable to stop herself. "How dare you! What the hell do you think you're…oh, oh, oh."

Her words bled into a moan as he stepped back away from her and held the gun back up.

Aimed at her.

With her pretty hair hanging limp from one of his hands, his gun hand tensed, and his finger tightened.

"Oh, sir, oh, oh—"

The bullet caught her in the chest, and she flew back against the wall.

Though she felt herself sliding down, Lorena couldn't breathe. She couldn't hear after that deafening blast. She couldn't feel except for a flash of heat and the hammer of shock running through her, centered on her breast.

Her nostrils stung with the smell of sulfur and oil piled

on top of the cigarette stink from before, and in a daze, she wondered if the paramedics would even know she'd put on perfume earlier in case Angelo came in to apologize.

She tried to look down, but realized she was lying limp on the floor, one arm bent awkwardly beneath her getting soaked with blood, just like her turquoise blouse.

This can't...this can't be happening.

She couldn't move, and the effort to breathe got harder every time she tried. Her chest grew tighter with pain, and wetter with the blood draining from her body.

And the man in the green mask waved at her with her own hair. He picked up his bag of money, turned, and jogged away.

A moist wheeze emitted from her lips, and she shut her eyes. They felt glued shut with either tears or blood. She fought for one more breath and didn't find it.

20

E mma pulled into the front parking lot of the Municipal Bank of Samson Creek. At first, she wasn't even sure the place was open. A lone Camry sat near the road, but the vehicle could just as easily have been left there by a bar patron from the night before.

It was nearing half past nine, though.

If it's open, the management can't be worth a damn. They're probably in violation of plenty of protocols, security or otherwise. Great.

Still, Emma pushed open the door of her Charger and stepped out, patting the vehicle on the roof as if to reassure herself it would be there for her when she needed it. She'd picked up the vehicle from the Bureau's motor pool that morning...no way was their gearhead robber going to outrun her again if she had to chase him down.

But right now, she just wanted the reality of the vehicle to ground her. Even though the nearby road hosted plenty of traffic, the lot was eerily quiet.

It was odd. And cold.

Colder than it was at the Bureau…

Shit.

Emma's lungs had chilled with the air temperature already, but her breath came a little bit faster as she examined the bank entrance.

On the bank's front walkway stood Trisha Terrence, white-eyed and grimacing. The ghostly mother, recently killed by their robber, couldn't have been clearer in message if she'd spoken. One of her hands pointed at the bank's front door, closed and shaded against the morning light.

A pit settled in Emma's stomach. Ten minutes before, she'd been focused and optimistic in the wake of a fabulous night's sleep that had been dreamless and deep. Just what she'd needed after baring her heart to her mother.

But the thickening cold around her and a ghost pointing at the bank's front door whisked away all of that in seconds.

A quick scan of Emma's surroundings offered no glimpse of a pickup, let alone the old model she and Leo had chased through a field. In the road, traffic hustled by as if nothing were wrong. No sirens screamed, no other ghosts gathered, and no bank robber sat waiting for her handcuffs.

But he could be inside.

No telling what vehicle he's driving or where it might be hiding, Emma girl. Don't expect patterns where you aren't sure they exist.

Keeping her eyes on the ghost of Trisha Terrence, Emma radioed the team that the bank seemed wrong, and she was going in.

Jacinda's voice came back immediately. "Emma, wait where you are. Do not engage. We'll be there in five minutes."

Emma's breath plumed from her lips in the cold. "We could have another body in five minutes, Jacinda. I'm going in." Rather than waiting for another reply, she flicked off the radio and drew her weapon.

Jacinda would definitely rip into her for this, but their bank robber had already killed one woman, injured two others, and done who knew what else.

She wanted to stop him today. Now, if possible.

And with Trisha there reminding her that the woman he'd killed had left a child without a mother, Emma had no intention of waiting for backup.

"Trisha, is he still in there? The man who killed you?"

The ghost's white eyes roved side to side before settling on Emma. "He cut it. Just cut it all off."

"Super helpful there, Trisha. Thanks." The cold numbed Emma's exposed skin as she angled around the ghost toward the bank door. She listened for a moment but heard nothing. Nobody and nothing else—besides her and the ghost—moved around the bank's perimeter or lot.

The door gave way easily, unlocked, and she slipped inside with her gun up, eyes wide as she rotated to the right and checked her near corner. A loud *ding* chimed above her, stopping her heart for a half second. She swept her aim around to the left, scanning the lobby as she flattened herself against the wall.

Nothing moved. The room stayed still and silent but for her own breathing.

The hardwood floor gleamed in the fluorescent lighting, and everything in the lobby looked to be in place. No broken glass, no fallen pictures, and no blood. No bodies, either, ghostly or living.

She re-scanned each corner of the space fast, paying special attention to the set of office doors at the back of the space. Frosted glass prevented her from seeing inside two of them, but the third was open and clearly empty. If the robber was still there, he could have shot her when she'd entered or when her attention had been elsewhere.

But the building felt dreadfully empty, which was a problem. Nobody opened a bank and then left it sitting unstaffed for any Tom, Dick, or Harry to wander in.

Somebody should've been there, but the place remained as quiet as the parking lot outside.

Emma relaxed her aim. If their robber had been there at all, he was gone now. Still, she held herself steady and put her back to the wall beside the door, holding her gun close to her body with the muzzle angled toward the floor. Something was obviously off.

"Hello? FBI! Is anyone here?" She waited one beat, then another, but got no response. "I'm Special Agent Emma Last. If you are here, come out now, hands raised!"

She gave another scan around the small lobby. It held a waiting area with a few chairs in the nearest corner. A hallway wound around beside the last office, heading farther into the building.

Keeping one eye on the hall, in case anyone appeared, Emma made her way to the tellers' windows. She froze midstep when she spotted the unmistakable mark of blood spatter against the back wall.

Damn this man. Damn him.

Moving to the counter, weapon raised again, Emma snuck a look into the tellers' area. A pretty woman in her twenties lay bloodied on the floor, her blouse soaked in a way that suggested she'd been shot or stabbed. Her eyes were shut, and her head twisted at an awkward angle so that Emma could see her hair had been cut off.

Just like Trisha Terrence's.

Emma's instinct was to check for signs of life, but she quickly realized there was no point. The woman's ghost sat cross-legged on the floor beside her body, rocking in place. Her white eyes stared forward, focused on something Emma couldn't see.

But she did speak. "She can see you."

A breath jittered out of Emma's throat. "Shit."

OUTSIDE THE BANK, Emma glanced at Mia's phone, which Mia held up for her own viewing pleasure.

A message box from Vance stared outward like a harbinger of germs.

Can't get out of bed. Sorry, but you do not want me there when I'm like this. Good luck with the bank robber.

Leo slid his phone into his pocket with a grunt. "Denae just texted. She thinks it might be pneumonia."

Jacinda grimaced as she waved them on toward the front of the bank, which Emma had already cleared. "Let's get in there, then, since this is all of us. Sloan may be able to join us later, but she's not up to it right now. Just watch where you step and what you touch since we beat forensics."

"They usually this slow to get to a violent crime scene?" Keaton raised an eyebrow.

Their SSA shrugged before answering. "They're still at one-quarter strength because of the flu. Make sure you're taking your vitamins as long as you're here in D.C."

Emma rubbed at her temple as her teammates slipped on shoe covers and gloves. That done, the group filed into the bank like a string of ducklings with Jacinda in the lead. Jacinda knelt beside the body and read the name badge. "Lorena Diaz."

Rest in peace, Lorena.

At least the ghosts had disappeared and left the FBI agents to their own devices, but that was little enough to ask for. Really, she felt like spraying the whole crime scene with disinfectant now that they'd verified their missing team members were mostly worse, if anything.

Her low-grade headache had nothing to do with oncoming illness, though, and she knew it.

No, the hum of discomfort resounding in her skull was built of pure frustration.

Leo gazed over the counter at Lorena Diaz's still body and the pool of blood soaking into the carpeting that covered the teller area. "Our timeline to catch this guy is tight. Two banks in twenty-four hours? He's gathering funds for something, and he can only have so much more he needs. At least, I think. Or hope."

"I'd love it if there wasn't so much doubt surrounding those words." Emma grimaced at the body. "But one way or another, you're right. Either we need to catch him to stop him, or he needs to reach his goal and stop himself."

"Before he drops more bodies." Mia halted a few feet from the victim, nodding at Jacinda when the other woman gestured that she was taking a call. Her eyes were hooded with concern when she glanced back at Emma and Leo. "I'll say one thing for him. If he's old, like we think based on the truck, he's got stamina and energy. I wish he didn't, but look where we are."

Keaton crouched next to Lorena's body, near the spot where Emma had seen her ghost sitting earlier. With one gloved finger, he traced the air along the back of her head as he craned his neck forward. "She's missing hair, just like Trisha Terrence. Cutting it seems like a necessary part of these crimes. That's how we're going to catch him."

Leo scoffed beside Emma. "Little early for identifying a killer based off a couple of haircuts, Holland."

Emma forced a small smile for Leo's benefit. "Keaton and I had been looking at a possible connection to a cancer patient, but he's clicking his tongue. That means he's got something else in mind." The explanation hung in the air until Mia laughed a little.

Then Keaton got to his feet. "We'd been so focused on the cancer angle...I wonder if we're looking in the wrong place."

Mia frowned down at the body. "You mean there's another bank with a dead woman in it we should be looking at?"

Her biting tone, of course, did not faze Keaton. "Well, this bank wasn't on Georgie Treadway's list, so we can probably count on that list being falsified even without digging into his employment history."

The SSA had her phone out and was texting. "Even so, Agent Holland, I'll alert local authorities near the other names on that list. I doubt the Bureau has any assets we can devote to surveillance, but at least we know where we might be called to provide aid."

As if everything Jacinda said was of little consequence, Keaton shrugged.

Not for the first time Emma noticed Leo casting a dubious glance at the Richmond agent.

For his part, Keaton seemed not to notice as he turned to Emma. "What are some other reasons a woman would need a wig? Cancer isn't the only one. We could be looking for someone with alopecia or even inherited female-pattern baldness. Or someone who is just very vain."

Giving a grunt of what sounded like irritation, Leo took out a notebook and pen. He began writing and spoke without looking up. "Okay, but how does this help us look in the right place? I'm still waiting for the magic trick."

Keaton didn't seem to be listening, focused on his phone. He tapped something in and scrolled along as though none of them were in the room.

Mia shook her head at him. "The car dealer. You said he got handsy with a woman in a wig, and her husband went bananas."

Emma nodded. "I was about to mention that."

Jacinda rejoined their group and *ahem*ed. "Did you bring enough for the rest of the students, Agent Last?"

Emma brought the SSA up to speed, then explained what she and Keaton had learned from Barry Meldrum's former employee, Davy Delko.

"He said that when Meldrum stroked the woman's hair, it came off because she was wearing a wig. And Meldrum's story corroborates. He said he'd been shot by a man who told him to keep his hands to himself."

Keaton stepped around Lorena Diaz's body and turned his phone to show Jacinda. The smile on his face was out of place given the circumstances, but Emma took comfort seeing her old partner acting like she remembered.

Clueless to just about everything going on around him, but he still brings in results.

"Mary Karen and Kenneth Grossman," he narrated. "Bank robbers from the seventies. She had alopecia and wore her hair super short. Together, they robbed twenty banks across the South over four years, and they used the victims' hair to build her wigs."

Emma scanned the page he was showing them, scrolling up to read the details.

The Grossmans were notorious in their day but were caught and jailed. There was a huge hullabaloo over what to do with the wigs once things went to trial. Prosecutors and law enforcement couldn't decide whether the wigs ought to be separated out by victim to be returned to their families, maybe buried, or just locked in an evidence box forever.

"The Grossmans would have to be, what? In their late sixties? Early seventies? You can't really be thinking we're looking for a geriatric Bonnie and Clyde."

Leo grunted. "Or even just a Clyde. We only have one

killer, decidedly male if we put any stock in voice, height, and build."

Mia crossed her arms, ignoring the exchange and looking at Emma. "Plus, they were caught after killing people in the act of robbing a bank. That's a life sentence. And this is the South we're talking about. They might have received the death penalty."

"I'd think so." Emma frowned. "But we can at least check, and it shouldn't take too long to find out if the Grossmans are still doing time, or if they're even still alive."

Leo's phone pinged. He slipped it out and gave the message a look. "We asked Georgie Treadway's warden to get us information on current parole officers and parolees. He's just sent it on, for whenever we're ready to go hunting."

"Okay, folks, let's get serious." Jacinda waited for all eyes to turn to her. "I'll manage the on-scene investigation and make sure forensics gets all the evidence gathered before anything's contaminated. With this body dropping on top of yesterday's, I should be able to put a rush on ballistics. While I'm waiting for those units to arrive and do their thing, I'll see what I can dig up on Treadway's employment history to confirm which other bank might be our perpetrator's next target." She pointed at Emma and then Leo. "I want you both to focus on that parole list. And talk to Meldrum again. Get a description of the couple Delko mentioned."

Emma nodded. "Yes, ma'am."

Jacinda aimed her phone at Keaton. "Find out where the Grossmans are now. Behind bars, in the ground, or other-wise. And make sure you confirm the facts. Mia, you review this bank's footage."

Mia headed back toward the manager's desk and security equipment they'd found earlier.

Emma met Leo's gaze and jerked her head toward the doorway. "Ready to get started on that list?"

"Thought you'd never ask. And I rode with Mia, so you're driving, unfortunately." He shouldered his way past a recently arrived tech, who was holding the door open for Emma. "That your muscle car I saw outside?"

"The Bureau's, yeah." She kept up with him, taking a deep breath of the cold air as soon as they were on the sidewalk. "No way is this guy losing us in another car chase. If we get him in our sights, his taillights are mine."

Leo laughed out loud, a bit more high-pitched than usual, but headed straight for her latest ride.

Sounds like a nervous laugh. Maybe he really doesn't trust my driving.

The Charger glittered black in the sunlight, just waiting for the fast-driving bank robber to make her take advantage of its speed. And suddenly, that didn't seem so far-fetched. This case actually felt a hell of a lot more in hand than it had just the night before.

A plan was in place. Her steps felt suddenly lighter, her headache a little bit more manageable. Closer to the state of mind she'd enjoyed on waking up that morning.

And as Leo climbed into the passenger seat of the Charger, Emma assured herself that having a plan was all her instincts were reacting to. A game plan on the heels of a good sleep. That was why she felt better all of a sudden.

Even when Leo's determined brown eyes met hers across the space of the car, and her belly settled down for the first time since entering the bank, she repeated to herself that she was just glad to be doing something. Glad to have a lead to follow.

She absolutely *did not* feel safer, or steadier, with Leo at her side. That was nonsense.

Just as much nonsense as seeing the dead, Emma girl? Kind of like that?

She stuck her smile in place and clicked her seat belt home as Leo pulled up their next destination.

If she could ignore ghosts threatening her, she could damn well ignore an annoying little voice in her head. No matter how true it sounded, or how confusing that truth might be.

21

W ith a list of over twenty parole officers in hand, Leo and Emma spent the rest of the morning on the phone, camped out in a musty office at the nearest police station. Georgie Treadway had a lot of so-called friends among recent parolees, or at least he thought he did. Any of them who would have admitted to knowing the man hadn't mentioned him to their parole officers.

Call after call, they got roughly the same reply.

"Treadway? Haven't heard the name, but my parolee's minding his p's and q's. Got a job. Never misses an AA meeting. Gets home on time."

Emma called another parole officer and tried another angle, to see if any of the recently paroled offenders had been even more recently un-paroled because they'd tried getting back into the game using Georgie's "system."

"Nope, he doesn't have a car or a truck."

"This morning? He's been at work since eight. I was just there getting a cup of coffee."

The few times Treadway's name came up from a parolee, it wasn't complimentary.

"Oh yeah, my guy knew Treadway inside. Said he's a jackass."

Some replies went a little further in their critique.

"Treadway? I hope he doesn't fuck this up for our guy. He's holding down a job better 'n most of 'em do. Volunteering with a church day care and everything."

All the parole officers either knew where their recent parolees had been during one or more of the robberies or could verify that location with a simple phone call.

The police station in Samson Creek was housed in an old multistory building that had originally been a schoolhouse. Wide hallways, decorated with faded mass-produced paintings and laminated signs, made for a labyrinth of doors leading into classrooms that had been converted into shared offices, storage spaces, and, like the space she and Leo occupied, interrogation rooms.

Emma's first breath of fresh air came with a blast of ghostly cold. When she went to the bathroom, she encountered a grumpy ghost reading a tattered newspaper on a toilet.

"Um, sorry?"

The ghost *harrumph*ed pointedly and ignored her.

She excused herself and tried the next stall, finding it blessedly empty. As she peed, she shivered at the idea that, only a handful months ago, she would have used the other toilet, never knowing she occupied the same space as the ghostly figure.

Ignorance is bliss.

Or was it?

Still pondering that question, she leaned against the wall of another drab hallway and sighed as Leo pulled up the list yet again.

"Back to phone banking?" Emma groaned, dreading the thought of returning to the dim corner of the station where they'd spent the last three hours. "How many do we have left?"

"Not many." Leo chuckled. "Robberies committed at nine in the morning make for some easy alibi finding, at least."

"True enough. I bet we'd be having more trouble if our guy was robbing banks at closing."

Her partner's eyes narrowed, and his smile tightened a touch as he turned his phone around so that Emma could view the screen. "You see what I see?"

"Officer Lina Vernon." The name was familiar, and it took Emma only a couple seconds to place it. "She's a parole officer in this building. Let's—"

"Go." Leo turned on his heel and headed farther down the hall to the office marked as Vernon's. When he knocked, a tired voice told him to come in.

The frizzy-haired woman behind the desk pouted. "I don't see a bag from Subway, so I'm guessing you're not here to deliver my lunch."

When Leo flashed his identification along with his signature grin, the woman waved them to the two chairs before her desk.

"Special Agent Leo Ambrose, and this is my partner, Special Agent Emma Last. Any luck, we'll be out of your hair before your lunch shows up."

"Naw, it's fine. Go ahead and take my mind off my stomach. What can I do you for?"

Emma shifted in her seat, trying to get comfortable with the lack of padding. "We're looking into the bank robberies and checking into parolees. You have anyone with a history of hitting banks? We understand you have Marco Schwab and Edgar Millard on your list, both of whom were on the same block as Georgie Treadway."

"Schwab and Millard are idiots, but they're behaving themselves, 'less you count Schwab getting a parking ticket last week. If you want to waste your time, I can give you their addresses."

"What about someone else who's struggling to keep their nose clean? Someone who might be in touch with either guy and heard about Georgie Treadway from them."

Officer Vernon tutted. "My parolees are all staying in line...I make sure of it...and I don't know the name Treadway."

Leo leaned forward, putting every ounce of charm into his voice. "Any bank robbers among your crowd?"

She smirked and gave Leo a shake of her head. "I have one bank robber on my list, which has twenty-four names on it, and I need to be getting back to checking on them, on top of everything else I have to do today."

Emma pulled out her pen. "We need that name." To take the edge off her order, she added, "We can confirm his whereabouts for you and at least save you that task."

Officer Vernon twisted sideways and pulled a file from a nearby cabinet. "You got a deal. But that name I got...well, *she* ain't your guy. For one thing, Mary Karen Grossman's sixty-five, she's fighting a cancer diagnosis, and is barely five-one."

You've got to be kidding me.

Emma sat up straight, sensing Leo doing the same beside her. "Did you say Mary Karen Grossman? The bank robber from the seventies? And she has cancer? I thought she had alopecia."

"That's right. Cancer came on fast, and she was paroled because of it." The officer waved a file, offering a small smile. "But you and me both know she's not the one you're looking for. Chatter says your robber's pretty tall in addition to being a man. And let's remember, Mrs. Grossman is dying of cancer. Last time we spoke, it didn't look good. I doubt she'll be around more than another six months. No way does she have the energy to be running around robbing banks."

Leo typed something into his phone. "Do you know why she and her husband were serving sentences instead of receiving the death penalty? Capital crimes in southern states tend to go in one direction, especially when the perpetrators commit serial crimes."

Vernon stared at him, deadpan. "I can offer you my opinion, but it won't even buy you a cup of coffee down the hall. Good defense attorney? Hell, I don't know how the trial went because I was barely out of diapers when it happened."

The officer's gaze wandered to her door, as if searching for her lunch, then tracked to an open appointment book on her desk. She closed the book, gave a resigned sigh, and shrugged. "I can tell y'all have a burning desire to know about Mary Karen Grossman, so go ahead and ask your questions."

Emma got right to the point. "How often do you see her, and does she come in with anyone?"

"Every month, without fail. She never misses an appointment. And lately, she's been coming in with her husband. You want a tall bank robber, I guess he'd fit the bill, but that man's got to be close to seventy and spends all his free time taking care of his wife, so I doubt he's your perpetrator."

Emma swallowed. Playing caregiver to his dying wife or not, Kenneth Grossman could certainly be their perpetrator. They had to at least consider him a real possibility.

"Well?" the officer pressed. "Something I need to know about my parolee?"

Leo sat back, glancing over at Emma. "What do you know about her husband?"

Rather than reading from a file, Vernon tapped at her keyboard this time. "Parole officer is Tim Lee."

Leo mouthed, *On our list.*

"Grossman's been out of jail for three weeks." When a noise came from the open doorway, she gestured for a delivery carrier to come forward with her sandwich, barely taking her eyes off the screen before her. Apparently, the idea of lunch had paled in relation to a little bit of excitement. "He's sixty-seven years old, but healthy. Made every appointment with Tim so far, and is currently looking for employment, applying for jobs in between making sure Mary Karen gets what she needs. No negative marks on his record so far. They're living together, and I take it you want their address?"

"Yes." Emma tapped her pen on her notebook. "Where was Kenneth released from?"

Another glance at the computer. "Jackson Federal. Oh, and hey, you mentioned a Treadway. They're known associates from what Lee's marked down here. Not friendly in a suspicious way, but crossed paths enough for it to be noted in the files. Looks like Kenneth might've roughed him up for something that...wasn't disclosed."

"Shit." Leo sat back in his chair, the curse hanging around them as Emma took a fast-track approach to explaining that Mary Karen wasn't a suspect in their case at this time, but her husband most definitely was.

"We need that address and any known aliases."

Vernon nodded and began composing an email to Emma at her Bureau address and double-checking everything before hitting send. Emma appreciated the effort. If they finally had an actual suspect, she wanted to make damn sure they didn't end up spinning their wheels over a typo.

Finally, it felt like they were getting somewhere. Not enough so that she could celebrate...but a long, boring morning had, for once, actually gotten them results.

Maybe.

Emma checked her phone and confirmed the email had arrived. Vernon was already eyeing her sandwich as Emma and Leo stood up. "Thank you for your time, Officer Vernon. Enjoy your lunch."

Speaking of which, I think maybe we've earned ours.

Leo shut the door behind them once they got into the hallway. "Could we really be dealing with the same Grossmans who hit banks in the seventies?"

"We've seen weirder things." The words were out of Emma's mouth before she could catch them, and she felt her cheeks warm. References to the Other were not what she needed to be offering right now. Not at the moment and definitely not with Leo Ambrose. She tried for a save, surging forward before Leo could catch her slip. "You know...knife-throwing circus killers, crazed vigilante prophets living in a cultish little town. Things haven't exactly been run-of-the-mill since you joined the team."

Leo grinned in acknowledgment. "True. I guess the Grossmans are almost tame by comparison."

"You call Jacinda, and I'll call Keaton, all right? Tell them we have an address for the Grossmans, and what we've found out. I know Jacinda will still want us to head to the car emporium for an ID on the couple, but we ought to get a uniform over to the address even if it's likely to be a bust. If it is them, they won't be staying at their address of record."

"I agree. Unfortunately. But we'll work on it. I'll ask if Jacinda can pull files on this Bonnie and Clyde pair before they hit another bank too. I think our last few parole officers can wait, assuming we even need to talk to them."

"What about Kenneth's PO? Shouldn't we try him too?"

"We have an address, and Mary Karen's PO confirmed they're together. I say we check that first. Call his PO on the way, maybe, but I don't want to give these two any more breathing room than we have to. The faster we get there, the faster we catch them."

Leo punched the speed-dial on his phone to call Jacinda. Although Emma didn't particularly like the knowing glint in his eyes. No matter how she backstepped, they were going to be talking about exactly what weird things she'd seen, and soon.

But not now. We've got a bank robber to catch.

She dialed Keaton as she led the way back toward the stairwell. It was time they revisited Barry and had a conversation about this couple of ex-cons.

EMMA PULLED into the parking lot of the dealership and shot the oncoming salesperson a discouraging look. He didn't get one foot off the curb in front of the entrance.

Realistically, this was not where she wanted to be, but a uniform had already reported that the Grossmans' on-file address was a dead end for now. They'd keep surveillance running, but the little home looked closed up and empty. She couldn't say the same for their current location, though.

Crazy Barry's Car Emporium was busy enough but appeared even more dismal than before, all its tackiness on full display in the afternoon sunlight. Outside, a slick-haired salesman argued with a man over the worth of a trade-in.

Just inside, Barry Meldrum himself stood flirting with an admin specialist who was doing her best to be polite while also remaining focused on her computer. Her modest blouse left *everything* to the imagination, just short of a loose-fitting turtleneck, and Emma could imagine why.

She'd have stayed buttoned up tight, too, if this jerk had been her boss.

"Mr. Meldrum, could we steal a bit more of your time?" Emma considered giving Leo a formal introduction to the man, but doubted it was necessary. True to form, Meldrum had eyes only for her as he nodded. Still, she whispered to Leo as they followed the man toward his office. "Enjoy the show."

He let out what sounded like a stifled hiccup as he held back a laugh, but Meldrum was already escorting them into his little office.

Emma took the same seat as before but kept to the edge. She wanted to make this quick. "We spoke to Davy Delko, and he mentioned a couple you had something of an altercation with outside. A woman wearing a wig and her husband?"

May as well hold off on the mug shots. See what he remembers without their benefit.

Meldrum's face grew red as he scowled. "Sure, I remember them. What do you want to know? You gonna arrest them for causing trouble around here?"

"Just tell us what you remember, Mr. Meldrum." Leo waved his notebook at the man, as if to make it clear he'd write down all the details. "Then we can figure out arrests on our end. Sound good?"

Meldrum's eyes narrowed at Leo. "Sounds like a fucking fairy tale to me, considering you haven't caught the guy who stole my money, but sure."

"The couple?" Emma prodded when he remained silent and glaring.

"Yeah, yeah, yeah. The *freaks*. I mean, don't get me wrong, the woman was lovely for someone so long in the tooth. Beautiful blond hair and a cute little dress I'd have liked to—"

"Mr. Meldrum..." Emma was inches from shaking the man. "What happened?"

"Right. Well, you get the picture." Meldrum straightened in his seat, adjusting the tie that looked a touch too tight for his neck. "But the husband? The husband was a dickhead, through and through. He used to buy parts off Davy at the repair shop, so I knew him on sight. Guy was one of the reasons I had to fire Davy for making bullshit side deals on my property. Side gig, my ass. Kid needed to keep it in the scrapyard."

Leo traded a look with Emma. "Guess Davy forgot to mention that."

"Either that, or he's afraid of what might happen if he talks too much."

Turning back to the car dealer, Leo gestured with his pen. "So you knew the man? The husband?"

"Not by name." Meldrum's lips flattened into a scowl as he adjusted his arm in its sling. "I don't normally deal with that type. I've got a reputation, ya know?"

Emma held in her inner eye roll. "What do you mean by 'type' if you don't mind me asking?"

"Tattooed prison type. Redneck, through and through."

Pulling out her phone, Emma brought up the email Jacinda had sent just before they'd arrived. The most recent mug shots of the Grossmans stared up from her screen, and she held the device up to display them for the car salesman. "Could this be them?"

Meldrum squinted at her phone, his lips pursing for a few seconds before he nodded, albeit hesitantly. "I think so? I mean...the broad, I don't know. I mean, she had hair when I saw her, but then she didn't. I think that's her. The guy, though? That's him for sure."

Leo's notebook settled onto his knee, nothing much scrawled down. "So if you didn't get names, I'm guessing they never bought a vehicle from you?"

"Oh yeah." Meldrum's lips lifted a touch. "That day, in fact. Put it under the woman's name. Solid little car, a Toyota Camry or something."

The man gazed at the wall as if picturing the car or the money that had come from it, and Emma could practically feel Leo's ever-present smile twitching with the effort of being held in place. She understood the feeling.

Emma pointed at his file cabinet. "Mr. Meldrum, if you wouldn't mind. That means you have a sales record, right? Maybe an address on file for the car registration? That's policy?"

"Huh?" The man blinked at her. "Oh yeah, sure. That'd be helpful? You think they had something to do with me getting shot? My money getting stolen?"

Leo positively growled beside her, one boot near hitting the expensive desk in front of them when he uncrossed his leg and leaned in. Sarcasm dripped from his voice when he realized Barry was still waiting for him to respond. "Yes, Mr. Meldrum. That would be very helpful. Please."

Meldrum shrugged and rolled his eyes before rummaging inside a desk drawer and withdrawing a folder spilling out paperwork. He flipped through the papers one-handed, moved one on top, and then turned the folder around so Emma could view it.

As she leaned over the desk to read the bill of sale, the man's one good hand reached up and stroked the hair falling to the side of Emma's face. She froze in place, unable to decide whether to maim the man or laugh in disbelief.

Leo had no such quandary. He grabbed the man's wrist and yanked it away. And then his voice redefined the word "growl" for all of them. "*Stop. Touching. Women's. Hair. Without. Permission.*"

Meldrum paled, and Leo shook his wrist.

"Do you hear me, Mr. Meldrum?"

"Yes." The salesman choked on spit, voice cracking. "Yes, Agent. Sir. Yes. I hear you."

Leo released the man's wrist, and the car dealer pulled it back to his chest, probably thankful not to have come away with a second gunshot. But Emma barely registered the move.

Her pen was scribbling on her own notebook, triumph practically bleeding out her pores.

On the bottom of the bill of sale, right there in front of them, was one of the aliases handed over by Mary Karen's parole officer. And Emma had everything she needed now. Not just the alias and its address, but the couple's newest vehicle down to make, model, license, and VIN.

Boom, boom, Mr. Grossman. You hear the steps of the Feds at your door? Because we're coming.

She hoped.

She grinned at Leo, who looked slightly more relaxed after having taught their car salesman a lesson in courtesy that might or might not stick.

Notebook tucked safely away, Emma rose to her feet beside Leo, and then she acted before the cowed Grossman could react. With the tip of one of the man's own pens, she tugged the bill of sale from its folder and scooted it over the desk.

Leo plucked the page up with a latex glove held between his fingers. Then he slid it into a fresh manila folder taken from a stack by the door and waved their evidence at the sputtering salesman. "To protect any fingerprints. Evidence."

Aiming for a fraction of Leo's charm, Emma smiled nicely as she focused her attention back on Meldrum. "We'll also need you to come with us to the local precinct. We need your fingerprints, too, for disqualification purposes."

"What? Hell, no! We're only halfway through the sales day, and—"

"Mr. Meldrum." Leo's voice shut the man up in a breath. "I know you don't want us to end up having to charge you as an accessory after the fact to the robbery of your own car dealership."

Doing her best to feign sympathy, Emma shook her head. "Not to mention your own assault. That would be such a shame. And as for what that would do to your business insurance and any recent claims—"

"Stop!" Meldrum stood fast enough that his chair knocked into the wall. His good hand loosened his tie. "Just lead the way, okay?"

Emma held out an arm, as if to usher him past Leo and give the two men some distance from one another.

Meldrum scuttled by in a way that suggested he might just be sorry there wasn't a wire screen separating him from Leo on the drive, and somehow, Emma didn't quite blame him. She patted down her hair where Meldrum had touched it and gave Leo an honest smile.

He shrugged. "Big brother reflex. Think it taught him the error of his ways?"

"Ha." She scoffed, holding the door open for her partner. "Just don't break his wrist if he tries it again in the car, okay? We have a bank robber to catch."

22

Cardinals chattered at me from the half-dead tree branch hanging over the truck, but I ignored them. Far as witnesses went, they were the best I could ask for. If some birds and squirrels wanted to watch me work along the country highway I'd chosen as my drop zone, that was fine by me. Hell, they could invite a herd of damn elk if they wanted to. Long as everything else remained silent and still, we were golden.

Because this wipe-down had to be thorough. Too many idiots ended up in the joint just because they didn't have the patience to clean up after their own damn selves, and I wasn't about to be one of them.

I'd known more than one thief who got caught because he neglected to get his fingerprints off the trunk release or the window crank on his getaway car, which made my philosophy simple.

I wiped down *everything*.

Even if I was damn sure I hadn't touched it. Lucky for me, modern-day tech made that easier than ever. Disinfectant wipes were a damn godsend. And this country road I'd parked on was as isolated as could be. That meant I had plenty of privacy to take my time with the decoy truck, so I wasn't about to rush the process.

I wiped the truck down in the same order I used for painting, making it easy to keep track of my progress. Coming around the right rear panel to the tailgate, I found Mary Karen leaning against the hood of her newly purchased Camry. A pretty maroon, the car gleamed in the afternoon light, and my woman shined just as bright. Dressed in old-fashioned bell-bottoms like the ones she'd worn when we were kids, her waist looked even tighter than I remembered. What an hourglass she was.

"You about ready?" She leaned back against her car deeper, as if luring me away.

Rather than answer, I reached her in two long steps and kissed her, dropping my duffel and my plastic bag of used wipes in the dirt beside us. Chemo might have stolen some of her weight, but she still had the curves and softness to fill my hands.

Her lips opened under mine. Warm, sweet with her lip gloss.

When I pulled back, I kept my eyes on hers. "That answer enough for you?"

The blush that warmed her cheeks went down below the V-neck of her sweater, and she bent down to pick up my trash before I could. "Well, get in, then. I'm driving, you old robber."

I settled into the passenger seat with a sigh. Our fancied-up decoy gleamed green, and if it had been summer, the color might have bought us some extra time, but the field beside the road was brown with winter. It was a shame to abandon the vehicle this early in the run, but we weren't going to be hitting quite so many banks as I'd planned.

"In the old days, we would have been taking our time."

The mutter came out despite my best intentions. I hated complaining to Mary Karen. "Feds didn't have the manpower or resources they seem to now, and banks didn't have the security..."

Mary Karen's hand stilled on the radio. "Ken, we could keep going. We could pick our spots careful and—"

I put my hand on hers. "Not happening. Time's a luxury that got lost in the last forty-five years, and we both know it." *You don't have any time left, baby.* "Life's unfair, but we're making the most of it, and this is what makes sense."

She smiled softly. "Just sit back and enjoy the ride in my little car for a change. She's got a bit of zip."

I did as instructed while she pulled away from the side of the road. "It better. Guy who sold it to us was enough of a prick without giving us a lemon to boot."

That ass had actually had the gall to put his hands on my Mary Karen. Earned him a bullet when I went back to empty his safe. Part of me wished I'd killed him outright. I left him to suffer, thinking I might go back and finish the job later, but things had just gotten hot too fast.

Beside me, Mary Karen started singing along to an old Dire Straits song, and I let myself get lost in her voice. *Man, how I missed this.* The confidence of a woman easing around turns like she owned them, one hand on the wheel and one hand resting against the window, tapping out a tune. Foot on the gas instead of the brake.

Time and chemo sure hadn't taken her ability to drive. Hell, she loved cruising along almost as much as I did. One more reason we were such a good match.

"Mary Karen, just you wait. Picture yourself in some sweet, little antique convertible. We'll be cruising like this in Belize, enjoying the sea breeze."

She giggled, eyes on the road. "Sounds perfect."

"Meanwhile...I've got some Valentine's presents for you."

Her eyes darted my way. "You don't think it oughta wait 'til we get to the restaurant? When I can really *appreciate* you...I mean *them*." She batted her lashes at me, and the insinuation was about as clear as a bird dog on a trail, but there wasn't time for that right now.

I waved her ahead toward a big-box store's parking lot. "Pull off here if you want to focus on me. I ain't waiting any longer, baby."

At the edge of the lot, she put the Camry in park. Then she angled herself toward me, a little purse to her lips. "It's your show, then."

I already had the manila envelope I'd tucked into my duffel for just this moment. Opening it up, I fanned out the contents for her viewing pleasure.

New passports, licenses, and vaccination records with brand-spanking-new aliases, courtesy of a guy I met inside and who got out a few weeks before me.

"We're set." I passed her the license with her image, the name she'd chosen emblazoned beside it. "One more good-sized bank will get us all the capital we need to start a whole new life in Belize."

Her eyes had been lit up a moment ago, but now the fire died. It broke my damn heart.

She handed me the license, brushing her fingers along the other documents before she met my gaze. "Kenneth, thank you. This is the best Valentine's heart you could get me..."

"But?"

"But. But...well, except for the present of letting me do it with you." Tears sprang to her eyes. "One more time."

The knot in my throat went wider. I closed the manila envelope and tucked it away again, giving the task more focus than it required.

"Ken, babe, I want to do it with you—"

"It's too risky." I double-checked the zipper on the bag

needlessly. "Your energy goes up and down. You haven't done it in ages, not since before we got caught. I'm back in practice. Plus, they see me with a partner, that'll be one step closer to them figuring out who we are. All the trouble I've gone to make sure they can't track me could be out the window. It's just too dangerous, and you know it."

Mary Karen's silence was about the only answer required. She sat back in her seat, hands gripping the mushroom patches she'd sewn onto the knees of her bell-bottoms, just like old times. It wasn't nerves radiating off her, I knew. My baby didn't get scared. She was just stuck in her own head right now, teetering between frustration and logic.

And then she started crying, little hard-fought tears leaking from her eyes. "It's just…just that this cancer…fuck, I don't mean to cry. I'm sorry. It's just that…"

I shushed her and wrapped her in a sideways hug, and her crying got louder around her words as the tears bled into my shirt, each damn one shredding my heart a little bit more.

"It's stolen so much. Time. I need…I need one more high-throttle moment. Before I'm gone. Please, Ken. Time's going. And sometimes I feel fine, and we get to be a couple. And sometimes…"

A louder sob hiccupped out of her chest, and I clutched her closer. She didn't need to finish.

Sometimes, you're not even yourself, you're so sick. Curled in bed, and I can't do anything but watch you suffer. Sometimes, we've got nothing but breaths that are already dying out.

I swallowed a knot in my throat. I'd been denying it, but the two of us pulling off one last heist together meant more to her than any escape or beach vacation. She wanted to feel alive, the way she used to feel. The way I'd felt running from those Feds with the pedal to the floor. I'd wanted her beside me in that moment…and she deserved nothing less.

"Okay, Mary Karen." I nearly choked on the words,

holding her tighter, but I kept going. "We'll do it together, one more time."

Mary Karen shook harder, the emotion flooding through her now built of relief and gratitude. I petted her hair, shiny, blond, and oh, so special.

She didn't wear this one much anymore—that was how much it meant to her, to us—but she'd put it on for today. For us. The gorgeous blond locks had once belonged to seventeen-year-old Elisa Miller, who we'd killed during our first spree. This had been the first wig my Mary Karen had made that ended up living up to the real thing, a true work of art.

The wig had been in storage, but just for today, she'd pulled it out and brushed it 'til every bit of its old sheen had returned. It took me back to more than four decades past, fogging up the air in the car and my memory like a damn time machine.

If only I could give my baby that. The gift of time.

I couldn't, but I did have one more gift for her.

When her sobs quieted, and she started settling herself back in her seat, I put my hand into my coat and pulled out the something special I'd found just for her. Tugging the envelope open so she could see inside and dip her fingers in, I let her joy warm me up as she teased out some strands of the thick purple-red hair that all but glittered between us.

"Oh, Ken. Oh, this is gorgeous. Thank you."

I grinned, watching her play with the hair as if it were the only treasure in the world. "Happy Valentine's Day, Mary Karen. You deserve it."

Mia popped another ball of fried mac and cheese into her mouth, just refraining from humming with the warm coziness of the cheese coating her tongue. She'd have preferred going home to cook Vance some chicken noodle soup, but if she had to eat with the team, this gastropub hadn't been a bad choice.

Of course, the joy of a good meal wasn't enough to lift the team's mood. Their leads on the Grossmans turned out to be a dead end. Neither address they got was valid. Not the one from Officer Vernon nor the one Mary Karen supplied on her car purchase paperwork.

Leo finished off his taco and sat glowering at the other one still on his plate.

"You had to know they wouldn't put their real address on the paperwork." Mia snagged a sweet potato fry from Emma's plate and swiped it through some of the mac and cheese that had dripped from her burger.

"A girl can hope." Emma raised an eyebrow after she finished chewing. "It would've been easier to stomach that creep Barry's presence if we'd gotten more out of it."

Jacinda waved a piece of bread dipped in clam chowder. "Come on, everyone. Eat up so we can get moving on the night. We know Treadway was 'blowing smoke'," she aimed her bread at Leo, "and now we have the banks he really worked at to keep an eye on. His employment history included a total of eight banks. Four we already know about because either he or Grossman robbed them. Treadway's were Green Community, Union National, and Sundial Trust. Grossman hit Municipal Bank of Samson Creek this morning."

Leo reached for his taco, then put his hand back in his lap, apparently having lost his appetite. "What were the other ones Treadway cased?"

"His first employer was, fittingly, the First D.C. Bank. Then he worked at Monument Reserve, Bank of the Potomac, and last of all, Farmers Bank. It's in a somewhat exclusive and semirural community called Watson Ranch. We only have enough personnel to stakeout three of those four, so I'm putting Farmers on the sheriffs."

Mia looked pointedly at Emma's plate, which was set off by little app plates of Cuban egg rolls, chicken wings, and seaweed salad with tomato garnish. She'd ordered half the appetizers on the menu. "Somebody might need to take first watch while Emma digests."

Her joke didn't exactly fall flat, but the best she got was a half grin from Leo.

Jacinda agreed with her, at least. "Mia's right. Stakeouts aren't naptime, and with two people per bank, I need everyone on their toes. We know which jobs Georgie Treadway planned out in advance, and I want to make use of that information before it goes out of date. These stake-outs are important. We'll trade out with local police at midnight so everyone can get some sleep, despite limited coverage. Sloan's feeling better and we have her on loan until everyone feels better, so we'll have three teams of two."

Mia sighed in relief. Sloan had become ill as soon as they'd gotten on the same page, and Mia had wanted nothing more than to sit down and start investigating Ned's death. The two of them were both anxious to make up for lost time —Mia could hear it in Sloan's voice even through the flu— and having her back in play meant time for that, as well as another set of eyes out for the Grossmans.

Grabbing another sweet potato fry from Emma's plate, she wondered if Sloan's return meant they might have Vance and Denae back soon too. Talk about a game changer. She dragged the fry through the remains of her soup. What was a gastropub for if not experimenting? Too bad she couldn't take some of this soup to Vance.

Jacinda gestured at Keaton with her fork. "You and I will take First D.C. Bank." She thanked the server for refilling her coffee, then kept going down her list. "Emma and Leo, Monument Reserve. Mia, you and Sloan will take Bank of the Potomac."

Mia caught sight of a figure heading toward them over Jacinda's shoulder and waved. "Speak of the devil."

Sloan offered a smile that didn't come close to her usual bluster and pulled up a chair from a nearby empty table. A thick cable-knit sweater blanketed her turtleneck, and her skin looked a shade too pale, but at least she was on her feet again.

"It's good to see you." Mia pushed her untouched water toward the woman.

Sloan grabbed the glass and paused with it raised toward her mouth. She held Mia's gaze and gestured in a toast. "You too, Mia. It's been too long."

Jacinda glanced her way. "You sure you're up to this, Sloan? If not—"

"I'm fine. Feeling a hundred times better than yesterday. And," she held up a finger, gazing pointedly around the table, "if anyone tries to tell me to go back to my couch, I will not be responsible for how I react."

Mia bit back a laugh and returned to her soup. The other agent might look like a teenager in her oversize sweater, but she was anything but that. Sloan was fierce…a reminder of why Mia's brother Ned had loved her so much, Mia thought with a quick pang of regret.

Keaton pulled his coffee closer. "Now that we're back to the case…I looked into the Grossmans and confirmed they're in town."

"You've gotta be kidding." Leo dropped his last taco from his hand and glared. "Emma and I figured that out already, remember? Or were you not listening to the conversation earlier?"

Mia's mouth dropped open, and when she saw her shock reflected in Sloan's expression, she hurried to stuff her lips with a fried ball of pasta.

Though Leo might be offering a tight grin now, as if to suggest he was joking, the antagonism in what he'd just directed at Keaton had been anything but a joke. Even Jacinda had her eyebrow raised, coffee stilled halfway to her lips.

Keaton just smiled, but his focus was on only Leo as he answered. "And as a good agent, you know we can't rely on one source of information that hasn't been verified, particularly when that source is an overworked parole officer who's not even the primary contact for our main suspect. If I remember right, you spoke to Mary Karen's parole officer, not Kenneth Grossman's, which makes it all the more important we source check. So I verified."

When Leo frowned, Emma's elbow hit his pointedly enough that he didn't argue. Not immediately anyway.

"May I continue?" Keaton raised an eyebrow at Jacinda, wiping his hands on a napkin.

After a pause that was a touch too long to be casual, she gestured him on.

"I dug into the Grossmans' crimes and came away with a few things we ought to keep in mind. They never hurt anyone younger than seventeen, no kids, and all their victims were women with long hair. It seems that wig-making was always part of their signature, even from the start. Later in their spree, Mary Karen was always seen wearing wigs that could be traced back to earlier victims. Some men were wounded, but the kills all seem to relate to the wigs, as if the hair isn't useful unless its previous owner is out of the picture."

"That's twisted." Sloan frowned, one hand fondling her own long hair.

Leo passed Sloan the plate of his own remaining fried mac and cheese bites before turning back to Keaton. "Did you find anything we can *use?*"

Man, he's got a bee in his bonnet tonight. Holy shit.

"They're sentimental." Keaton let that pronouncement hang in the air before continuing. "For instance, they were caught at Mary Karen's parents' house celebrating Christmas. Even though the heat was high, they risked going back to visit family. That's probably something we can exploit."

"I've been doing my own reading, Holland. Sentimental might be stretching it." Leo pushed his plate away and leaned over the table. "Look, we're talking about cold-blooded killers here. The pair killed three women in the seventies... one of them just seventeen, as you pointed out. The only reason they weren't serving life is that the prosecution teams couldn't prove which one of them actually pulled the trigger in those crimes. They pointed the finger at each other.

Doesn't seem very sentimental to me." He huffed and sat back in his chair, as if satisfied.

Emma opened her mouth to respond, but Keaton spoke first.

"That's where you're wrong, Ambrose." He narrowed his gaze. "They did not blame each other. You read too fast. They each took the blame, claiming responsibility. The prosecution couldn't prove it either way, but that selflessness is what made the case difficult. Therefore...sentimentality. Need me to define it?"

Emma coughed as Jacinda broke in to ask for more detail about the Grossmans' crimes, with Leo and Keaton talking over each other to provide the details.

Mia couldn't stop watching them angle to outdo each other. As Emma all but shrank into her seat while studying a dessert menu, Mia watched her fellow agents as if they were engaged in a tennis match. She didn't know whether to be worried or impressed by such a display of machismo from two men who normally kept their egos in check. Finally, though, she decided she had to say something before one of them started hurling street corn or fried tomatoes.

"Guys, everyone..." Mia glanced to Jacinda for help, but their SSA seemed to be studying the exchange rather than intervening. "We have some addresses. For the Grossmans' old family, even if the ones you got from Barry and Officer Vernon didn't pan out. We can check those first thing tomorrow. That's something. No need to get testy when we've still got leads, right?"

Swirling his coffee, Keaton shrugged. "Odds are the addresses are bullshit. This pair's like a couple of ghosts."

Emma flinched, pulling Leo's gaze, but Keaton kept going without noticing.

"We have to anticipate where they'll be, and the banks are the best bet right now. Fitting, right? We tell the future to catch some ghosts." He laughed at his own quip, pulling Jacinda in with him.

Mia couldn't help glancing at Emma, who ignored her and munched on a dragon-hot chicken wing. Better than flinching.

Heck, all that said, I guess we're lucky we have someone who can see ghosts.

AFTER DINNER, Mia sipped hot chocolate in the driver's seat of the Expedition, Sloan doing the same in the passenger seat beside her. The other team members had all opted for more coffee, but this and some bottled water had won the day for the two of them.

And honestly, the creamy chocolate was such a perfect finish to the night. More for the comfort than the caffeine.

Kenneth Grossman, or whoever their guy was, clearly preferred opening hours, first thing in the morning, so they weren't expecting him to strike.

Sloan had more than cold medicine and hot chocolate to keep her ruminating, though, and Mia knew it.

Her brother, Ned, had died in a car accident, but it wasn't really an accident. His car had been forced off the road, or tampered with before he left Sloan's place the night she refused his marriage proposal.

"I told him I had met someone. I told him I'd been unfaithful."

Mia had been stunned to learn that truth, and especially as she, Sloan, and Emma faced off against a distraught, bomb-wielding woman hell-bent on taking all four of them out.

By comparison, the conversation Mia just had with Sloan, where she laid out what she knew about Ned's murder, felt like a cakewalk. And when Sloan turned her gaze to Mia, eyes distant, Mia knew that was what still held her focus.

"I never knew much about his work. I don't know if it was because it sounded boring, or he thought it would bore me, or…" She fiddled with her sweater, teasing apart some of the weave in a way that made Mia want to turn mother bear and grab her hand. "But he said it kept him busy and challenged his mind, and that was what he wanted. I guess we left it at that. I can't believe we're the FBI agents, and it's his work that might've gotten him…"

Tears tugged at the backs of Mia's eyes, but she drowned them in another sip of chocolate before giving in to her instincts and grabbing Sloan's hand, stilling it. "Please, please, please don't start blaming yourself for something else. Neither of us should've ever blamed you, and I'm…I'm so sorry I did."

Sloan gripped Mia's hand back, a thin smile surfacing and then disappearing. "It's okay. I just…three years. Even if we couldn't have stopped it from happening, we could've been working on this three years ago. That's hard to accept."

Sweeping her gaze back across the front of the bank—the focus of their stakeout, after all—Mia fought down the lump of emotion in her chest. "I know. I keep thinking that, but at least we're on it now. That's gotta be enough."

Even if I have to keep certain Other details out of the story. For Emma's sake, if nothing else.

24

E mma and Leo sat in the Charger across from the Monument Reserve Bank. She'd popped open her to-go container the minute they arrived, and now, over two hours later, was finally scooping the last bite of her black-berry bread pudding into her mouth. She shouldn't have ordered it—her meal had more than filled her up—but it had just been too hard to resist.

Apparently, a great night's sleep followed by the shock of the morning had grown her an extra stomach.

Leo stretched in the passenger seat and shook his head. "How are you not already asleep after that meal? I dare you to do that again tomorrow."

"Dare accepted." Emma closed her to-go container and added it to the one already discarded in the back seat. "And how was your grilled pineapple s'more?"

He grinned around his coffee cup. "Point taken, but I didn't fill my hollow leg at dinner."

Emma sighed and settled into her seat, willing the food in her stomach to lighten up fast. This bank was larger than the previous two, which wasn't saying much.

Another small-town setup that probably didn't keep much cash on hand but also didn't have much security as a result.

And probably doesn't give half enough attention to who they hire to offer that security. Case in point...our Georgie.

She took a gulp of her coffee, not worrying how it scalded her tongue. The day had been a long one, and the food was taking its toll after all. She needed something to help keep her awake.

Leo's relative silence wasn't helping either.

For a moment, she thought to ask him what was on his mind. It was either the same thing all of them were thinking of—the Grossmans—or else her own behavior, which she did not want to get into. Not tonight, at least.

He shifted in his seat. "You think these two criminals love each other?"

"What?"

"The Grossmans." He licked his lower lip, eyes remaining on the quiet bank. "You think they're in love, even now, after all the time apart with prison sentences?"

What the hell?

"I mean...I guess. They might be. She's dying of cancer, and he's taking care of her through her final days. That sounds like love to me. Why?"

"I was just wondering if they're in love in the way that makes you crazy for the other person, or in the way that makes you do crazy things."

"Like robbing banks, you mean."

"Yeah, like that."

"But it's just a one-man show right now. We have no evidence there's a woman involved, and we only saw one person in that pickup we chased and in all the security footage we've reviewed."

Leo rubbed his knuckles against his scruff, remaining

silent for another few seconds before he shrugged. "Never mind. It's probably just Valentine's Day."

Emma's instinct was to laugh, but then it hit her.

Valentine's Day.

Tonight.

"Shit, shit, shit, shit."

Tugging her phone from her coat pocket, she fumbled for the door lock. There was no time to get her gloves on or explain either. Nearly stumbling from the muscle car, she half shut the door behind her on Leo's question of what she'd forgotten.

Oren's name came near the end of her contact list, and she clicked on it so desperately fast that at first the phone dialed and hung up. She clicked again and brought the phone to her ear.

Waiting for him to pick it up, she couldn't help thinking back to that first day they'd met. How self-assured he'd been. His unruly brown hair and arresting blue eyes had been the first thing she'd noticed on walking into his studio. And the way he'd led his class, with his graceful body folding into every pose so effortlessly...but without judging someone like her, who'd stumbled in as a beginner.

He'd had such a gravity to him, she'd been a goner from the start. And here she was ruining things before they had a chance to get off the ground. She wouldn't blame him if he ignored her call after she'd stood him up tonight.

But, on the third ring, he answered. "Happy Valentine's Day."

"Oh, Oren, I'm so sorry." She closed her eyes, leaning back against the Charger. "I'm not going to make it."

He chuckled—of all things—and her grip on her phone loosened just a touch. "I guessed that about forty-five minutes ago, but at least that means I don't have to share my apple strudel."

Her stomach flip-flopped the bread pudding and meal she had consumed over the last few hours…without a single thought to the man who was waiting for her across town. "Oren, truly, I am just so, so, so sorry. I was so excited to meet you tonight, and then this case—"

"I get it." His voice had a deeper timbre, but the sincerity was still there. The man was too generous and understanding to deserve someone like her. "You have an important job, and planning ahead outside of it isn't possible. I knew that from the beginning. It's okay. I'm just glad to know you're safe."

"Oh gosh, Oren. You were worried? I'm so—"

"I know you can take care of yourself, Agent Emma Last. I do."

Emma swallowed another apology. She could repeat herself ad nauseam, but it wouldn't change anything. And it wasn't like she had the ability to offer up details of the case in explanation either. "You have to let me make it up to you. As soon as this case is over."

"Promise?"

Emma's mouth went a little dry, his voice had gone so husky. "Promise."

"Well, I should get back to my apple strudel and let you get back to your case, then. The sooner you solve it, the sooner we make that promise a reality."

"Happy Valentine's Day, Oren. Thank you for being so understanding…a woman couldn't ask for anything more."

He once more told her it was fine before they said their goodbyes and hung up.

Emma stood at the side of the Charger for just a moment more, allowing her heart to slow in the chill night air. The man was so zen. Not much rattled him, but still. That reaction to her literally forgetting their date existed? Unbelievable. Oren Werling might actually be the one man on Earth who could put up with her work schedule.

When she settled back into the seat beside Leo, he gave her a knowing look, but she still apologized. "Sorry that was so sudden. I just remembered I was supposed to be somewhere else."

"A date." He gave her a wry smile. "Been there. It's the job. There's no need to apologize. You salvage things?"

Emma smiled, mostly to herself. "He's a special person. Wasn't even angry."

"That's good. I'm glad for you." Leo twisted open a bottle of water and sipped at it, gaze going back to the bank. "It's good to have loved ones to reach out to."

Loved ones. Is that what Oren is?

She didn't know. Was that the right word yet? She could imagine it becoming possible, which was a new enough feeling in itself. Right now, though, he was maybe more of a comfort. That felt a bit more right. Albeit a very sexy, deep-voiced, handsome comfort.

"Yeah," Leo mused. "I guess I do wonder about the Grossmans and their 'love.' I'm finding it hard not to. They seem to have found each other after their releases. That has to mean something. Like, they were looking for their family and found them. I miss that. Having family, I mean. Parents in particular, though, more than romance."

Emma didn't feel entirely confident that Leo had meant to say *any* of that out loud, his voice had gone so soft. They were all tired, after all. But she also couldn't not ask.

"Your parents aren't in your life? To reach out to, I mean?"

Leo jolted in his seat, proving she'd been right. He'd all but forgotten she was there, from the looks of the startled expression on his face.

"I...sorry. That's more personal than I meant to get. But yes." He sighed. "You might as well know, since it will come up at some point. My parents died in a car accident when I was in elementary school, on the way to my Christmas concert. I was playing the little drummer boy and had a solo. They died because of me."

Emma's throat closed, blood thundering through her veins in response to the emotion in her partner's voice. She nearly choked on her words when she tried to respond. "Not because of you, Leo. You can't really think that."

His eyes hooded, and he looked back through the windshield.

Gods, he does think that.

"Your parents wouldn't want you to live with that."

He seemed to sink deeper into the bucket seat, though she wasn't sure he moved. Leo just…deflated. "You're right that they wouldn't, but I do. If they hadn't been rushing to get to me, if I hadn't had the concert to begin with, if I hadn't pitched a tantrum to guilt-trip them into coming…those are a lot of *ifs* to dismiss, even a few decades later."

"Leo, I'm sure your parents wanted to be there and would've been on that road whether you'd said anything. Maybe it felt like a tantrum to you, but you probably didn't even need to ask."

Emma ran her tongue against her teeth, visions of her mother's picture overlaying Leo's scruffy visage beside her. Guilt was so loud in his voice, so heavy in the car.

Emotion weighed down her next words. "I know what it's like to lose parents. My mother died when I was very young."

His gaze darted to her, narrow-eyed. "I'm sorry, Emma. You don't have to—"

"No, it's okay. There's no reason you shouldn't know. And I still had my father after that. He was a demanding man, but he loved me, and he did his best. He died just a few years ago."

Leo's lips formed a small smile, but it held none of his

usual laid-back charm or ease. The expression was only sad sympathy. "It never ends, does it? The grief? I try to go visit their grave sites every year, but mostly on their birthdays. I can't stand to visit around Christmas."

Emma found herself nodding. She'd never known a real family Christmas. But to have those memories, and then lose one's parents right at that time of year...that had to be a special kind of pain.

Conversation's gotten a little too real, Emma girl. You're not careful, you're going to be crying on this poor man's shoulder.

A gulp of coffee steadied her pulse just a touch. She put the cup in the cup holder and zipped her coat tighter. "I don't know about you..." She coughed, her voice a moment away from cracking. "But I think I need some air. How about we walk the perimeter?"

Rather than answering, Leo twisted his loosened scarf tighter around his neck and gripped the door handle beside him. A moment later, he was out of the Charger and waiting for her.

Hurrying from the car, Emma locked the vehicle as they started their circuit around the building. The bank took up half the block, but trees and a closed diner were the only other things occupying it. Traffic on the street was so infrequent as to be nonexistent.

"Now I know what people mean when they talk about towns that roll up the sidewalks."

They were passing near the drive-through when the air went colder, thickening.

Emma glanced around, darting a hopefully casual glance over her shoulder. Sure enough, striding along together, the ghosts of Trisha Terrence and Lorena Diaz were approaching from behind. Like demented twins, with their hair chopped short and bright-crimson bloodstains covering their expensive blouses. They seemed to be focused on one another…though the direction of their steps betrayed the real reason they'd appeared.

Leo's elbow nudged her. "Something wrong?"

"Nothing," Emma bit out. "Just the wind. Let's keep going."

Focusing her gaze ahead of her, Emma willed herself to finish their little stroll and get back to the Charger. Hopefully, the ghosts of the two victims wouldn't land themselves in the back seat of the car unless they really did have something to share.

The first clear words sounded from behind them on the sidewalk.

"I have a poem about motherhood running up my thigh. I thought it would hurt like hell, but the tattoo artist was a genius. You know how it hurts more when they have less experience? Well, this guy must have been a tattoo artist for decades. His needles barely stung. Just hummed along 'til that poem was embedded in my skin deep as a birthmark."

Same voice as the ghost in the ambulance. That's Trisha talking.

"Mine wasn't that easy." This voice was louder, slightly accented.

The ghosts were catching up to Emma and Leo.

"I got five. All monarch butterflies, clustered together. They were my mama's favorite. The orange practically glows on my shoulder, it's so pretty. They represent me and my siblings. And you just have the poem for motherhood?"

Emma scowled into the night, wondering why the ghosts couldn't at least give her meaningful information if they had to be there. Who cared this much about tattoos? Yes, they symbolized things to the people who got them, sure, but why did they matter now?

If I ever get a tattoo—a big if—it'll be a "shut up" on the back of my hand so I can wave it over my shoulder at moments like this.

"Oh, I've got the dramatic masks on my shoulder also," Trisha Terrence giggled, "from my college days. The happy and sad masks, you know? I was scared stiff for those. Skin is so close the bone there, that one hurt."

"Oh, yes, I remember that pain. I'm glad I got the butterflies, but, uh-uh, I would not want to go through that again."

Emma tried to tune the ghosts out as they kept talking about their tattoos, but their voices shot her concentration. As did Leo's gaze. He kept raking her with his eyes full of suspicion.

He wasn't the type to get a tattoo any more than she was, she guessed. What would he say if she told him a couple of ghosts were rambling about theirs in the background?

Talk about a conversation starter.

No matter how the ghosts prattled on behind her, tonight was not the night she'd be telling Leo about the Other. She wouldn't acknowledge the ghosts either. What was the point? Almost every ghost she'd ever spoken to had done nothing but tease her with warnings. Not to mention what Leo would think if she did attempt to engage them.

But Emma did appreciate that the ghosts had grown more verbose and articulate, even if they still spoke in riddles. Or maybe it was her, and she was starting to hear them more clearly. Was she becoming fluent in ghost speak?

Just get back to the Charger. Worse comes to worst, you blast the radio and wait for backup. Midnight's coming. Let the Other take care of itself for one damn night.

25

I hated cruise control. Whoever invented it had to be the dumbest person on the planet.

It was for lazy asses who didn't know how to handle an automobile. The kind of people who'd be happy to let some robot drive the car for them someday. But I had to suck it up and deal with it. Cruise control had its good points, I had to admit.

It was good for one thing and one thing only. Even when my blood was pumping loud enough to attract lights and sirens all on its own, I could keep rolling along under the speed limit with no chance my foot might get heavier at the wrong moment. Anything that could eliminate human error meant less of a chance we'd get caught. I'd have been a fool not to take advantage of it.

We were coming up on Monument Reserve Bank, speedometer pegged just a few miles below the posted speed limit. A Charger rumbled down the road beside us. The heavy beat of the muscle car's engine put a grin on my face, but I kept my eyes forward, focused on the next target.

When the Charger turned off the street behind us and

disappeared into the darkness, I let out a sigh of relief. Anyone out at this time of night was either headed home from the bar or up to no good.

I took my eyes off the rearview mirror and glanced at Mary Karen. She sat curled up next to me in a sweaterdress and long shawl. She was spoiled as a housecat at the moment, and stuffed full of hundred-dollar lobster. She smiled lazily in the darkness, and I knew it was going to be a good night for us. Just like it used to be, and just like my Mary Karen deserved.

"Bank's up here on the left." I needn't have whispered, but I did anyway. "And lookie here. You see them?"

Mary Karen tensed in her seat. "Yeah, I see 'em."

Two police officers were stationed outside the target bank, smoking beneath a tree. Their roving flashlights made it clear they didn't like sitting on their duffs any more than I did.

I kept driving, making sure to leave the cruise control in play. "Don't sit up, darlin'. No reason they oughta notice us."

When we'd gotten a mile away, I pulled into the parking lot of a bar that thumped and echoed with bad music. Drunken twentysomethings congregated around the outside, daring one another to be stupider than they already were. One lifted a can of beer to his lips while his buddies chanted for him to "chug" it. A few ladies giggled and hooted nearby.

Damn kids don't even know how to have a good time without acting like idiots. Me and Mary Karen never did stupid shit like that.

Adjusting my gloves, I glanced over.

She had a pinched expression to her face but forced a smile when she saw me looking. "Ken, do we have enough money already? You think?"

Her voice held more hope than confidence, which was about how I felt.

"Nah, baby, I think we need one more score."

And I did think that. I'd been doing the math in my head —all over again just in the last few minutes, too, after seeing those uniforms. We just weren't there yet. Maybe our haul so far would have been more than enough for normal people. But for us? Needing not just to get away clean but also to make sure the time we had left was as good as it could be? Not so much.

She ran her hand down my arm, bringing up a shiver of cold as she did. Then her hand landed in mine and squeezed. "You remember Savannah? How good we did there?"

"Do I ever." The grin I let spread could have stretched off my cheeks, and I knew it. "Two hundred thousand in one go. And we blew it on diamonds and crab boil, knowing there was more where that came from. We could always get more."

She scooted over beside me. "The good times."

"The good times." My echo sounded happy, nostalgic, but I was already thinking forward to what had happened a few months later.

Christmastime. We'd been so shaken after our baby's loss. Little Angela. We'd had her just three days before losing her to SIDS, and I still didn't know how we'd survived the pain.

Everything about life had gone fuzzy, blurred through the lens of grief. So much joy from having that little girl, and then, all of a sudden, we were lost. Hopelessly lost, wilting under the weight of crushed dreams.

That Christmas would have been our little one's first, but that hadn't been the plan of either God or the Devil, it seemed.

The music outside got louder. Maybe someone opened a side door. Then it went softer again, and I spotted a guy standing near the back of the building, lighting up a cigarette.

I closed my eyes, trying to anchor myself in Mary Karen's

soft warmth beside me and the hum of the car's heater. But it was no good. Christmastime was calling again. That memory that never quite let me go.

Our family had been around the tree that fateful night at her parents' house, me playing Santa Claus. The night had been a full one. Filled with gifts we'd splurged on to overcome what wasn't there. A crying baby, first pictures with Santa, a new crib, and an endless supply of clothing. All the stuff, I knew, had been packed into the attic so it wouldn't serve as a reminder of little Angela not being there.

The gifts had been good ones, though. Jewelry, and a new television and radio for Mary Karen's parents. We'd even gotten her dad a genuine Rolex that had about floored him when, *wham*.

Feds knocked the door in, tearing Mary Karen's brand-new shotgun out of her hands and coldcocking her. She was on her fanny in shock, and I screamed something awful. If I'd ever in my life roared with rage, it'd been that night. I could still feel the branches of that Christmas tree in my hands as I raised it and hurled it at the people flooding through the front door.

And Mary Karen, bless her, had somehow pulled herself conscious again and gripped onto one of the Fed's legs, pulling him down to the ground and nearly wrestling away his gun before another Fed wrapped an arm around her throat and put her to sleep. At least he hadn't killed her. I could still be thankful for that. That we'd both survived the night.

We'd put up a fight, no matter how bad a day it'd been, and we could be proud of that.

Mary Karen's fingers gripped mine tight, bringing me back to her like she always did. "You're thinking about that night again, aren't you? Please don't." She reached up and wiped away a tear I hadn't been aware of, putting it to her lips before she kissed me where it had fallen.

"You're all I need, Mary Karen. You're what matters."

She kissed me again, on the lips this time, and I sank into her.

This is what matters.

When she pulled away, I kept my fingers interlaced with hers before putting the car back in drive.

We'd turn around tonight and go back home and to bed. But we'd come back to that bank, sure enough. And then... then, we'd be gone.

26

For the second morning in a row, Leo's phone buzzed him awake at a little after six. And, for the second day in a row, Warden Payne was the early bird caller. *Does the man not sleep?*

"Warden." Leo stretched, arching his back. "This is becoming a habit, but if it means you've got news for us, I'll take it."

"Yeah, sorry about that, but I figured you'd want to know ASAP that Georgie Treadway's ready to talk. Now, I'd say."

"And you think he's on the level? This isn't just some 'let's waste the Feds' time while I have their attention' ploy?"

The warden grunted but didn't take long to consider the question. "It's possible, but I'll tell you, Treadway's as twitchy as I've ever seen him. Doesn't seem like himself. You ask me...either he did some hard thinking after the talk he had with you and your partner or something scared him. He's not himself now, so I'd say this is the real deal. Hard to tell how long his generosity will last, sure, but if you want to get over here, we'll have him ready."

"Fair enough." Already out of bed, Leo hurried toward the

kitchen. "Be there as soon as we can. Thanks for the heads-up."

Leo made coffee while calling Jacinda, and then shot Mia a text. They'd been paired for the first interview with Treadway, so he was sure she'd want to be along for this one too. Treadway wasn't exactly reliable, but Leo'd sit through a hundred more of the felon's break-dance moves if it led to their killer.

By the time he met Mia at Jackson Federal Max Prison, he'd hashed and rehashed what Treadway might want to talk about. Leo wouldn't put it past the man to simply be messing with them. Having some federal agents chomping at the bit for information, at his beck and call when he gave the word to come, could be a power trip for the guy. If Treadway gave them nothing, Leo wouldn't give the idiot any satisfaction by letting his frustration show.

If, on the other hand, Treadway was ready to talk, there was no telling what he knew. The next target? Confirmation that it was Grossman they were hunting down and where the man might be hiding?

Mia shoved her hands into her pockets as they approached the prison. "Think this is the real deal? The lead that'll break the case open?"

"It's possible." Leo pulled open the heavy door and held it for her. "I'm not holding my breath, but the warden seems to think something's changed. That could certainly work in our favor."

Mia grinned in response and hurried forward, clearly just as optimistic as he was, even if he was attempting to tamp down the excitement. They were due a break, and with bodies falling, it couldn't come soon enough. He wouldn't be picky about the source.

The same likable guard as last time signed them in and cut straight to the chase. "Treadway's ready for you, already in the room and waiting, like he's got ants in his pants. Hope it's worth y'all's trip out here."

Mia took a deep breath and led the way. Leo fell into step behind her. His excitement went up a notch. Treadway must've been driving the guards crazy if they'd let him go to the interview room first.

"Georgie, nice to see you again." Leo paused in the doorway, only moving forward when Mia had taken her seat.

Across from her, Treadway was red in the face. Fidgeting too. No more dance moves, not yet...just nervous energy radiating from him everywhere. He bounced one leg beneath the table as he clenched and unclenched his fingers.

"Warden Payne said you've got something to tell us."

"If we coulda talked on the phone, that woulda been best, but yeah, I got something. I need you to catch this mother-fucker now. You got me?" He ran out of breath and finally caught it just as Leo sat down. "Unless you got him last night? Did you? 'Cause, man, I want my hands on him. You get him in here with me, gimme five minutes with him, I'll—"

"Whoa, Georgie, whoa." Leo glanced sideways at Mia, whose mouth hung slightly ajar. Treadway was primed to erupt in a way they hadn't seen before. And that meant they had to err on the cautious side, making sure he wasn't just setting them up. "Let's go back a second. What makes you want to talk to us now when you weren't willing to do so before?"

Treadway gritted his teeth, both his hands clenching against the table, face going redder with anger and something else. "Because Kenneth Grossman...yeah, that's right, the shithead son of a bitch Kenneth Grossman...killed my mom to get to that safety deposit box. *Killed her.*"

Leo's doubt over the morning's errand drowned in Treadway's repetition. There was no way to disbelieve the animosity boiling across the table from them. And no way to doubt a motive like that either.

Their killer had murdered the man's mother, the one person they'd seen Treadway show any affection for since they'd first encountered him. Pity wouldn't do this man or his mom any good, but Leo couldn't help feeling it for him. Losing a parent was bad enough. Losing one while behind bars? That had to be infinitely more difficult.

"Bastard betrayed me. Broke the plan." Treadway leaned his head down against his forearms on the table, shaking as he spoke. "I shoulda known. I shoulda fucking known. My mom didn't deserve…"

Despair flowed from him as he spoke. Georgie Treadway would very likely tell them everything he knew, but Leo found it hard to feel triumphant. An innocent woman had died to get them to this point.

Leo sat back in his chair, torn between sympathy and shock.

At his side, Mia sighed. "Georgie, tell us what the plan was."

A muffled groan broke from the man collapsed over his own arms in front of them. He turned his face to the side so he could be heard clearly. "Ken was supposed to meet up with my mom in West Virginia, where she lives. I gave him the address and told her I'd tell her to expect him. I did, too, during her last in-person visit. You can check the visitor logs. He or a representative he sent was supposed to just go get the key from her. For the box."

Treadway shuddered, snot leaking onto the table, and Leo tugged a tissue from a box a guard had left here. Now he knew why, protocol or not.

"Here, Georgie. Take this." When he leaned deeper over the table to take the tissue, though Treadway's tears kept coming, Leo prodded him to keep going. "And the deposit box had your notebooks? Is that right?"

Treadway nodded, more snot dripping over his upper lip, shining and pitiful. "Plans and codes. For eight banks." He sniffled. "Scouted it all myself and hit two of them by my lonesome. Tried for a third and got busted. I wound up here, where I met that asshole, Grossman. I thought...I thought he was a god when I met him. I'd been a big admirer of his work."

When Treadway went silent, Mia leaned in, speaking softly. "That's probably natural, he was so well-known. Anyone could understand that. And then you found out he was being paroled after forty-five years...?"

"And would need some starter money, yeah." Treadway heaved a breath, clenching his fingers around the table's edge tight enough to turn his knuckles white and his fingertips red against the metal surface. "Him needing funds after parole, we agreed he'd commit the robberies I'd already planned before the info went totally stale, and then he'd bring my mom my part of the take. Then he was going to leave the country. Simple."

Simple. Maybe if you're not talking about a hard-nosed killer and setting yourself up to rely on his good graces.

Leo almost wanted to laugh at Treadway for having thought Grossman would honor the deal, especially with him being behind bars and in no position to demand his share. But the man before them was broken. He'd not been big before, but he seemed to have shrunk over the last few days, imploding with the force of his grief as tears kept leaking down his face.

Now that he'd let his rage bleed into sorrow, it seemed he couldn't stop the grief from overtaking him.

Leo gave him another minute, and another tissue, and then he proceeded. "Do you know where he was going?"

Treadway all but trembled, shaking his head. "That's why you gotta catch him and bring him here, so I can get to him."

Like that's gonna happen. You're really not the sharpest knife in the drawer, are you?

"We had it all planned," Treadway muttered, bouncing his fists on the table. "Mom was gonna give him the key. But he *stole* it and killed Mom and left her dead in the middle of her own kitchen. You believe that? I'm her only family, and she's all the way back in the middle-of-nowhere West Virginia. Took weeks for someone to find her. I heard the news last night."

"I'm sor—"

"You *get him*." The convict shoved himself upright in his seat, straightening his spine in one quick movement that left him staring at Leo. Tears leaked out his eyes as anger took over, and he sneered. "I may be a shit, but my mom didn't deserve that. Ken needs to pay. I want to shank him with my own two hands. He wasn't s'posed to kill anybody. That wasn't in the plans! I'm gonna shank that moth—"

Mia shoved her notebook his way. "Write down each of the banks you scouted."

He smirked. "Figured you guys'd put two and two together and come up with *Georgie's a lying piece of shit*. Yeah, I gave you bad intel last time you were here. So sue me."

Leo leaned forward and swiped the notebook back. "Georgie, we checked your employment history. We know which banks you cased. Agent Logan was just giving you a chance to appear remotely cooperative."

"Hey, I'll cooperate 'til the cows come home if it gets me back on the street where I have a chance to put a knife in between Grossman's ribs."

Mia *tsked*. "Keep making threats of murder, Georgie, and 'back on the street' will be nothing but a dream to keep you occupied in here. Let's talk cooperation again. Do you have a way to contact Kenneth?"

Treadway frowned, looking down at his shaking hands. "Don't know. I'll give you his burner number, but the last time I called him, he told me to fuck off. So who knows if it's good anymore?"

Leo forced a smile. A number was a number. "Worth a try."

If they were lucky, this robber from the past wouldn't switch up phones like criminals did nowadays.

Mia waved her phone, making it clear she was ready to take down whatever number Treadway might offer, and her smile finally did the trick. Just like that, they not only had a number to investigate, but at least one address that could p be connected to the Grossmans.

Sitting back in his seat, Leo thought forward to what the day might bring. If this information led somewhere...

He tamped down excitement working to bubble over. He couldn't afford to move too fast, to get so hyped up at the possibility of taking down Kenneth Grossman—*the* Kenneth Grossman—that he made a misstep.

Since being paroled, the man had already killed three people that they knew of. After everything he'd done, Grossman would have no hesitation about pulling that trigger on a federal agent either.

27

Emma glimpsed Keaton even before she pulled the Charger to the curb of his hotel. He stood just inside the glass doors, zipping up his coat and staring off into space, probably thinking deep thoughts. It took her honking to get him to glance up and see she'd arrived.

"Didn't recognize you in this thing." He yanked the door shut and rubbed his hands together in front of the heating vent. "Feeling the need for speed?"

"You got it." Emma swung the muscle car out into traffic and hit the gas, maneuvering into the next lane and speeding up to avoid a yellow light turning red. "No way do I want to be top-heavy the next time I run into Kenneth Grossman. The Expeditions are great, but not so ideal when it comes to car chases through fields and around corners."

Keaton overexaggerated leaning sideways into her space. "Your driving habits haven't changed, that's for sure."

She forced a smile but kept her focus on the road. There'd been a time when him invading her personal space like that wouldn't have bothered her a bit...but the smell of his aftershave wafting over the driver's seat reminded her she wasn't with Leo. She could banter with Keaton endlessly over dinner, but they were on a case now, and she wanted the serious focus of a man on a mission to catch a killer.

"Leo and Mia are over at the prison questioning Georgie Treadway again." She cut across a lane, opting to take a side road rather than the clogged Beltway. "Warden Payne called first thing this morning and woke Leo up. Said the guy's ready to talk."

"Well, at least we're not the only ones getting an early start. Oh, hey, you said you're doing yoga now?"

Emma's eyebrow raised without meaning to. What did yoga have to do with their case? "Yeah…"

"So you'll love this. I was watching this movie last night, and this character starts running a chop shop out of a yoga studio. You ever heard anything more ridiculous? This guy's in downward dog and talking on the phone to guys running a container ship…"

Emma glanced at the GPS, willing herself not to cut Keaton off and just focus on her driving. So much for shoptalk.

Beside her, he prattled on, apparently keen on going through the whole synopsis of whatever comedy he'd been watching. The tension encircling her own shoulders could've strangled her, but he didn't seem to notice. Maybe she was imagining the awkwardness between them, but their attitudes were so different right now. The situation was laughable.

Had he changed? She wondered. He'd seemed the same. They'd once been in sync. Both of them in the mood to joke around, or both of them ready to focus.

Maybe it was just the overly honest talk she'd had with Leo last night, about loss and pain and grief. About a desire for family built from trauma and heartache. She and Leo were on the same page when it came to many big-picture issues. He carried grief with him like a safety blanket, just like she did.

Keaton, though, seemed entirely unscathed by his past, generally speaking. And that was on full display today, when he could joke like this despite their larger case.

If he hadn't changed, was it her?

He'd remained silent for a few seconds when Emma realized that was her cue. "Sounds like a funny movie."

"You have no idea." Keaton laughed at whatever he was remembering, eyes crinkling. "I'll have to look up the title for you."

Please don't.

Emma swallowed the words and nodded at the GPS instead. "Uniforms never saw Grossman's truck coming and going, but this is Mary Karen Grossman's listed address we're headed to, in case you were wondering."

The man shrugged as if he hadn't remotely wondered where they were heading. "Bet you twenty dollars it's a false address."

"It's registered to a Courtney Cowie, no criminal record or relation to the Grossmans, but that doesn't mean she doesn't know them."

Keaton scoffed and leaned back into the bucket seat, settling in to watch the scenery. Silence wrapped around them, making her itch to reach their destination and escape the car.

When she finally pulled the Charger into the driveway of a little brick house at the end of a cul-de-sac in an old neighborhood on the outskirts of D.C., it was about all she could do to keep from clapping in celebration.

Even banging on the door of an empty house would be better than one more minute of awkward silence or B-list comedy synopses.

But despite feeling that way, she couldn't be particularly

hopeful about this errand bringing results. Standing at the head of the little sidewalk with Keaton, Emma didn't sense any sort of movement there, and she saw no place where one could hide a truck. The house was a cracker box, peeling paint where there wasn't brick, and no garage. "Barely big enough for two people, huh?"

"As long as they like rubbing shoulders." Keaton pointed to the bay window some fifteen feet from where they stood. "Notice the curtains are open?"

"Yeah." Emma sighed, realizing she'd hoped against hope that they'd been wrong. Finding the Grossmans here would've made for a fast solve. "Criminals don't leave their curtains open for bystanders...or Feds...to peer in and catch the action. And this house doesn't have any curtains closed."

"Let's get it over with, then."

On that note, Keaton headed up the cracked concrete pathway. He lifted and dropped the worn brass knocker and stood to one side while Emma called out to announce their presence.

"Mr. and Mrs. Grossman? This is the FBI."

She got no response.

Emma leaned in toward the door and heard the muffled sounds of a television turned up loud. Frowning, she lifted the door knocker and slammed it down on the metal twice. If that didn't get the homeowner's attention, nothing would.

Sure enough, a woman's voice called out a few seconds later.

"Sound like 'coming' to you?" Emma grimaced as the seconds stretched on, but finally the door creaked open.

The woman staring at them wore an oversize sweatshirt, which buttoned down the front, the likes of which Emma hadn't seen in decades. And she was most definitely not Mary Karen Grossman. Probably ninety years old.

The bent over, squinty-eyed woman leaned heavily on a

cane and stared at them as if they were aliens, giving little notice to the badge Keaton held up for her viewing pleasure. "What do you two want?"

"Ma'am, I'm Special Agent Emma—"

"Speak up!"

Emma forced a smile and raised her voice. "I'm Special Agent—"

The woman huffed and knocked her cane into the doorway for emphasis, interrupting again. "I said, speak up. I can't hear you!"

Giving up, Emma went into full shouting mode. "I'm Special Agent Emma Last! This is Special Agent Keaton Holland! We're FBI!"

We'll be lucky if we don't wake the neighbors this time of the morning.

Finally, the woman pursed her lips and nodded. "Good. I hear you now." She pointed at Keaton's badge, still held out for her viewing. "Put whatever that is away. I'm about blind. Now, what do you want?"

Half deaf and half blind. What luck.

Emma took a deep breath, preparing to shout. "Ma'am, are you Courtney Cowie?"

"What?" The woman gestured with her cane, ready to knock it against the doorframe again.

Emma nearly screamed her question this time, which finally did the trick.

"'Course I am. Who else would I be?"

"Who else, indeed." Keaton muttered under his breath what might have been a curse, and then took his turn serving as a megaphone. "Do you have anyone staying with you?!"

The woman's nose crinkled as if Keaton smelled bad. "This house look big enough for me to have anyone staying with me, boy?"

Emma fought down a giggle. Maybe this visit had been

worth it after all, to hear that retort and see Keaton's eyes go as wide as pool balls. "Ma'am, do you know the Grossmans?"

"Do I know someone gross?"

Courtney Cowie's cataract-filled eyes seemed to examine the agents again, so Emma repeated the question. When it registered, however, the elderly woman only leaned more heavily on her cane and mirrored Keaton's grimace.

"Well, my favorite newscaster is Richard Gross, over on Channel 5, but I don't know him personally, and his name isn't *Gross-man*. Maybe the neighbors in the blue house on the corner? They've only lived there about ten years, and I haven't bothered to learn their names yet. Nice young couple with three kids. Keep their yard clean too. I baked them brownies when they moved in."

Keaton glanced at Emma rather than repeat the megaphone routine. That response said it all. *Only about ten years.* This woman didn't know the Grossmans and would've called the cops if she did. Heck, she'd probably called the cops on neighbors who forgot to abide by the county's restrictions on operating lawn sprinklers off schedule.

Before either of them could continue, Keaton's phone rang, and he held it up in apology as he stepped away.

Emma sighed and raised her voice once more. "Thank you for your time, Ms. Cowie!"

Once she'd closed the door, Emma rubbed one hand across the front of her throat. "Talk about a rough start to the morning."

Keaton slipped his phone back into his coat pocket with a wry smile. "Blessedly saved by the bell. That was Jacinda."

Emma cocked one thumb at the Charger as he continued, as she'd known he would. Some aspects of their old partnership seemed to remain in her instincts after all.

"Says they've located the truck and sent me the address. It was abandoned on a rural road not too far from where we are now. We're to meet the forensics team there and process it. Ballistics results are in also. Wanna venture a guess?"

"With my scratchy voice?" Emma slipped into the Charger and got the engine running before continuing.

Beside her, Keaton was already typing the address into her GPS.

Emma clutched her throat comically and spoke in a wheezy, hoarse voice. "But sure, I'll take a shot. Whoever shot Trisha also shot Barry and Lorena, meaning that all the robberies are definitely connected."

"Bingo." Keaton hit go on the GPS and sat back, chuckling at her show. "Jacinda's been in touch with the detective in charge of investigating the murder of Marla Treadway, Georgie Treadway's mother, as well. They're rushing the ballistics now, since she was found killed in her home."

And so the body count rises, Emma girl. Which means you'd better step on it.

E mma pulled onto the shoulder behind the truck but didn't get out immediately. The quiet road stretched into the countryside around them, and the truck looked as if it had been parked neatly to the side. No flat tire, no open hood, no sign of him having been forced to swerve. Likely he'd simply abandoned it.

"This feel right to you? That he'd abandon his truck? And do it where we'd find it so easily?"

"No." Keaton shoved his hands into his gloves. "I buy that he'd paint it a new color...that's on-brand and easy enough for a guy like him...but get rid of it? The way you talked about him driving after that first job, I'd say his truck's an extension of him. An extra limb. You don't cut off an arm and leave it on the side of the road...especially after having been away from it for so long."

"Not your own arm anyway."

Gallows humor aside, this truck looked to be the same make and model as the red one she'd chased. "Let's take a look."

Keaton led the way to the vehicle, leaning in at various

points to see into the truck bed or the windows. It did appear identical to the one she and Leo had chased, minus the color, but Emma still had difficulty understanding the drop.

"Didn't you say they were pretty religious about their vehicle in the seventies? Painting it, yeah, but also souping it up and making sure they had the best of the best when it came to parts?"

"Yeah." Keaton sighed and took a step back, standing in the middle of the road to view it at more of a distance. "I can't imagine they'd switch if they're really planning on hitting more banks. He wouldn't risk all that money on a vehicle he didn't have absolute mastery over."

Emma waved at the forensic team just driving up and parking behind the Charger. "Even if it's this distinctive?"

As he bent to peer beneath the vehicle, Keaton shrugged off the question. "Especially if it's really distinctive. Grossman has no other skills outside of driving and working on cars. Driving is his superpower. Painting a truck is one thing. Heck, stealing a truck is one thing. But getting one in condition to where you can maneuver it on instinct and outrun federal agents…that's something else."

"What about the car Mary Karen purchased? The Camry. Or do we think that purchase was intended as a decoy, or something to cover for the two of them casing Barry Meldrum's dealership?"

"That's probably closer to the truth. We've had a BOLO out for the vehicle and so far gotten nothing for our trouble."

The tech approached from the back—they were down to one forensic tech now, it appeared—and began unpacking his satchel, laying out evidence bags. Emma recognized him as Jeremy Kornher, one of their senior techs, and nodded a greeting. "Glad you're still standing."

"Ha. One of us has to be."

She gestured toward the front of the truck. "You mind if

we go ahead and pop the hood?"

Technically, this was their crime scene, but especially when half of D.C. was down with the flu, no way did she want to get on the bad side of the only tech left at their disposal.

Jeremy shrugged and came over to dust the front door handle. "Gimme two seconds." When he was done, he headed back to his van to retrieve whatever else he needed. "Make sure to use gloves if you touch anything."

Emma obediently gloved up and opened the driver's side door, then reached in and popped the hood. "During the chase, that truck picked up a lot of speed fast. I'm a hundred percent sure Kenneth tricked out the engine."

Keaton walked around the front of the vehicle with her, using the hood strut to prop it up for easy viewing. He whistled. "Emma, I'm going to say that this truck is roadworthy *only* because it sure as hell got here from somewhere. If not for that, I'd say this thing wouldn't run without a magic wand and some fairy dust."

Emma knew nothing about engines, but the truth was, she had to agree with him. The truck's guts looked rusted and ancient. The battery was corroded, and some of the wire casings were fraying, others cracked. "Looks like they used its last gasps to get it here, huh? I mean…assuming it's even the Grossmans."

Keaton scowled and took a step back from the truck, giving it another once-over. "Seems like way too much of a coincidence for a truck identical to Kenneth's to get washed up on a country highway with no apparent reason."

Leaning in, Emma gave the battery another look to see if the old thing was recently planted in the truck's guts to steer them astray. "But?"

"But look at the new paint job." Keaton pointed along the side of the truck. "Totally at odds with the truck's inner workings. "You don't end up with a truck that looks brand-new on the outside and decades old on the inside just by happenstance. Somebody did that on purpose."

Emma sighed. "So this was just meant as a red herring. Planned in advance. Which means Mary Karen must've followed him and picked him up, possibly in the Camry or another vehicle. This was just a decoy."

Keaton pushed aside the hood strut, letting the hood slam shut with a bang that echoed through the still air. "They just dropped this off to keep us busy. If we're busy looking at a vehicle, we're not looking at banks."

"I'm gonna call Jacinda." Emma stepped aside and dialed the SSA. She didn't wait for a greeting once the other woman answered. "Jacinda, this truck couldn't outrun one of our Expeditions if you put a jet pack on the back of it. Forensics is here, but I'm telling you, they're not going to find anything worthwhile. We should double down on the BOLO for that Camry, too, just in case."

Jacinda cursed on the other end of the line. "Figures. All right. You and Keaton get over to the Farmers Bank in Watson Ranch. Check in with their head of security and be ready to act if Grossman shows up. Should be an hour away if traffic's good."

"We know that's where Grossman is headed?"

"It's one of our best bets. Despite being semirural, it's the most central bank on Treadway's employment history. We'll be able to scramble more effectively from there."

They disconnected and Emma crammed her phone into her pocket.

Two leads down, more than an hour into the day, and they were no closer to catching Kenneth Grossman. But they might be closer to one more robbery, which would likely mean one or more dead bodies on top of the count they already had, unless they could get there first.

29

F armers Bank in Watson Ranch might've been the smallest on Georgie Treadway's list, but it looked barely miniscule in the early morning hours. Like another decoy if she'd ever seen one. But using this as their meetup location made sense, and it might be where Grossman decided to strike next. According to Treadway, at least.

Of course, Grossman'll bail the instant he sees all these govern-ment plates and patrol cars on the street.

Emma fought down her frustration as she parked. A tired-looking cop stood guard outside the entrance. He waved her and Keaton inside as they approached the front door.

The rest of the team already awaited them in the bank's lobby, gathered in a circle with phones in their hands. Leo held up his own phone in greeting. "Still waiting on ballistics from the West Virginia PD. Anything on your end?"

Emma exchanged tired looks with Mia before shrugging. "Truck was a decoy."

"We should've known." Keaton leaned back against the

counter beside Sloan. "And the address we had for Mary Karen Grossman wasn't any better."

Jacinda nodded, shifting her long red hair around one shoulder. "Every address we find is going to be a fake. I think we've established that well enough now, unfortunately."

Emma played with the zipper of her coat, fighting the urge to tug it higher even in the warmth of the bank. She'd look like an idiot, since she was the only one feeling the chill in the air. The very *unnatural* chill in the air.

Because, sure enough, Trish and Lorena's ghosts were there again. Emma's whole team stood arrayed in a little circle, and the two dead women had come up right behind her, as if to join the huddle and offer input on where the Grossmans would pop up next. Unfortunately, they remained focused on their damn tattoos.

Trisha let out an overly dramatic sigh that reminded Emma of every tired romance heroine ever put on film. "I got this tattoo right after Chelsea was born. It means the world to me, symbolizing the connection between mother and daughter."

Emma gritted her teeth. The woman had left a motherless daughter behind. *That* was what should mean the world to her. Why was she still talking about tattoos? Was that really her biggest concern?

Fighting to remain focused, Emma kept her eyes on Mia and listened as the other agent recounted what they'd heard from Georgie Treadway. Meanwhile, Lorena began talking about her siblings' tattoos, actually cataloging them by sibling age as she described them…in detail.

"Agnes has a little sparrow beneath her rib cage. I can't imagine how that hurt! It means so much to her, though. She talks about how it symbolizes her connection to the earth more than material things. You should see it…it's so pretty."

Emma steadied her feet and closed her eyes against the

onslaught, thinking she could better block out the ghosts in that fashion, but the women went on.

"My daughter wants a rose on her chest." Trisha Terrence grunted her displeasure. "And a rose, fine, but on her chest? Chelsea says it symbolizes the beauty in her heart and how she'll always be the person she is now, though I can't imagine where that came from. I told her she had to wait—"

"Good!" Lorena's exclamation seemed to come from right inside Emma's ear. "My mom gave me permission when I was seventeen, and I hate to think about how much it cost to cover that boy's name up."

This was absurd. Sure, everyone wanted to tell the story of their own tattoos—what they meant, the heartbreak or triumph or obsession behind them—but why now? *And what's the point?*

Because there had to be a point.

Which meant there had to be something else.

Mia mouthed concern to her. *Are you okay?*

Emma jerked her head in a nod, gesturing for Mia to go back to listening to Sloan, who was talking about where green suits and masks might be bought and whether that could get them anywhere. Talking this out wouldn't get *Emma* anywhere, though.

She just needed to think. About tattoos, it appeared. So the ghosts were now talking in complete sentences, and had been all week, but their messages were still cryptic. Emma had to play the game, simple as that.

Sentimental. Tattoos are sentimental, just like our killer.

But this was like trying to remember an actor's name in a movie when you couldn't quite put your finger on it.

Jacinda had just begun speaking, but Emma ignored the SSA's annoyed frown and raised her voice anyway, eyes on Keaton. "You said our guy's sentimental."

Though the edge of the counter had to be cutting into his

back by now, Keaton didn't shift position as he nodded. "Sure, yeah. To break down and go celebrate Christmas when he and Mary Karen were definitely smart enough to know better? Absolutely."

Emma stepped closer to her team and raised her voice again, drowning out the incessant ghosts as the agents all focused on her. "The Grossmans are reliving their heyday, right? Going back to what they know. But one thing's different. Kenneth's got that tattoo."

She took a breath, expecting the ghosts behind her to fill the silence, but they seemed to have disappeared.

They got what they wanted. You're on the right track, Emma girl.

"The date from the tattoo was February 15, 1978." She glanced around the group, making sure they were following her train of thought. "We have to figure that out. It's significant to them. What is it? Wedding? Birthday?"

Mia's eyes widened. "That's forty-five years ago *today*. Emma, you're right. That has to mean something."

Shifting onto the balls of her feet, Emma whirled on Keaton. "When we were at dinner yesterday, what were you saying about us needing to know where the Grossmans would be instead of where they'd been? Anticipating their moves?"

Keaton nodded. "Well, right. Because we'll never get an accurate, truthful address, we need to either catch them on the move...if we can...or be able to predict where they're headed. That's why staking out the banks is important."

Emma turned her eyes back to Jacinda. "We need to know what that date means."

Jacinda squinted in thought but was already directing traffic. "Mia, Keaton, the two of you start calling records offices...Social Security, DMV, you name it...and make sure we have all addresses and relevant dates on these two. See if the tattoo matches up with anything. Leo, you check hospital records and see if we find anything family related. Sloan and Emma, the two of you start searching news articles and see what we can find online. I'm going to get in touch with the detective originally on their case and see if the date jogs anything."

Around their circle, everyone pulled forth phones and iPads, focused on the date, shifting into action now that they had a new direction.

Emma began with Mary Karen Grossman, thinking her husband might have been focused on her when he wrote the date. Her birthday was in April, though, and their wedding date was in July. She searched the name "Grossman" alongside the date instead, leaving off "Mary Karen" to see what that might get her.

And just as a death certificate popped up, Leo shouted in triumph. "Gotcha!"

The rest of the team froze, and Emma grinned at them. Thinking she and Leo had found the same thing, she gestured for him to go first.

"They had a daughter, Angela Mary Grossman. Born on the twelfth of February in 1978. We find the daughter and—"

Emma held up a hand, stopping him mid-sentence. They'd almost found the same thing, but not quite. "Angela Mary Grossman died three days later, on February 15, 1978."

She gazed around her group, barely holding in the grin that had no business following such a pronouncement. If the Grossmans' little girl had died on this date, they'd be spending at least a portion of today honoring her. And the cemetery where she'd been buried was less than an hour away, right on the outskirts of D.C.

"I know where they are, or at least where they'll be, and it's not at a bank."

30

I dug my fingers into the bark of an old oak tree, the roughness of it serving as a sort of anchor. In a place this pretty, I needed something hard, something real, that didn't look quite so heart-wrenching as my Mary Karen kneeling down in front of a little angel statue. An angel herself, she was so pretty.

Cedar Grove Cemetery had been her choice for our daughter, Angela. We'd chosen that name because she was our little angel. Hokey, but true.

This little grove of old-growth oaks and dogwoods was set aside for children like our little baby. Kids who'd been taken too soon. Their monuments stood in the manicured landscaping, with low-cut grass around each headstone and figure. It was all so perfect, I could almost—almost—believe our little angel was at peace, and that, by extension, we led a peaceful life too.

Beyond the trees, a wide and empty lawn separated this place from other grave sites. Expensive mausoleums lined the edge of the grounds not so far away. We were way back in the cemetery, where you couldn't hear traffic, and where mourners rarely came.

Mary Karen's prayers hit a higher pitch, and I glanced over my shoulder, but saw nothing. Nobody to interrupt us. Truth was, I hated coming here...despite the quiet. The place was a bit too peaceful, even with the weight of my gun on my hip and the sight of Mary Karen's trusty shotgun by her side.

Not to mention that we were a bit too far away from the truck for my liking. I hadn't exactly been able to drive it up into the mourning grove, so it sat more than sixty feet away, on the side of the closest dirt lane. True, that wasn't far off, but it wasn't close. Not like it would've been if we'd been fleeing a bank.

I had to remember that didn't matter here. We were supposed to be at peace in our little girl's resting place. Right at this moment, it was just Mary Karen's needs that mattered.

Anything for Mary Karen. She needed to say goodbye one final time.

Soon after getting out of the joint, I'd dropped by the cemetery late one night. There'd already been a plan in my head to take Mary Karen away to Belize, so I'd said my good-byes then. And hard as it was, I couldn't make myself go through that again. Being here for my Mary Karen was about as much as I could do, even if I did stand a few feet away so I didn't have to read Angela's name engraved on the stone.

Mary Karen hunched over in the grass, sobs interrupting her prayers. She said her faith comforted her, and I hoped that was true. What she told herself, over and over again, was that after three days on Earth, our little angel had decided to go and be an angel in Heaven instead. It was bullshit, obviously—no infant *decided* to go to Heaven—but Mary Karen was a devout Catholic, through and through.

Well, more power to her.

I anchored myself to the solidness of the oak, putting our little Angela's face out of mind for the moment. I'd seen enough of the world to understand that bad things, terrible things, did happen. The world was simple in that way. And while I didn't have any sort of faith to comfort me, accepting that meant something.

And like I told Mary Karen, I did have action. I'd take action over faith any day of the week. Because in the end, that meant I had control.

I shifted my eyes from my sweetheart, glancing beyond the trees. Nothing moved. Nothing but the occasional branch in the light winter breeze. Shaking it off, I leaned heavier on the tree. It made sense that I was uncomfortable, I guessed, since we were moving a fair bit slower than I would've liked.

But after this next hit, we'd be gone. Belize had our name on it. We'd hit the biggest bank on Georgie's list as soon as Mary Karen said her goodbyes. Getting the biggest buck for our bang, as it were.

Mary Karen sat up from her prayers and went into the second part of her routine. It was always like this. She'd start off like she was in her old Catholic church, praying with her hands together and her eyes closed and then get all personal. I dreaded this part. She brought tears to my old eyes, even though I fought it every time.

And yet, I still couldn't help but listen in.

"...last time we'll be here, Angela. But, baby, soon we're gonna be together. You didn't have enough time on this Earth with me and your da. But we would've been such good, good parents to you, and you'll see that soon. I love you so much. So does your da, baby. You just gotta watch the way he looks at me and talks about you to know that. I hope you've been watching. We think about you every day. But I'm coming to you now. I don't have long on this plane, so I'll be with you soon. You've got my word, baby girl."

Mary Karen's voice broke on that promise, and my gut clenched. Hearing her say out loud that she wasn't long for this world...it was too much. To think of what life would be like without her, without us sharing our morning coffee and lying in bed at night, talking about our plans. Beginning and ending each day together...

I stepped away from the shade tree and laid my hand on her head, petting down some of the flyaway blond strands. From this vantage, she could still be the sixteen-year-old I'd fallen for all those years ago.

She reached up and put her hand on my wrist, gripping me like I'd gripped the old oak. For a little while yet, we had each other.

I heard her swallow, and then she bent down and kissed the top of the marble angel's head. "Goodbye, baby girl. I'll be seeing you soon."

She reached for my arm again, and I gripped her and pulled her to her feet. Some more weight had fallen off her over the last week, so her turtleneck hung loose on her limbs under that heavy corduroy coat. I tried to ignore that as I pulled her in close, mindful of the shotgun hanging loose in her hand, letting her cry into my chest.

She feels like she's just barely here. Like the cancer's taking her faster than it was supposed to.

Maybe we should just go. Just take what we have and run. Forget the final score.

There was no point to it if Mary Karen wouldn't be alive to enjoy it with me, and with the way she felt...I wasn't so sure I had her for months yet. We could only spend so much in a matter of weeks. The question was how to tell her that.

But I opened my mouth to try, only to hear a voice like the crack of a gun.

"Kenneth Grossman! FBI! Freeze where you are!"

31

Emma's gun remained trained on Kenneth Grossman as she stepped out from behind a mausoleum. She'd already radioed the rest of her team that she'd found them. Jacinda had initially suggested she and Leo go to the cemetery together, but with multiple banks still "up for grabs," the team had instead divided to cover as much ground as they could.

Sure wouldn't mind Mr. Charming Smile watching my back right now though. Kenneth and Mary Karen are both armed.

Trees dotted the landscape—between her and the Grossmans as well as between them and their truck, parked perhaps sixty feet behind them—and made for a less-than-ideal confrontation, but at least they were isolated. The Grossmans would have to put their backs to her if they wanted to make a run for that truck.

Emma worried about gunfire being sent in less-controlled directions, where a round could get through the trees to the road beyond the cemetery perimeter or where pedestrians might approach.

Jacinda had balked at the idea of clearing the cemetery

grounds when Emma radioed in because that would alert the Grossmans. Mourners and cemetery staff remained in place, going about their business like normal, but all on one side of the grounds.

If the Grossmans did open fire, the best option was for that fire to be directed toward Emma's current location. She had nothing at her back but national park grounds and gravestones.

Emma only hoped the caution would pay off in their favor, and the Grossmans would simply surrender.

Aiming between the oaks, Emma had a clear shot, but Kenneth's options for cover were the reason she'd waited until the man and woman were embracing. Maybe this way, he'd make the smart decision. For Mary Karen if not himself.

She'd heard the woman's prayers carried on the breeze. Seen the love in him, the way he'd touched her and then pulled her to her feet. Emma's heart had ached to see that love, and the way it seemed to lift the two of them up even at a time like this when they were running for their lives.

But murderers in love were still murderers. Taking advantage of that might be her best chance of getting this couple to surrender.

"The two of you have nowhere to go, nowhere to run!" That earned Emma no response, not even a flicker of movement to show they'd heard her, beyond the fact that they'd frozen when she'd first called out. "Mary Karen Grossman, put your weapon on the ground. Kenneth Grossman, raise your hands high. *Now!*"

Emma waited, anxious for the sound of sirens to begin filling the air. Anything that might mean back up was on the way. But the grounds, and the murderous couple, remained silent. Mary Karen held her shotgun just as she'd gripped it when standing. Kenneth Grossman's arms remained wrapped around his wife's body, but his angular face positively glowered at Emma.

I've seen the faces of men and women prepared to surrender. Kenneth's isn't one of them.

In the little clearing of trees, Kenneth Grossman twitched, cricking his neck, Emma realized. Maybe flexing his muscles.

Getting ready to make his move. Like a painter choosing his next brushstroke.

Emma braced herself. That little movement had reminded her that Kenneth Grossman had committed crimes and served time for longer than she'd been alive. He'd enjoyed only two decades of freedom in his near-seven decades among the living.

Taking a quick chance, she glanced around her. No civilians lingered in the immediate area, but a maintenance crew was making its way down the access road Emma had arrived on, behind a row of mausoleums. "Kenneth and Mary Karen, this isn't the time for a blaze of glory. Put your weapons down and your hands up."

In one smooth motion, Kenneth's hand moved from his wife's back to his own hip. It reappeared between them, with a gun aimed in Emma's direction. A bullet ricocheted off the mausoleum beside her even as Emma dove behind it, landing in the dirt. She quickly rolled to her left, crouched and aimed around the side of the building, firing.

"Get in the truck, Mary Karen!" Kenneth screamed as he returned fire.

Emma ducked around the other side of the building. Mary Karen moved surprisingly fast for a sickly woman with only months to live. As the grieving mother ran, she brought up her shotgun and fired wildly behind her, forcing Emma to duck back behind the mausoleum again.

Though she wasn't visible to the criminals, they were

both firing as they fled, making it impossible to keep an eye on where they were going.

Emma shoved away the memory of Mary Karen's prayers and gripped her gun tighter. She moved low and away from the mausoleum, heading toward her vehicle parked behind those near the maintenance crew.

The cemetery staff had all retreated and lay flat behind some gravestones. Emma waved at them to stay low as she rounded a large grave marker and spotted the Grossmans. The couple was at their truck now, Kenneth screaming curses. Emma couldn't help remembering what Keaton had said about this man and his vehicle.

Kenneth was that truck's master. He knew it like an extension of himself. And if he was in that truck, they might just get away again.

That man murdered a mother in front of her child. He's killed and he's killed, and he will kill again. You can't let him get away, Emma girl. Not this time.

The truck roared to life, practically purring. This was the real escape vehicle, the one that had outrun federal officers through the seventies, and, more recently, Emma herself earlier that week.

"Not this time!" Emma's shout echoed behind her as she sprinted for the Charger. Another engine roared from nearby, and Emma spotted Mia wheeling a Bureau SUV down the road with gravel kicking up behind her.

The Charger could keep up with the Grossmans. It *would* keep up with them. She knew it was wrong to go off by herself. She should wait for Mia, but the SUV was top-heavy and had already failed to stop Grossman once before.

Emma yanked open the door and threw herself inside the Charger, the slam cutting off Mia's scream for her to stop.

It was too late for that. Emma wouldn't be stopping until Kenneth did.

32

Emma sped down the gravel-strewn lanes winding through the cemetery, desperate to catch the Grossmans as they kicked up stones and dust doing, Emma estimated, at least forty-five miles an hour. Escape was clearly all they cared about, but the way Kenneth was driving, they'd be lucky if they made it out of the cemetery alive.

A strip of tire tread flew out to one side of the truck, bouncing off a monument. A family of mourners a few yards away ducked and took shelter behind the gravestones. More chunks of tire were flung from the speeding truck, and still, Grossman kept them at chase speeds, clearly not caring for anyone's safety.

He's got at least one flat now. That should slow him down.

Emma growled in frustration, knowing that what should happen and what would happen were very different things where Kenneth Grossman was concerned.

She pushed the Charger forward, hoping to ram the truck and send it into a skid. At the same time, she did her best to keep an eye out for mourners who might end up in harm's way.

The old cemetery was a labyrinth of narrow lanes, mostly of bare earth but with patches of worn, overgrown pavement here and there. The softer dirt surface made it easier for Kenneth to keep control of the truck. A flat tire, and now mostly bare rim, on full pavement would've rattled him and Mary Karen right out of their seats.

Emma pressed the Charger to go faster, skidding around corners and praying that the front gates had been barricaded with patrol cars after Mia's arrival.

Swiping the radio handset from her dash, she called Mia to confirm that. All she received in reply were shouted demands to slow down and wait for backup.

"You're out of your mind, Emma! Stop before you or someone else gets hurt!"

Emma dropped the handset to the seat and swept the muscle car around a curve, narrowly avoiding an old pine tree. She was gaining on the Grossmans, but Kenneth had found a lane hidden between two ranks of monuments. Dust and gravel flew up in rooster tails behind the truck, pelting and clattering against the Charger's hood and windshield.

In another moment, the Grossmans took a turn that hid them from view. Even though their trail of dust told Emma which way they'd gone, not having eyes on the truck was enough to add weight to her foot.

The Charger roared ahead, slowing strategically around the same curve. Bringing the truck back into her sights, she accelerated forward.

No letting up on the gas now, Emma girl. He is not getting away again.

The Charger thrummed beneath her as it resettled from taking the turn. She gave it a little more gas and focused on her goal of getting Kenneth Grossman off the damn road.

They'd wound up on a curving, dirt road that ringed Cedar Grove Cemetery. Gravestones and monuments lined the lawn to their right, so tightly packed in this area that the Grossmans had only one path to follow now.

Emma gunned forward, pulling in tight against the truck. She aimed for the rear bumper and gave a punch to the gas.

The angry crunch of metal made her flinch backward in her seat even as the impact jolted both vehicles. The truck fishtailed, but Kenneth had it back under control a split second later.

On a downhill slant, Kenneth maintained his pace, despite the one flat tire now having a mate on the opposite side. Sparks kicked up as bare metal rims screeched across a small strip of cracked pavement before racing ahead along the dirt road, kicking up dust and pebbles in their wake.

Emma's whole view became a cloud of brown, obscuring the truck for a moment.

Furious and fearful, Kenneth would find a way to escape again. Emma pressed down on the gas, planning to ram the truck through the screen of dust, even though she couldn't see exactly where to aim. She'd adjust if she had to. The truck couldn't be more than a few yards ahead of her. With a final stomp of her foot, the Charger surged forward.

Emma braced for the impact as she entered the brown cloud, and her muscles tensed at the first sound of grinding metal.

But it was farther ahead, and she hadn't hit anything yet.

The dust billowed away just as the truck gave a violent jolt to one side. The right rear axle separated from the gearbox and spun away among the grave sites. Kenneth was trying to keep control, but the truck had given all it could.

The Grossmans skidded, swerving toward the iron fence that enclosed the cemetery. The downward slope increased their momentum until, with a sickening screech, the truck spun to the side, then flipped and began a violent descent, rolling over gravestones and finally crashing against a mighty oak tree.

Dust and grass circled the air between Emma's car and the immobilized truck. She stopped, set her car's front tires against the slope, and all but leapt from her seat.

The shouts from her fellow agents in the distance broke through the hazy air so she didn't bother radioing in her location. Emma drew her weapon and advanced toward the truck.

The battered vehicle had come to rest upright against the tree, with the driver's side facing Emma's direction. Every panel was a crumpled testimony to the path the Grossmans had taken. The tailgate hung loose. Wisps of steam or smoke rose to mix with the settling dust.

Staying twenty feet back, Emma lifted her aim at the driver's door and yelled ahead of her, taking no chances. "Hands in the air, Grossman! Now!"

Within seconds, Jacinda and Leo both echoed Emma's words, and she solidified her grip on her weapon, stepping toward the wreck.

An anguished scream erupted from the truck, and Emma froze in place, still aiming ahead of her. The shade from the overhanging oak branches obscured the cab's interior except for the figure of Kennth Grossman, slumped against the steering wheel.

Mary Karen's desperate screeches split the air, unintelligible but for an occasional "Kenneth!" Emma spotted the woman, lying half across her husband's form. Her hands fluttered up and down, coming to rest on his hunched back.

With no weapons in sight, Emma relaxed her stance, but only enough that she could keep Jacinda's and Leo's positions clear in her peripheral view.

She followed the path of broken glass and shattered gravestones, yelling out one more time. "FBI! Get your hands in the air, Mary Karen, now! Kenneth Grossman, please comply and place your hands in plain view, slowly!"

The only response was more desperate screaming from Mary Karen.

Leo's or Jacinda's footsteps crunched along the dirt track behind her. Emma continued her advance, finally reaching the driver's side door.

Kenneth was folded over the steering wheel, and it was obvious that he presented no immediate threat. His forehead was a ragged, bloody mess, with slivers and pebbles of glass embedded in his flesh. His mouth hung open, with his upper lip torn away, revealing bloodied teeth. Emma checked his eyes, expecting a dead stare. But Kenneth was alive, drawing stuttering breaths, and his eyes blazed with rage.

Mary Karen sat in the passenger seat, shaking and bruised, with only a trickle of blood running from one nostril. She'd avoided the worst, though Emma could only imagine how. Maybe in the last moments before the truck began to roll, Kenneth had tried to shelter her beneath him.

The woman stared through the spiderweb of cracks in the windshield, taking slow, halting breaths, before turning back to her man.

"Kenneth, wake up. Get us out of here, baby. Kenneth, please."

Emma still had her weapon in hand but held it close and with the muzzle lowered. Kenneth was dropping in and out of consciousness, waking up to express rage and stare at Emma in one moment, then slipping back away. He didn't seem to hear his wife at all.

He certainly wasn't in any condition to pull an escape maneuver, not that the smoking truck could be counted on.

"Place your hands on the dashboard, Mary Karen." Emma maintained her relaxed stance but was ready to snap up her muzzle and take aim on the woman if necessary.

Leo stood close by, in her periphery.

Mary Karen whimpered her husband's name. She looked and sounded like a woman whose last good day had long since come and gone. Her skin was pulled tight against her bones, and as she placed her hands on the dash and turned to face Emma, the eyes that peered out from deep, gray sockets were all but haunted.

She was too aware of what awaited her...both in this life and possibly the next.

She looks like she's seen ghosts. And she knows she's dying.

As Mary Karen's mouth twisted into a smirk, she moved one hand from the dashboard. In a flash, she snatched at Kenneth's hip and had his pistol in her hand before Emma could open her mouth to speak.

Emma's muzzle came up, but Mary Karen wasn't directing his gun at her or any of the agents.

"Bury me with my daughter."

Emma lunged across Kenneth's form, reaching as far as she could into the cab.

The gunshot cracked loud and violent in the still and wintry air. Blood spattered against the top of the cab and the shattered rear windshield.

Emma forced herself to look away from the grisly sight, focusing instead on the man stirring beneath her outstretched arm.

He groaned, his red-eyed gaze coming to rest again on Emma with a look of knowing that he had run his final race. She stepped back from the cab and brought up her weapon.

"Put your hands up, Mr. Grossman."

If he heard her, he didn't give any sign. His eyes wandered past her, over her shoulder, and then he pushed open the door and stumbled sideways. She backed up to give him room as he fell, landing on his knees. He wavered there, and then slurred his wife's name as grief and agony poured from him.

Swallowing, Emma repeated her command. "Hands up, Mr. Grossman."

Maybe his eardrums got blown out when the truck tumbled over. Or maybe he's just out of his senses.

Leo joined her, holstering his weapon and taking out his cuffs with his other hand.

"Want me to do the honors?"

Holding her aim steady, Emma nodded for Leo to proceed. Jacinda approached from behind him, adding her aim and attention to the struggling figure on the ground.

Emma didn't say it out loud, but the man was no longer a threat. She knew it just as well as they did.

Kennth Grossman rolled onto a hip, falling backward onto his bloodied hands. When he got himself turned around, facing the truck again, he reached for the mangled step bar hanging beneath the driver's door.

With the agents watching from a short distance away, Kenneth pulled himself up and got a look into the cab. The sight of Mary Karen jolted him back away from the truck, and he landed on his ass in the dirt, hands up in front of him.

A low murmur of pain built into a growl that trembled out of his throat. He waved his hands frantically, as if warding off the memory of what he'd just seen.

And then he screamed. "Gahhhh!"

Emma holstered her weapon and turned away, waving off Keaton when he tried to say something to her. She couldn't right now. She just couldn't.

Pure anguish echoed around them, and the cold presence of Mary Karen's ghost wailing above her husband's shattered figure was no source of comfort.

33

Mia busied herself on her phone while Jacinda lectured Emma. Although the SSA's voice had dropped in volume, that only made her frustration more evident. But everything she said was true, and with each accusation and criticism added, Mia's own annoyance grew closer to becoming anger.

Because, really, what had Emma been thinking, chasing Kenneth Grossman on her own at high speeds with their suspects known to be armed and dangerous and with civilians present?

Jacinda felt the same way and made no effort to disguise her feelings.

"I don't care if you do know how to pursue a suspect at that speed. You can't tell me you're familiar with this environment! What if a grounds person had walked out from between the trees or come around a corner in their own vehicle? What if we'd had mourners coming up the slope as the crash was unfolding? Or if you'd been the one to spin out after nudging Grossman's vehicle?"

When Emma attempted a protest, Jacinda held up a hand to stop her.

"You don't know what might have happened, Agent Last."

"Agent Last." Maybe that'll make her realize how stupid she was, if nothing else will.

"Not to mention Grossman's injuries." Jacinda lowered her voice again and pointed back to where Sloan stood guarding their perpetrator, waiting for an ambulance. "A high-speed chase that seriously injured one of our suspects? When we could've waited for that truck to break down on its own or collide with the barricades at the entry gates. Even if they'd somehow gotten past them, we could've followed at a distance."

Mia winced at Emma's tone when she replied. "You can't be serious. They were both firing on me. You think a couple of patrol cars and uniforms would stop them from unloading the rest of their ammo? I had to follow him."

"Not by yourself, Agent Last."

Leo grunted, clearly tired of listening, and stalked off to join Sloan and Keaton. Personally, Mia was waiting for her chance to holler at Emma for being so reckless.

She bit down anger, punching out an update text to Vance. Emma had earned this ass-chewing, no question about it. She and Jacinda exchanged a few more words, none of them easy to hear. They finally called it quits when the ambulance pulled up, lights flashing red against the broken gravestones littering the ground.

Mia turned in a circle, remembering the last visit her team had made here. They'd spent more time than she cared to think about examining smashed crypts, and the bodies Renata Finwick-Flint had desecrated in her bizarre attempt at resurrecting her dead husband's spirit.

A normal case, for once, would be great. What am I saying? This is normal. I just need to get used to it.

Kenneth's growls had grown louder as his grief gave way to the fury he seemed to always have just beneath the surface. He let loose a steady run of agonized screams through his ruined mouth, even as a team of EMTs maneuvered him onto a gurney.

As the group got closer, Jacinda signaled to Leo. "Go with him to the hospital. Do not leave him alone except for surgery. I'll make sure someone joins you soon, so you're not on your own. Understood?"

Leo shot a glance at Emma but nodded and headed after the others walking toward the ambulance, hands buried in his pockets.

That decided, Jacinda turned back to Emma and let out a monster of a sigh. "You, stay right where you are. I'll finish dealing with you in a minute."

To Mia's surprise, and concern, Emma didn't bat an eyelash at the SSA's sternness. She simply stood there, hands at her sides and her eyes neutral, like she'd just been told lunch would be delayed.

The SSA stalked off toward some uniforms getting out of their cars back behind the ambulance. Mia remained where she was, struck by the debris field of metal and stone littering the graveyard. Even Emma's Charger hadn't gone unscathed. Its front fender was bent in, and angry scratches stretched away from it like a monster's claws had raked the vehicle before going after Grossman's truck.

A flashback to Ned's death suddenly left Mia weak at the knees. The way his car had glistened in the sun of the impound lot, smashed in as if the thing had imploded. The funeral director apologizing and repeating that they'd had no choice but to hold a closed casket service.

And then her own part in the aftermath, sitting at her parents' kitchen table as they wailed, she herself stunned and heartbroken, wondering how her world had fallen apart so quickly.

I could have lost Emma in the exact same way. Just like that. I almost lost my friend just because Emma had to jump out ahead of things by herself.

There was nothing else to think about. Mia's boots carried her forward almost before she realized she'd pocketed her phone and begun stalking into Emma's personal space.

"You were irresponsible, Emma. Own it."

Emma's mouth dropped open, her eyebrows drawing together as if she were about to argue.

"No!" Mia gripped her upper arms and physically turned her, pointing at the crumpled truck still tucked against a tree in the cemetery. "Look at that, Emma. Look! That could've been you, dammit."

"Mia, I had to—"

"Stop it." Mia gripped her tighter and stared up into Emma's sky blue eyes, willing her friend to listen. She was yelling now but didn't care anymore who heard her. "You could have died! And it wasn't necessary. You have people who love you, and you should never be so careless with your own life. Do you hear me?"

She breathed in, ready to start all over if that was what it took to get Emma to understand, but Emma abruptly shook her grip loose and pulled her into a hug. Mia's breath was coming hard, and it took her a moment to realize that Emma's own pulse was racing in the same fashion, her breath warm near her ear and a touch too fast.

Emma's heart pounded, and Mia finally felt her anger beginning to die in her chest. Emma did understand. Still, she didn't let the other woman go. Not yet. Not until she was sure she'd convinced herself that the flashback to Ned's car accident was only that—a flashback from the past—and today everyone had survived.

Everyone on her team, everyone she loved and had begun this day with, was fine.

Jacinda's voice intruded on the moment. Firm, but with a bit less anger than before. "Mia, take Emma up the hill and make sure you're both calmed down and focused. Then you can come back and help her catalog the scene. We're still shorthanded."

Swallowing down words that probably would've come out half formed, Mia pulled away from Emma so the two of them could walk up the hill a bit. She'd seen a concrete bench near an old-growth tree and led Emma to it. When they sat, she let out a small laugh. "I think I'm the one who needs calming down now, more than you."

Emma's arm settled around her shoulders. "I get it. I'm sorry I went off like that. You're right. I couldn't let him get away again. I kept seeing Chelsea Terrence's face. That poor girl will never see her mother again. I just wanted—"

"I know what you wanted. It's what we all wanted." Mia sighed and gripped her friend's knee, jiggling it a bit as if for emphasis. "The point is, you're part of this team, and the team comes first, okay? So if you have to rein in your super-hero instincts in order to make us happy and allow us to keep you around, that's another sacrifice you have to make. Got it?"

Emma huffed a laugh, tightening her arm around Mia's shoulders. "I love you, too, Mia. And, yeah, I got it."

For a few seconds, they sat together silently. Mia felt the cold seeping up from the concrete bench but relished it. They were alive to feel the cold, to feel the anger and frustration they'd just expressed.

They were alive, and that was what mattered.

She released a deep breath, glancing down the hill to where Sloan and Keaton were helping the lone tech extricate Mary Karen from the wreck of her husband's truck. "I talked to Sloan about everything, by the way. And asked her to help investigate Ned's death."

The "finally" was left unspoken between them, but Emma rested her head against Mia's. "I'm so glad. I was hoping you would. How do you feel about it?"

"Good." Mia nodded to herself, watching the other agents work. For so long, she'd blamed Sloan for Ned's death. But no longer. "The resentment's gone. It was misplaced all along."

"She's smart. Together, I know we're going to figure this out. We're going to get justice for Ned, Mia." Emma's voice had softened, but the steel of her friend's resolve was there, backing it up. Mia was glad to hear it.

Because it was past time for Ned to have his justice. Way past time.

And regardless of what she'd just told Emma about putting the team first, what that translated to came down to family. Putting family first.

Putting Ned first, before she ran out of time to do so.

Before she could voice the thought, an Expedition edged past the other vehicles lining the road, paused, and then kept on coming up the lane toward where Emma and Mia sat.

Squinting, Mia could just make out Vance's determined smile behind the wheel. In the passenger seat beside him, Denae's curls bounced with their progress up the little dirt road.

Oh, thank goodness. Finally. It's been way too long since we've all been together.

By the time the agents had parked and gotten out of the vehicle, Mia and Emma stood waiting for them. Mia couldn't help herself. She burst forward and hugged both of them, holding onto Vance just a few seconds more than Denae, absorbing some of his warmth to combat the cold.

When she looked up, his green eyes glinted with amused concern. "What'd we miss?"

34

Emma adjusted the heater in her car, glad to be back in her little Prius. Maybe the Charger had been fun for a while, when she hadn't been focused on why it was necessary, but this car suited her just fine. Especially with their bank robber back behind bars.

Beside her, Keaton flipped through some radio stations. Probably looking for some of his endlessly annoying pop music. She let it go and just focused on driving. This had been a long day. It had taken hours in the cold to process the crime scene and fill out the appropriate reports. Then Jacinda had considered putting her on forced leave for behaving so irrationally, but ultimately decided not to.

If only because the Bureau's so short-staffed. But I'll take it.

"Congratulations on a job well done. I'm glad you could come fill in with us." She glanced sideways at one of her oldest friends. "It was good to have you back in D.C. You sure you have to leave tonight?"

Keaton's brow creased, but he nodded. "Yeah. I wish I didn't and we could grab a drink, but Hailey's receiving her first award for something she did in the line of duty. I thought I was going to miss it, but since we've wrapped the case, I'd rather be there, you know?"

Emma waved him off. "I get it. Family calls." The words sounded so natural on her lips, she couldn't believe she'd said them. And without her voice breaking. "What was the award for?"

"She wouldn't tell me." He grunted in annoyance. "Which probably means it was for something as stupid as what you did this morning."

Shooting him a grin, Emma pulled up in front of his hotel. Shifting the Prius into park, she turned and gave him a fast hug. A moment later, he was gone, hurrying through the hotel doors.

The fast goodbye stung. That morning, with the awkwardness between them, she might've preferred it to a more drawn-out farewell. But as the day had gone on, the friction she'd felt with Keaton that week had dissipated.

So what if he was more casual than Leo? He didn't live for his work...and when a case was closed, she could respect that all the more easily.

All day, she'd kind of looked forward to the two of them having a drink and talking about old times together. Catching up. Emma's plans originally were to visit Marigold, but the psychic had rescheduled for fear of contracting whatever had hit Emma's colleagues.

"This is a nasty flu going around, and I can't risk coming down with it. Let's try next week instead."

Maybe she and Keaton could have spent time watching a movie on her couch or half paying attention to a hockey game on some sports bar's television.

Instead, he was headed off to Richmond to be with his little sis, and the next time they saw each other, they might have to get over their newfound awkwardness all over again.

And meanwhile, her mind kept on drifting to family. To

the wound she felt, real as a gunshot, that ached within her. The lack of family was an absence that had bothered her for a long time, maybe for as long as she could rightly remember. But lately, it was hard to ignore the loneliness when she didn't have a case to focus on.

She wouldn't admit it to her team, but in some ways, she admired the Grossmans. Was even jealous of them.

Sure, they were murdering sociopaths, but they'd managed to find each other, fall in love, and maintain their own kind of love for each other. Over more than fifty years, with distance and prison walls between them for most of it. It was hard not to be impressed by that.

Tendrils of fog drifted across the city street ahead of her, and she slowed her speed just a touch. Pools of lamplight guided her way alongside her headlights, but somehow, tonight, she felt as if she were the only person in the world. The idea of pulling into her lonely apartment complex felt excruciating.

To do what? Eat a snack on her couch by herself, or maybe go for a run and then shower off the sweat before sitting on her balcony and waving at a ghost? She had nobody to share a late-night snack with. Nobody to curl up next to under a cozy blanket. How on earth had it gotten to be the case that murderers could have that kind of comfort, and she couldn't?

Tears pricked her eyes, and she swiped at them, biting down the sudden anger she felt at herself. Talk about a pity party. She was jealous of the Grossmans? The idea was absurd.

And to top it all off, guilt angled for her attention. She'd almost definitely screwed the pooch with Oren. Making him wait for her at that German restaurant for an hour, eating by himself, right up to a Valentine's Day dessert of apple strudel?

He did sound like he forgave me.

And maybe he did.

Emma palmed her phone, building up the nerve to call him. Oren was a good guy who was interested in her. Or at least, he *had* been interested in her. It was possible he'd hang up on her, or it was possible he'd allow her to try to make it up to him. Either way, she had to shoot her shot.

She tapped on the icon for his name, holding her breath. He picked up on the first ring. "Emma? How are you doing?"

"Oren, hi." She felt her pulse ease, just a touch, and let up on her grip on the steering wheel. "It's good to hear your voice. I'm doing okay. What about you?"

"Fine, Emma, fine, but are you safe?" Concern crackled in his voice—he was more keyed up than she'd ever heard him —and his words came out a touch too fast. What on earth was going on?

"Yeah, I'm fine. Safe. What's the matter?"

He sighed audibly and took another second before answering. "I was watching the news and saw the lead story about the Grossmans. *The* Grossmans. The reporter talked about the FBI being involved in a high-speed chase and having been focused on them all week. It's only been a few hours, but there are already specials being rerun about them, social media is blowing up with old articles...I was worried."

Emma swallowed. Worry. Having someone sitting at home worrying for her. This was what it felt like. An ache in her gut that felt good and bad all at once. "I was involved, but with the case where it is, I can't tell you much. But I'm fine. And Kenneth Grossman is back in custody."

"And Mia?"

He even remembers my friend's name after meeting her once. He really does pay attention.

Emma smiled into her phone. "We're all fine. And, hey..." She trailed off. She'd just pulled up in front of her apartment complex, getting ready to turn into the little parking lot across from the building, and thought her eyes were deceiving her. But they weren't.

Oren was leaning back against the building with a bouquet of hothouse sunflowers in his hand. The foggy night had left dots of moisture on his skin and hair. She stared through the windshield at him, and he gave her a little wave with his phone before speaking into it. "Thought I'd stop by and make sure you were okay. I've been waiting for you."

She couldn't help echoing him needlessly, frozen. "You were waiting for me."

"Right. Not in a stalker-y way. Promise. Want to park and then decide if you want me to come in?"

His laughter tickled her ear through the phone speaker before he ended the call. She watched as he tucked his phone into his coat and then waved her toward the parking lot.

In a blur, she did as directed. She parked, grabbed her bag, locked her car, and barely remembered to look both ways before crossing the street to reach him. The man who'd been standing out in the cold waiting for her, not even knowing when she'd get in. Just wanting to check on her, and with a bouquet of flowers in hand to boot.

"Oren, I—"

He hugged her, cutting off her breath, and instead of trying to think about what she might have said, Emma simply hugged him back. In fact, she nearly melted into him, leaning into his tall frame and relishing the comfort of his arms.

"I worried about you, Emma Last. God, how I worried today."

His voice tugged at something in her chest, but she couldn't quite find the words to answer. She was too focused on fighting down the tears suddenly threatening to erupt all over him.

"I need you to know something." He pulled back from her, hands moving to her waist and holding her in front of him. His brown eyes shined down at her, nearly glistening, and she realized she wasn't the only one who might have been close to tears.

The thought scared her as much as it thrilled her, but her fast-beating heart told her the thrill was winning out over the fear, at least today.

"I genuinely care for you, Emma. Deeply. Will you be my girlfriend? Officially?"

Emma's legs nearly gave out, she was so shocked. Of all the things she'd expected tonight, it hadn't been this. "I...I..."

"Go for it, Emma. Do it!" The familiar voice of Mrs. Kellerly's ghost echoed in her ears, and Emma nearly laughed out loud.

Then, when Oren grinned at seeing her smile, she did laugh.

"I'd love to, Oren. I'd love nothing more."

35

Emma sipped stale coffee in the VCU break room, hoping the tickle at her sinuses wasn't a sign of the flu. It would be just their luck to have the other half of the team out with the flu once the first half recovered.

You will not get sick, Emma girl. Don't even think it.

"It's allergies. Gotta be allergies."

Who knew what had been kicked up into that cemetery air, the way their case had ended? Barely forty-eight hours had passed since then, so if some of those particles were still playing havoc with her nasal passages, that shouldn't be a surprise. She hoped.

Emma went back to typing on her laptop, trying to remain focused. Her eyes nearly crossed with every added word. The paperwork on this Grossman case had been a bitch and a half from start to finish, not least of all because it seemed like someone had screwed up by allowing Grossman out on parole to begin with.

She sighed, closing out the latest form and letting herself sit back in her chair to rest her eyes for just a minute. Stale coffee was better than no coffee, after all, and she deserved a moment's breather.

Maybe now they could *all* get a breather, once paperwork was finished up. She could only hope. Mia and Sloan were certainly eager to focus on Ned's case, however much time it required. And Emma couldn't have been happier that they were finally on the same page, the truth starting to come to light. With resentment and bad feelings gone, they could focus on getting justice for Mia's brother.

The idea of the old mystery being solved brought Emma back to her own troubles, though. Especially now that Oren was a decided part of her life—her official boyfriend, who'd have thought?—she was all the more anxious to get herself in order and stop being held down by the past. But that meant being able to put to rest her own mystery.

Finding out the truth about this awareness of the Other that she'd somehow developed. Finding out what her mother wanted to warn her about after all these years of being silent.

And, more than anything, finding out what all these ghosts wanted and whether there'd be any way of putting them behind her.

With that thought, Emma opened up a new document on her laptop. She'd start a to-do list, and that would put her one step closer to getting her life in order. So she could focus on the future, not the past. Maybe to-do lists weren't normally her thing, but breaking from her own patterns couldn't hurt. Not when her own patterns had just been leading her into more and more ghosts along the way, without offering any answers.

Something new had to work, if her old habits wouldn't. Or, at least, she hoped that was the case.

In another moment, she began muttering out loud, thinking through what had to get done before her life could be cleared up.

"One, I need to find out what more I can about the Other. The dead can't keep throwing me off my game, and that's all there is to it. Two, Mom. She didn't show up to warn me for nothing. That warning *meant something*. Three, if my new psychic can't help me—"

A little tick of metal on metal caught Emma's ear, and she turned.

And there was Leo, crouched right outside the door in front of the vending machine, selecting some lunch.

Present, and staring at her with his eyebrows raised.

Shit.

The End
To be continued...

Thank you for reading.

All of the Emma Last Series books can be found on Amazon.

ACKNOWLEDGMENTS

How does one properly thank everyone involved in taking a dream and making it a reality? Let me try.

In addition to my family, whose unending support provided the foundation for me to find the time and energy to put these thoughts on paper, I want to thank the editors who polished my words and made them shine.

Many thanks to my publisher for risking taking on a newbie and giving me the confidence to become a bona fide author.

More than anyone, I want to thank you, my reader, for clicking on a nobody and sharing your most important asset, your time, with this book. I hope with all my heart I made it worthwhile.

Much love,
Mary

ABOUT THE AUTHOR

Mary Stone lives among the majestic Blue Ridge Mountains of East Tennessee with her two dogs, four cats, a couple of energetic boys, and a very patient husband.

As a young girl, she would go to bed every night, wondering what type of creature might be lurking underneath. It wasn't until she was older that she learned that the creatures she needed to most fear were human.

Today, she creates vivid stories with courageous, strong heroines and dastardly villains. She invites you to enter her world of serial killers, FBI agents but never damsels in distress. Her female characters can handle themselves, going toe-to-toe with any male character, protagonist or antagonist.

Discover more about Mary Stone on her website.
www.authormarystone.com

facebook.com/authormarystone
twitter.com/MaryStoneAuthor
goodreads.com/AuthorMaryStone
bookbub.com/profile/3378576590
pinterest.com/MaryStoneAuthor
instagram.com/marystoneauthor
tiktok.com/@authormarystone

Made in the USA
Middletown, DE
09 October 2023